DEDICATION

This is for all my Reylo shippers.
Get ready.

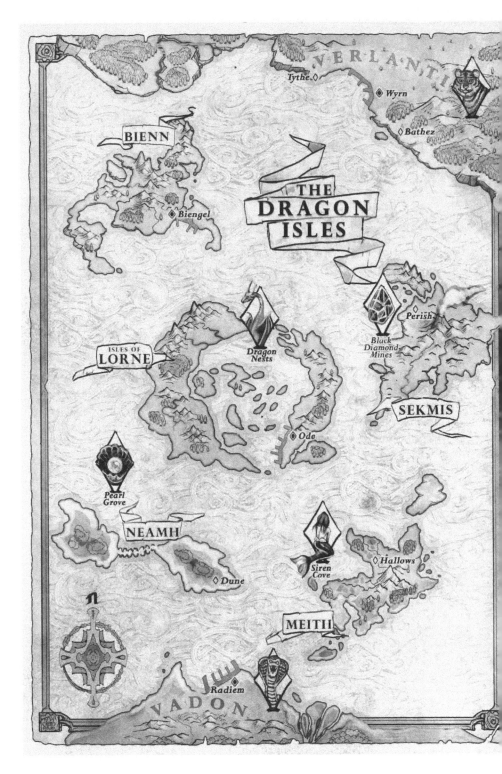

TABLE OF CONTENTS

PROLOGUE

Trust your heart.

Three little words that would lead anyone to ruin.

My mother taught me early to never trust my heart. It was a treacherous, fickle thing that would eventually lead to downfall. Her scars proved it. Every time I looked at her face, I was reminded of the pain the heart could cause.

Trust your mind.

Now, these were three words that would save my life over and over.

My heart wanted to believe the young elven sailor when he promised he loved me, but I *knew* better. He wanted my body, my access to the throne, and *my* dragons. He didn't want me—Wren—the wild girl who fought like a man and screeched like a fish monger's wife.

When I turned sixteen, the southern delegation tried to woo my family and people with gifts of friendship. While I longed to experience new cultures and make new friends, I put my dreams aside and used my head. The dark elves were only here for one thing. Our throne. It was the way it had been for five hundred years.

COURT OF DRAGONS

The fables say we are all born from the flora and fauna of the world. It's a pretty thought for bedtime stories, but I know the truth.

We were born from greed, jealousy, selfishness, and desperation.

We were born warriors.

My heart longs for fairytales, but my mind knows our reality.

The elves are coming.

The sand people are coming.

I am the only thing standing between the enemy and our dragons.

I will not fail.

@_ArtJake_

CHAPTER ONE

WREN

The sun shone brightly, the sky clear and blue on the morning of Wren's wedding, which was a bloody miracle in Lorne. She tipped her head back, basking in the afternoon warmth. If her granddad were there, he'd say the weather was a very good omen indeed.

Cracking an eye open, Wren glanced toward the southern beach. The waves lapped calmly along the black sand beach. A lucky day indeed. The weather for the last month had been atrocious. The sea had been stormy and unsettled, tossing waves, salty foam, and debris across the beaches that lined the shores of the island. It had been nearly a fortnight of gray skies and pelting rain. The night prior, the wind had railed and howled, but when she'd woken this morning, the clouds had finally parted, giving the sun a tiny, blessed chance to shine down upon this most auspicious of days.

"Have you finally tired yourself out, Daughter?" Her mother's melodious voice carried to her.

Wren sat up and fluttered her fingers across the tiny purple flowers that grew along the moor and peeked at Anneke through her tangle of red locks as her mum crested the nearest hill.

"Never," she called. Her mum grinned and picked her way down the incline.

Wren flopped back, the spongy plants cushioning her spine as she inhaled deeply, enjoying the fresh air and quiet time before the festivities began in a few short hours. The wind, sea, and land spoke to her, always urging her to run faster, dive deeper, push harder. Her papa said she had a wild spirit, and, on that, they both agreed.

A shadow blocked out the sun as her mother's soft steps paused. "Enjoying your meadow, I see."

She cracked a smile. Her mum always knew where to find her. Wren patted the ground on her left side. "Sit with me for a bit."

Fabric rustled, and the shadow disappeared. She sighed as Anneke ran her fingers through Wren's hair, her eyes closing for a moment. She rolled toward her mother and opened her eyes. Her mum lay on her side, facing Wren with a smile. Her mother was a beautiful woman. Deep-auburn hair, creamy skin, and fawn-like eyes. The only things that revealed her age were a few silver hairs and crow's feet around her eyes. Many of their people had mistaken Wren and her mum for sisters.

"I wish I had hair like yours," Wren grumbled. Her blazing, bright red hair had been the bane of her existence for years. She could never blend in or get away with anything, because someone always recognized her.

Anneke chuckled and ruffled Wren's hair. "We all wish for what we do not possess."

"I could have been born with any shade of red: copper,

auburn, rust, pale orange, but not me. No one has hair as bright as mine in the isles."

"It suits you. Bold just like you, and it's lucky, too."

Wren rolled her eyes. "For our people, the color of red is lucky, but it hasn't brought me any good luck. Just a lot of punishment."

Her mum snickered and cupped her cheek. "Now that, Daughter, had nothing to do with your hair and everything to do with your actions. You just can't keep yourself out of trouble." She wiggled her brows. "But you are almost no longer my responsibility. Soon, your husband will have to deal with your mischief and antics."

The nervous jitters in Wren's stomach tumbled about at the reminder.

Husband.

In just a short time, she'd be married. Be someone's wife.

"Love?"

She focused back on Anneke.

Her mum studied Wren, pulled her hand from Wren's cheek, and pushed back her own hair, securing it behind her slightly pointed ear. An elven ear. Her mother hailed from the northern kingdom of Verlanti and possessed the prominently pointed ears of the elves. Anneke had once told Wren that her sire had not been native to Verlanti. Instead, he had belonged to the kingdom of Vadon, which lay well to the south of Lorne, the sand kingdom so hot you could taste spices on the air. It was hard to imagine.

Anneke fiddled with her simple earring, pulling Wren's attention back to her mum.

"You know some of my history," her mother stated softly, her gaze becoming distant.

Wren swallowed hard. Her mum's origins were a dark tale. Stolen from her family's farm, she'd been taken to a high lord to be his concubine. Anneke had fought, but it hadn't been enough. The lord brutally took her innocence, and when he was through, he gave her to his men. Even thinking about it made Wren sick. She was a product of force, of ravishment.

"I know what it is to feel trapped. To feel like there is no other way out." Her mother focused back on Wren, her expression grave. "We've made a good life here in the isles, with your father."

"Papa is a good man," Wren said. He loved her mother fiercely and had raised Wren as his own.

"He is, but I would spirit you away right now, if you wished it."

Wren's eyes rounded as she gaped at her mother. "What?"

Anneke held her gaze. "You and your sister are the most precious gifts I've been given in this life. I know you've made promises to Rowen, and that your father has certain expectations for your future, but they mean nothing if you want out."

"Do you think I don't want to get married?"

Her mother sat up and picked a leaf from Wren's dress. "No. I believe you love the boy. I just want you to know you will always come first, and, that if you have any doubts, I have a ship in the harbor we can board now."

Wren sat up and pushed her hair from her face. "You would leave Papa?"

"I love your father dearly, but it will never surpass the love a mother has for her child. I will do what I must to protect you."

Wren reached for Anneke's hands and squeezed them. To anyone else, her mother's offer would seem extreme, but, to Wren, it meant everything. Her mum had a dragon heart. No one and nothing would break the bond that they had.

"I truly want this," Wren murmured. "Any nervousness you see on my part is just normal marriage jitters. I've never lived alone with a man. It will be an adventure, to be sure."

Her mother's seriousness melted away. "I'm happy to hear it. I just wanted to be sure."

"Would you have really run away with me?" Wren asked.

"To the ends of the earth, Daughter."

"Papa would have searched for you."

Anneke quirked a smile. "He would have tried."

That put a grin on Wren's face. Her mother's skills at hiding her tracks were unparalleled. If she didn't want to be found, no one found her.

"Now we have got that discussion out of the way, I believe it's time to return." Her mum climbed to her feet, pulling Wren with her. "Our clothes will get wet if we lie here much longer," she told her daughter, lifting the damp hem of her dress to prove her point.

Wren chuckled softly. "It is hardly as if we will be wearing these clothes to my wedding," she said, picking at the sleeve of her threadbare shirt. She did not *need* to wear such rough, uneven quality fabric, but when she was running about, Wren did not see much point in wearing the higher-end garb. Why ruin someone's hard work or waste the gold?

Anneke snorted. "If I let you, I think you'd wear breeches to your own wedding."

"We do live in the isles," she pointed out. "Only elves have such strict fashion etiquette."

She dodged as her mother tried to flick her own rounded ear. While she was at least half elven, her rounded ears spoke of some human heritage, which was a blessing. The Verlantian people were known for their brutality, apathy, and selfishness. Wren didn't want to be identified as an elf.

"What would Rowen think of you if he could see you right now with twigs and branches in your hair?" her mum mused.

"He would probably be disappointed he hadn't put them there himself," she retorted.

"If you're trying to shock me, you'll have to work harder."

Wren winced. Her mum was a private person; however, she believed in education of *all* things, much to the chagrin of her father. Even now, there were some explanations and mental images she wished she could erase.

Brushing at her dirty clothes, she eyed the crushed plants beneath her bare feet. "I think Rowen would marry me just like this if I wanted it."

"I don't think he cares what you are as long as you are his by the end of the day," her mother commented wryly.

She blushed at that and patted her wild hair self-consciously. Dressing up wasn't a bad thing, but Wren just preferred a pair of trousers, lace-up boots, and a leather vest outside, because whenever she attended duties inside the keep, she had to wear dresses. That was the way her father had brought her up—like *a chameleon girl*, a trader from the mainland had once said.

She'd never seen a chameleon before, and when the trader drew her a picture of one, she laughed. The lizard had big, bulbous eyes, a shifty nature, and green scales that she was led to believe changed color depending on its environment, allowing it to all but disappear from view. Even now, she didn't know if the creature was real or if the old man had been pulling her leg. A creature whose color changed depending on where it was seemed ridiculous. Too magical. He had argued that dragons were supposed to be myths.

What rubbish.

Dragons were flesh and blood and bone, lurking beneath the waves or soaring above the clouds. There was no magic to them. They were simply creatures of nature.

"I would have thought Aurora would be bothering you by now," Anneke said, as if reading Wren's mind.

She scanned the beach and then the sky. Her dragon was nowhere to be seen. She was still awed that Aurora had chosen Wren to be her rider. Normally, a rider chose a dragon and had to conquer the dragon before they accepted the bond, but it had been clear from the beginning that Aurora had chosen Wren, too. They had bonded years before, when Wren had found the abandoned egg that hatched into Aurora. She had helped raise the dragon.

"I've no idea where she is," Wren said. Her dragon was practically glued to her side any time she ventured outdoors.

"I'm sure she'll show up soon." Anneke clapped her hands. "We should head back."

Wren nodded and tipped her head back once more to soak

up the sun. Lorne never got very warm, but a summer sun was still a summer sun. And though there were ever-present great gray clouds looming on the horizon, cresting over the mountains and threatening to expand across the sea, hopefully the sun would set before the storm hit. Plenty of time for it to shine over the ceremony.

All she cared about was marrying her best friend. She'd take him rain or shine.

She reached for her mum's hand, and they began walking through the moors toward the keep in the distance. A small shepherd's hut leaked curling smoke from its chimney as they passed by. Her mind drifted to old memories.

"Do you think Alec would have liked Rowen?" Wren asked, fleeting memories of the first man she once called father going through her head. She was sure he would have liked her husband-to-be. They were both salt-of-the-earth kind of men, after all.

"I like to think so," her mum answered. "He had a kind compassionate heart. I don't think there was a soul that Alec didn't like."

"I feel bad that I don't remember more of him."

"You were so very young when he died," Anneke replied. "When I fled to this kingdom, he was one of the few who showed me kindness, despite my Verlantian heritage. Alec offered me work, a place to stay with his family, and all the herbs I could take from his property. Never did he ask for anything in return." Her mum smiled. "As if that wasn't enough to make me fall in love with him, he cared for me when I grew gravely ill and never judged or scorned me when my pregnancy became apparent. We were lucky indeed to meet him and get to spend what time we did with him. The world is a grayer place indeed without him." A pause. "You were so young when he died, but I can still see some of him in you."

"How so?" Wren asked. For the longest time, she'd wished he'd been her true sire. Eventually, she came to the realization that it didn't matter if they shared blood—he had been her father through-and-through for the four sweet years they'd had together. They had been happy, Wren, Anneke, and Alec. They had been content.

"You have some of his mannerisms. It seems four years with him left an impression."

"Do you miss him?"

"The ache and pain are gone. I still long for his company and look back on our memories fondly." Her mother squeezed her hand. "He restored my faith in men. His love and generosity led me to your papa."

Wren still didn't know all the specifics of Alec's passing, but it had been swift. One evening he'd been fine, the next day he'd sickened, and by the third day, the life drained from his eyes. Wren knew her mother did not like to talk about Alec's death. Alec and Anneke shared fond memories, but his last few dark days were left in the past.

"I wish he was here," Wren said finally.

"Me, too," Anneke replied, her eyes gleaming with sadness. She had loved Alec deeply, but she had grown to love Wren's papa, too.

Wren loved her adopted father with his broad smiles and booming laugh, but it still hurt that Alec was gone and couldn't see her wed.

The breeze picked up, and she peeked at her mother. The scarf around Anneke's neck shifted, revealing the wraparound scars curling around her neck. Wren's thoughts darkened, and she focused her attention back on the keep.

Hate was a poisonous thing, but she couldn't help but hate the people who had done such a thing to her mother. The Verlantians had made Anneke so terrified for her life that she'd fled the kingdom. The northern dark elven kingdom needed to be dealt with. The people were cruel and untrustworthy and as sharp as their pointed ears. Their greed infected everything. It was only a matter of time before they waged war again for the isles.

Her jaw clenched.

They are not getting my dragons.

The Isles of Lorne were not huge, but they were wealthy and prosperous, thanks in part to the water dragons that bred there—and only there—and in even greater part to the black diamonds that were created from the underwater volcanoes which birthed Lorne itself. As a result, though small, the Dragon Isles were rich in fertile, verdant meadows and dark, volcanic soil. The black-as-night sand beaches were a sight to behold for any trader coming upon their shores, no matter if it was their first time visiting or their hundredth.

What the elves really coveted were the trade routes.

The oceans around the isles were too dangerous to traverse, so any vessel that wished to trade had to sail through the isles which the Lord of Lorne controlled.

Wren's papa.

He was a just man for all, but both the northerners and southerners hated his power of the trade routes. Which made the Dragon Isles a constant target of their enemies.

It was dangerous being related to the Lord of Lorne. More times than Wren could count, there had been an attempt on their lives or an attack on the islands.

That's when her papa had started paying the tithe, and it all stopped. At least, the very public attacks had. If she ever got her hands on one of those rock lickers, she'd...

"What is it, Wren?" her mother asked. "I can practically hear your thoughts from here."

"It's nothing."

"Out with it. You haven't been known to keep anything to yourself before."

She glanced at the wraparound scars that circled Anneke's neck once more. While Wren assumed that the scars were punishment for some perceived wrongdoing, her mother had never outright admitted what had truly happened. Pulling her hand from her mum's, she rubbed both her hands together and licked her lips, nervous at the mere thought of asking the question. Her mother was right; she never shied away from saying what she thought or wanted to know.

"Your scars," she ventured. "What...what happened to you? It must have happened before you reached Lorne. So wh—"

"Not all men are honorable." Anneke sighed. "The Verlantians enjoy owning slaves. Collars are quite the fashion statement."

Wren's hands curled into fists, and she wanted to hit something. Slavery was disgusting. No one had the right to own another human being. "They chained you like an animal?" she spat.

"Some things are best forgotten, Daughter. They cannot hurt me any longer." Her mum lifted her head high and jerked her chin toward the village, the keep, and the teeming mass of bustling people. "We should not talk about such grim things on a girl's wedding day. Our people will soon greet you. Let me give you one last hug before we are mobbed."

Anneke pulled her into a bone-crushing hug.

"M-mum!" She laughed against Anneke's neck. "I can't breathe!"

"I'm so proud of you, you know?" was her mother's response. Her voice was thick with tears. Wren's eyes heated. "You've grown into such a lovely lady. Fiery, like your hair, but so gentle and loving to your sister. I really could not ask for a better daughter."

The sentimentality was too much, and Wren pushed Anneke away in an exaggerated fashion, wiping at her watering eyes. "Who are you?" she mock-accused. "The mother I know would say I am the reason she has gray hair."

"You're not wrong," her mother quipped.

Wren snickered. "There you are. I was worried, for a moment, I would have to go hunting for my mum."

"Never. I wouldn't miss this day for anything." She held her hand out. "Let's make a pact not to cry anymore today, shall we?"

"Deal," Wren agreed, shaking her hand.

Anneke's eyes narrowed, and she scanned the edge of the moor. "How about collecting some flowers for the ceremony before we head back? All of your favorites are in season. The sun this morning has really helped them bloom."

Wren nodded eagerly; she was not quite ready to head back. "I can definitely agree to that." A shadow swooped over them. She held a hand over her eyes and turned her face up to the sky just as a telltale silhouette crossed the sun, becoming larger and larger above them as the dragon descended, stirring up grass, leaves, and flowers.

"And...it seems Aurora can, too," her mum commented.

Aurora was small and slight by dragon standards, though that did not mean she was not still giant. When she landed amid the flowers, the ground bumped heavily beneath Wren's feet, and she and her mother held on to each other to keep their balance until the earth was settled once more. Wren's dragon was resplendent, surrounded by the early summer flowers, her shimmering scales pale like the pearls that grew in the water she had been born in. They glowed in the sunshine. It was those very scales which made Aurora almost impossible to spot, both in the sea and the sky, which was deadly in tandem with the dragon's speed. No dragon who lived in and around the isles had so far been able to match her.

"You took your time," Wren chastised her dragon, closing the distance between them. She ran her hands over Aurora's muzzle and pressed her cheek to the slick scales. The dragon huffed out a breath in return, which ruffled Wren's hair. "Have you come to help us collect flowers?"

Aurora let out a series of whistles and clicks, which sounded odd outside of the water but were melodic and haunting beneath the waves. Wren had learned the language when she was young; almost everyone within the Dragon Isles learned it then. For what was a kingdom that coexisted with dragons if they could not speak to them?

The dragon stretched out and closed her reptilian eyes.

So that was how it was going to be.

"Fine, you big lizard. Just lie there in the sun."

Wren patted her dragon and joined her mother in collecting as many lilac, white, and blue flowers as possible. Together, they gathered: common chickweed, for they were delicate flowers with numerous leaves to bulk out the bouquets; giant knotweed, to add height; lousewort, white waterlilies, and heath-spotted orchids for their beautiful flowers; burnet roses to go around the edges; and lastly, violet pansies, some of them containing random yellow petals which acted as a startling and eye-catching counterbalance against the purple and white all around them.

Wren and Anneke sat beside Aurora to string them together to create garlands and flower crowns before Wren looped the leather rope around the assemblies and secured them to her dragon.

Anneke placed a delicate flower crown on Wren's head. "Daughter, the flowers look lovely in your hair. I can't wait for your husband-to-be to see you once you're all dressed up! But your papa will cry when he sees you."

"No more crying!" Wren exclaimed.

"I promised *I* wouldn't cry, but I said nothing of your father." A pause. "Are you ready?"

Wren fed a handful of daisies to her dragon when Aurora nudged her shoulder. "My stomach is fluttering like these flowers in the wind."

Her mum kissed each of her cheeks. "Nerves are good. They tell you that this is something you care about. That you want to get it right." She grinned at Wren. "Come on, dearest. We can't let the eldest Princess of Lorne be late for her own wedding. Your father would never let me hear the end of it."

CHAPTER TWO

WREN

The heat from the fire warmed Wren's skin. She stared at the dancing flames as Ethel, her handmaiden, brushed her tangled red curls. It almost seemed surreal that the wedding was today. From the moment she'd met Rowen at the tender age of fifteen, she'd known he was special. At first, he'd been a show-off who made her nerves grate together, but the more time she'd spent with him, the more she'd liked him. Wren wasn't really sure when she'd decided that she loved him, but one day it was just there, and it felt right. True, at nineteen, it was perhaps a little young to commit to such a binding promise of marriage, but it felt like she'd loved Rowen forever, and there was no sense in putting off her future with the man she adored, customs be damned.

She winced as Ethel pulled on her hair.

"Sorry, my lady," the handmaiden said.

Wren waved a hand through the air. Such was the life with hair as wild as hers. She paused and stared at her left naked wrist. Today, she'd receive her marriage mark. Excitement bubbled in her gut at the thought of Rowen's crest tattooed on the inside of her wrist. A feeling of smugness followed as she thought about her crest marking his skin. From today on, they would be bound, and nothing could tear them apart.

"If I may say so," Ethel said softly, "you're a lucky woman to marry the likes of the captain."

"Indeed, I am." Wren toyed with her robe.

Even though Rowen was older by four years, he'd waited for her. If it had been up to only her, she would have wed him two years prior. But the stubborn man wanted her to have more time to know herself. He could be so obstinate sometimes. Many would never see that side of him. For the most part, he was good-natured and goofy. Rowen was now first mate to the captain of the navy. But even that responsibility wasn't enough to make him more serious...at least on the surface. For Wren knew he deeply and seriously loved her and their country and would do anything to protect them both.

Her betrothed had a wicked sense of humor and an ability to swim with the dragons that Wren—and almost everybody else—had always been jealous of. She still hadn't been able to beat him at a race, and it ate at her. She grinned. But she could hold her breath longer than him, so she didn't feel too terrible.

"But he is even luckier because you *chose* him."

Wren reached back and patted Ethel's hand in affection. Her maid was one of her most precious friends. "Thank you."

"No need to thank me. It's the truth." Thunder rumbled in the distance, and Ethel paused in her brushing. "It's a good thing you got back to the castle before the rain started again, my lady. We'd never have dried you off in time for the ceremony!"

Wren laughed. "Let the rain come. I would marry outside in

the storm if I had to," she declared. A bit of water or dirt never hurt anyone. She meant it. Rowen wouldn't care if she walked down the aisle dripping from head to toe, looking like she had decided on an impromptu swim with Aurora. He always accepted her ever-changing moods with humor and grace.

The door burst open to her right, and Wren watched in amusement as Clara, her second handmaiden, bustled into the room, looking frazzled.

"You would not believe the chaos I just came from," Clara huffed, kicking the door shut behind her, her light-orange hair sticking to her sweaty face. She leaned back against the wood and flashed a smile at Wren, her arms full of fabric. "But, have no fear, I rescued your dress and not one inch is wrinkled."

"That's quite a feat," Wren remarked as her friend pushed away from the door and began to gently shake out the gorgeous swathes of fabric that made up the skirt.

"I can't wait to see you in that," Ethel said. "You'll look beautiful."

Clara glanced up from her work and winked at Wren. "I half expected your father to put you in a pair of leather trousers."

All three women burst into laughter.

Wren shook her head, which earned her a gentle reprimand from Ethel. "I'm sure he had that notion, but my mother steered him in the other direction."

"Your mother has been a good influence on him," Clara said, her sage eyes twinkling. "My mum used to say the keep was a filthy mess before he married the queen. He rarely even wore a shirt."

"What a barbarian," Wren teased. Even now, her mum was

barely able to keep the king dressed. That man loathed clothing. Said it was too confining.

"That he is, but that's why we love him. There's never been a fiercer or more loving king for the isles," Clara said.

"Don't let him hear that or his ego will get even larger," Wren muttered with a smile.

"Never, my lady," Clara retorted. "He has enough women to keep him in line."

That was the bloody truth. King Oswin was plagued by women. He was the eldest of five sisters, who almost all bore daughters. Wren had more female cousins than she knew what to do with. She eyed Clara and glanced at Ethel from the corner of her eye. These were her two favorite cousins. Sure, they were her handmaidens by title, but they were her best friends in all the world.

"How is my father doing?" Wren asked.

Clara arched a brow as she unbuttoned the back of Wren's wedding dress. "Trying not to lose his mind. I'm sure he was wishing he had a son at this point, so he could fade into the background."

"I'm sure." Wren massaged the back of her neck as Ethel began braiding her hair. "Not that he didn't try to make me into one."

The king may not have sired any sons, but he'd done his best to help raise his daughters and nieces with all the advantages afforded to men of the world. Wren hadn't minded; she enjoyed learning all the skills of the battlefront, how to hold her breath for minutes on end beneath the waves, and how to swim five miles without tiring, just as much as she enjoyed learning to read and write and dance and sing to the dragons. That was the way of the Dragon Isles. Your gender and sex didn't dictate what role you provided in society. Your skills did. Her mother had explained that it wasn't this way in the other kingdoms. In the Southern Kingdom, women were to be seen and not heard. Wren still didn't know how one could live that way. Just thinking of it made her want to rescue all the women and steal them away to the isles where they could be free.

"And my mum?" Wren asked, shaking off her thoughts.

Clara gently laid the dress on Wren's bed and walked back over to her, taking a seat on a small stool in front of the fire. "Calm and serene as ever. She handed Britta off to your father to keep her out of trouble."

"He has his hands full," Wren said wryly.

Her little sister was a handful on a good day. After so many years without children from their union, Britta had been a surprise for their parents. Wren was thirteen when her sister was born. As Britta grew, it became apparent that she was different from others. Speech didn't come to her as fast as other children her age, but her mind was so sharp. She could create intricate nets and finish puzzles faster than adults by the age of three. Britta had a habit of breaking things. At first her parents thought it was just a naughty habit, but the more Wren watched her younger sister, it dawned on her that it was something completely different. It wasn't that Britta was purposely being destructive, but that she was trying to figure out how things worked. Her brain needed something to keep it occupied. Once they discovered that, life became a lot easier for them all.

"My sister," Wren paused. "Is she okay?"

Clara reached out and squeezed her hand. "We all know she doesn't do well with a lot of people bombarding her. She stayed in her room most of the morning, and your father was taking her out for a walk just as I came up. I'm sure she'll be all right."

Wren nodded. Not everyone understood Britta's quirks. Her sister didn't like people touching her unless they were close family, and she was a quiet soul who preferred spending time with one person at a time. King Oswin had been a wonderful father to Wren, but when Britta was born, she'd changed him. He was much more compassionate and understanding for those who had been born with differences around him. Britta had made him a better king.

The thunder rumbled the pane of glass, and both Wren and Clara looked to the left, to the window that faced the bay. A fork of lightning flashed across the clouds closing in on the keep, followed by more thunder.

"Bloody rain. It was so beautiful this morning," Clara groaned. "I hope it doesn't ruin the ceremony."

"It's not as if many people are coming today, anyway," Wren countered. "The prior storm has been raging for days on end now. Everyone will have jumped on the small break of good weather to get their chores done." And she wouldn't have had it any other way.

A small ceremony sounded perfect to her. She'd never been one for fanfare, but there was no helping it when the daughter of the king—even an adopted one—was marrying. Wren could not find it in her to be disappointed that the storm had worsened.

It would not be Lorne if it didn't come with rain.

"Done," Ethel breathed.

Wren reached for her hair, and Clara slapped her hand away.

"Don't ruin all of Ethel's work," her cousin chastised. "Give us a moment to get you dressed, and then you can see the finished look."

"Very well," Wren drawled as Clara pulled her from her seat.

She groaned, rubbed at her rear, and then scowled at the old wooden stool. She'd sat on the uncomfortable thing for way too long. She glanced back at the bed and moaned when Clara held up an intricate corset and wiggled her brows.

"Not the torture device," she complained, even as she shed her robe and lifted her hands.

Clara slipped the corset over her hands and head, the cool silk settling down on her breasts, chest, and waist. "Think of it as wrapping paper. I know Rowen will," Clara joked.

Ethel gasped and placed her hands on her hips. "That's enough of that."

"Come on," Clara needled. "You're not so innocent as to how babes are created."

Wren grinned at her bashful cousin, who spluttered and then snatched hose and garters from the bed. She stomped over and knelt to help Wren put them on as Clara began to lace up the corset.

"Just because I have knowledge of something, it doesn't mean it should be talked about."

"It's a natural thing," Wren murmured.

"You're not wrong," Ethel said begrudgingly. "I just don't want to hear about Rowen and yourself." Her shy cousin mock-shuddered.

"I, on the other hand, want to know *all* about Rowen," Clara said cheekily, tying the corset tighter.

Wren tried to smack her cousin on the shoulder, but Clara danced out of the way and picked up a floor-length, see-through chemise from the trunk at the end of the bed. She carefully eased it over Wren's hair as Ethel finished tying the garters in place and stood. Her handmaidens reached for her wedding dress and held it out.

"You'll have to step inside it," Ethel explained.

Wren hitched up her chemise and carefully stepped into the dress. Fabric rustled as her cousins helped her slip her arms into the long draping sleeves that sat on the edge of her shoulders. She ran her hands along the deep-blue velvet bodice that cinched her waist and cut in a straight line across her bust.

"It's not as heavy as I thought it would be," she said, rubbing the midnight-blue velvet between her fingers.

"Your mother is a witch, I swear," Clara responded. "I have no idea where she conjured this fabric from."

"I love it," Wren whispered when she peeked over her shoulder at the flowing skirt that trailed behind her. There was no lace or gauze or revealing cuts to the fabric, but even without such mainland fashions, the dress was resplendent in its clean simplicity.

Her cousins spun Wren slowly until she faced the looking glass that rested in the corner behind her door. Her breath caught. The jewel-toned fabric, coupled with her fiery hair and the spring flowers, was a sight to behold.

She looked like a true Princess of Lorne.

Her eyes watered, and she willed herself not to cry. "Thank

you so much for your help."

Clara and Ethel crowded in on each of her sides and kissed her cheeks.

A door-shaking knock interrupted the moment. There was only one person who announced his presence like he was coming straight through the door.

"Come in, Papa," Wren called.

The king opened the door and froze, his coffee eyes widening.

Her father cut a striking figure in his ceremonial, embroidered teal jacket, white lace-up shirt, and tartan kilt. The royal tartan was all blues and greens shot through with silver—a beautiful yet stormy sea perfectly captured in the color of the threads. King Oswin was only a handsbreadth taller than she, but he, nevertheless, was built like a barrel. Summer after summer, he tossed the tallest and heaviest of logs during the summer games, despite his age. His long black braids were pulled back into a simple knot, highlighting the strong angles of his swarthy face.

Her cousins gave her one last hug before exiting the room.

He stepped away from the door and closed it. He twirled his finger in a circle. "Let me see the whole thing."

Wren grinned and slowly spun around, so he could see her entire ensemble. She gave her father a smile and held her arms out to her sides. "Better than the navy uniform, wouldn't you say?"

"I've scarcely seen you in a dress since you've come into my home. It's easy to forget how you've grown when all I see you in is trousers and men's shirts." He swallowed and rested a hand over his mouth, his eyes glassing over with tears. "Daughter, there aren't words for how beautiful you are. What a lovely woman you've grown into. Come here, love." He held his hands out.

Wren closed the distance between them and hugged her father. He held her tightly and pressed a kiss to the top of her head.

"How has this day come already?" he whispered. "Only yesterday, you were my little shadow, causing mischief everywhere in the keep."

"Don't worry, Papa," she answered. "I plan on causing a lot of mischief in the next few years."

"That I don't doubt." He laughed and released her, wiping at his eyes. "Rowen has no idea what is in store for him."

The king took her hand and led her to the chairs that bracketed the fireplace. He helped her sit and then knelt to make sure the train of her dress wouldn't get wrinkled. Affection warmed Wren.

She wriggled her brows at him when he stood and took his own seat. "Playing the lady's maid?"

Her father grinned, his white teeth stark against his skin. "Your mum would have my head if you rumpled that gown. It was for my sake as much as yours."

"I already was threatened by her this morning not to show up in trousers."

"Sounds like her. Would have been easier," he commented.

"I'll say." Wren grimaced as she shifted. "You're not the one wearing a corset."

"I do not envy you, Daughter. Women's fashion is a

nightmare. Sounds damned horrific." Her father's smile faded. "You do know I never wanted you to *be* a boy, don't you?" he asked, a frown of concern furrowing his brow. "I admit I may have gotten overeager in my attempts to train you like one—"

"Stop right there, Papa," Wren cut in. "I'm glad I didn't have to grow up as a stereotypical girl. I could only be who I am today because of you. How can I be anything but proud to be your daughter?"

The king's gruff face softened. "It is *I* who am proud of *you*. I could not have asked for a better daughter. You, Britta, and your mother are the lights of my life. You and I may not share blood, but you are mine in every other way. I hope you know how precious you are."

"I do not care for blood," Wren said. "Adopted or not. I do not care. We are a family, and that is it."

Her father's shoulders finally relaxed, though he still sat stock-straight in the chair—years of military training. "You're just at the beginning of your life, Wren," he said, his eyes shining, pride clear in his expression as he regarded her. "You have so many choices ahead of you. I cannot wait to see what you do."

They settled into silence, listening to the fire crackle and the storm grow closer. Wren closed her eyes and savored the moment. When was the last time she was able to spend time with her papa, just the two of them?

"Wren?"

She opened her eyes and studied his serious expression. The king sat forward in his chair, his hands clasped together, lips pressed together. It was a look that didn't bode well. Her gut clenched. What was wrong?

"Father? What is on your mind? I can tell something is troubling you."

"So astute. You've always been like that—able to sense other's emotions." The king rubbed his forehead and gave her a weak smile, shaking his head. "Today is a happy day, and I don't wish to make it otherwise."

A chill ran down her spine. "Tell me."

"As you know, our foreign negotiations aren't the best right now."

"When are they ever?" Wren wrinkled her nose. "You know how I feel about the damned tithe. What more do the Verlantians want from us?"

"Our kingdom."

And that was the ugly truth of it. The elves wanted control of the Dragon Isles. "Well, they're not getting it."

The king gave her a wider smile. "No, they are not," he murmured, looking at the fire. "I want you to enjoy this day, love, because the days coming may not be so easy."

Wren scooted to the edge of her seat and held her hand out. Her father grasped her left hand between his own and squeezed it twice. "No matter what, I am with you. Just because I will be someone's wife, it doesn't mean that I'm not your daughter or your rider. My sword is yours."

"I know that." He released her hand and cupped her cheek. "If things do not go well, do you remember the plan?"

Wren nodded. She was to get her mother and sister out of the keep and flee. She planned on getting her family to safety, but she wouldn't flee. Ever.

"I believe everything will work out, but you know how I like to be prepared."

"I know, Papa."

"Good." He released her and stood. "Are you ready to go? We don't want you to be late."

"You sound like Mother. She's been hounding me all day." Wren moved past the king and gave herself a final once-over in the mirror. She flicked a glance at her father, who stared blankly at the door. He was keeping something from her. Today, he didn't want to burden her, but, within the next couple of days, she'd needle the problem out of him.

Wren adjusted a few flowers in her hair before facing her papa.

"You ready?" he asked, giving her a warm, reassuring smile.

Butterflies took flight in her belly as her nerves returned with a vengeance. She closed her eyes, took a deep breath, and counted to three. Wren opened her eyes and nodded, going to her father when he opened the door and held his arm out to her.

She slipped her arm through his as he led her out of her bedroom for the last time.

"Let's go."

They descended the stone stairs slowly. Wren ran her fingers along the polished black stones of the wall as they reached the ground floor, the scent of spiced pies, apples, and savory meat in the air. Lorne Castle was not huge, by any means, but it was beautiful in its own way. The keep was grand and sturdy in its polished black stone and vaulted internal wooden ceilings, and, beneath the hewn floors, were a complicated series of underground tunnels, which were the true strength and defense of the castle.

She ran her left hand against an old tapestry as they strolled by, noting the draft. That was another secret of the Lorne Keep that she delighted in. The secret passageways. Even if the enemy managed to infiltrate the keep, they would never be able to figure out the labyrinth of interconnecting, hidden hallways.

"I can see your mind running," her father commented.

Wren glanced up at him sheepishly. "Just thinking about secret passageways."

The king rolled his eyes. "Mischief."

She grinned impishly as he led her from the tower that housed her bedroom and out into the blustery courtyard. The thunderous applause of townspeople calling her name crashed over her. All manner of flowers were thrown her way: blue, green, red, violet, pink, yellow, orange. Wren waved to her people, who were as brash and colorful as the flowers littering the ground.

They waded through the crowd, and Wren released her father when she spied her nanny Mary and Mary's husband Liam, the dragon master. The couple rushed toward them, and her nanny pulled Wren into a bear hug.

"You look so beautiful, my girl!" Mary cried, tears running down her wrinkled face.

"You'll ruin her dress, wife," the dragon master said, pulling Mary away. His gray eyes twinkled as he hugged his wife. "Don't let that Rowen get his way all the time, you hear me, lass?"

Wren grinned. "I hear you."

"You know how he can be with his food," the dragon master

clucked. "Fussy as a babe in—"

"Leave it alone, Liam!" Mary chastised, wiping her cheeks. "I'm sure the last thing she wants to hear on the day of her wedding is you complaining about her husband-to-be."

"On the contrary," Wren giggled, "It is helping a great deal with my nerves." She nodded in faux seriousness at Liam. "I shall make sure Rowen always eats his greens. But when has he *ever* gotten his way when it comes to me?"

Liam laughed uproariously and ruffled his white, curly hair. "I suppose you have a point. Oh, but what a sight you are today. A true princess, through and through."

"Such a bright, beautiful young woman," Mary agreed. "May your future with Rowen be long and happy."

"Thank you." She slid a glance toward her father. "I better head into the keep. Mum will not forgive me if we're late."

"Aye," Liam commented. "Best be getting on with ya."

Wren turned back to her father, allowing him to loop his arm with hers and usher her forward toward the main entrance to the keep. She looked at the spires of the keep with pride—the black polished stone, sea glass, and seashells made it formidable and stunning at the same time. It truly was a sight to behold—as was the great room that led to the chapel. An arched wooden doorway the size of a whale's ribcage marked the entrance, capable of allowing six people astride to walk beneath it.

The king drew to a stop by the heavy wooden doors and kissed Wren's cheek. "Are you ready?"

She stared up at her papa's soft eyes. "I am. Are you ready?"

"Never, love. A father is never ready to let his daughter go."

A surge of love filled her heart and warmed her insides. "I love you."

"I love you, too, Wren."

She faced the doors and straightened her skirt once more. "I'm ready, Papa."

The king signaled to the warriors bracketing the double doors. They heaved open the heavy wooden doors, and Wren and her father moved through the archway.

All her thoughts disappeared as she caught sight of Rowen waiting at the front of the chapel. Her nerves disappeared.

It was time to start the beginning of the rest of her life.

CHAPTER THREE

ARRIK

"Is it done?" Arrik asked quietly. He never raised his voice at anyone. He'd learned long ago that keeping his voice soft and low inspired more fear than any yelling ever did. Plus, he didn't want to be like his father.

"It is, my lord," Shane, his second in command answered. He was a tall burly man with more scars than Arrik and that was saying something. "The first ships have already made it into position."

"And the scouts?" he replied, eyeing the blasted storm. It would help give them cover but it was also a problem. It was perilous in of itself traveling through the Dragon Isles, let alone with a squall that threatened to dash them against the rocks or sink their ships with the sharp coral below.

"They've been taken care of," Shane confirmed, tossing his long black braid over his shoulder. "No one will be sounding the alarm."

Grim satisfaction filled Arrik. King Oswin had made a grave mistake crossing the King of Verlanti. The two kingdoms had held a tentative peace until the ruler of the isles decided not to pay his dues. He got too comfortable in his own strength, thinking that he could defy the elves. That was where he was wrong. No one defied the elf king and survived. It was a death sentence.

"And the palace?"

Shane grunted. "Your men are in the tunnels, waiting for the signal."

"Good." If all went to plan, it would be a relatively bloodless invasion. Arrik grimaced and brushed a piece of his stark silver hair from his face. That's if the people were willing. The inhabitants of the Dragon Isles were known to be barbarians. In fact, they even trained their women in combat. The very notation disgusted him and yet...it thrilled a very small part of him. A woman with fire was appealing indeed. "The royal family?"

"To be exterminated except for the heirs."

"Heir," he corrected. The islanders were secretive about the heir. The princess was to be married on this day. It was fortuitous for him. Arrik would have hated to leave her a widow. It was better for her if she wasn't attached to any man. His father would want her, either as his concubine or for other political intrigues.

Their ship groaned as the bottom scraped over some coral. He spotted several fins slice through the dark water. It was as if the beasts could sense the battle to come. Maybe it was a sign that there would be blood.

It didn't matter to Arrik either way. He was just a tool in his father's scheme to rule the isles. Everyone wanted them for their dragons, the diamonds, and control over the trade route. They held too much power. The King of Verlanti was a power-hungry monster.

And Arrik...well he was his father's son.

War was in his blood.

CHAPTER FOUR

WREN

A nervous walk down the aisle and a few whispered words, and that was it. After all the fuss, it was shocking how quickly the ceremony went by. Technically, the words were all a formality. They would only truly be sealed in marriage once their markings were complete and when they'd shared their first kiss as mates.

Wren inhaled deeply, Rowen's lemony scent filling her lungs. She glanced at the storm raging outside the windows behind the dais before looking up at her almost-husband. Rowen grinned at her as the holy woman gestured for them to face the crowd. Almost done.

She squeezed his fingers and smiled as he helped her face their friends and family, gently nudging aside the train of her dress. Her father stood from the first row; his deep eyes were glassy as he approached the dais. Wren's own eyes filled as the king took her left hand, and both men helped her to sit on one of the marking chairs.

She sucked in a breath as Rowen released her and moved to his own chair across from her. The king's hand settled on her shoulder as the holy woman set a table between Wren and her husband-to-be. Dara, the marking artist, rose to her feet and shuffled to the dais, a leather bag tucked under her arm. Bjorn Rowen's father, trailed behind her and took his place behind Rowen as Dara set her bag on the table and unfurled the tools and ink.

Wren eyed the wicked-looking needles and tried to regulate her breathing. She'd received two markings in her life, and, while they weren't horribly painful, she'd never been fond of needles.

"Don't pass out on us, lass," Bjorn said, a twinkle in his tawny eyes. He shook his head, and the movement emphasized how his black hair was streaked with white. Even at his age, he was a striking man. Not only that, but he was also still young at heart.

"Not planning on it," she murmured. *Hopefully.*

"You are looking a bit green," Rowen teased, his teeth bright against his swarthy face.

The crowd snickered.

"Shut up," she muttered.

"That's right, missy," Dara crooned. "Let him have it. No sense in letting him think he's getting a docile bride."

The king chuckled, giving Wren's shoulder a pat. "If he wanted a docile woman, Rowen would have run screaming for the seas already."

"Oh hush," she chastised, squirming just a bit in her seat. "Let's get this over with."

She laid her left arm across the table, wrist up. Dara's warm reedy fingers curled around Wren's hand, holding her still as the old woman lifted the needle. Wren locked eyes with Rowen.

39

This was it—the final sealing act of the ceremony.

No longer would she belong to one house, but two.

Not two souls, but one intertwined forevermore.

Her heart thundered with excitement.

Almost done.

From the corner of her eye, she watched as Dara leaned in, and then she couldn't help closing her eyes.

Thunder boomed, shaking the building.

Wren's eyes popped open. What the bloody hell?

Dara hesitated, and Wren looked around. Dust from the rafters fell from above, and, for a moment, everyone was still.

Bjorn seemed to shake it off first, his bushy brows furrowed. "What kind of storm—" But he broke off as another boom rattled the keep.

Wren's stomach dropped.

That wasn't thunder, but an explosion.

Her eyes widened as she stared at Rowen.

An attack.

Another bang went off, the vibrations rattling her teeth in her skull. The tension broke, and everyone went wild.

"Everyone, out!" her father bellowed over the screams of frightened children. "Stay away from the windows and move into the cellar, now!"

Numbness kept Wren rooted to her seat even as Rowen shot up from his own, his normally jovial face set in harsh lines of worry and anger. A high whistle filled the air as he reached for her, making to grab for her hand but not quite reaching it as the next explosion went off.

The blast tossed her from her chair. Wren tumbled to the

ground. *Hard.* Her palms stung as she tried to sit up, her ears ringing.

"Wren!" Rowen called out over the sudden cacophony of panicked screaming. Rubble began to fall from the ceiling. The wooden rafters groaned and swayed ominously. "Run!"

Horror filled her as one of her friends was crushed in his flight from the chapel. She grabbed the hem of her dress as she staggered to her feet, the floor rolling beneath her. Her eyes watered from the stench of smoke and debris in the air. Where was her family? Wren searched the chaos, not seeing any signs of them.

Move, Wren, or you'll die.

She lurched toward the nearest doorway as the telltale whistle filled her ears.

Get to safety. Get armed. Then fight.

One, two, three steps...

An invisible force slammed into her, and she catapulted into the stone wall. Wren collapsed, darkness descending.

Pain, blood, and ash.

All three things clued her in that something wasn't right.

Wren groaned as she turned her head to the side and spat blood. What had happened? She forced her eyes open and cried as pain spiked inside her head. Immediately, she closed her eyes again and attempted to breathe through the pain.

Just what was going on?

Think, Wren.

Jagged pieces of stone dug into her back, making it difficult for her to focus. The last thing she remembered was the ceremony. Her brows furrowed, and she lifted a shaking hand to her pounding temple. Hadn't she just been married? The marking...

Opening her eyes, Wren lifted her left arm. A bare wrist.

Her memories flooded back. An attack. The explosions.

You need to move.

She rolled to the side, wincing when lights flashed across her eyes. Her stomach rebelled, and, somehow, she found the strength to push onto her hands and knees to retch. Her body convulsed, and her ears rung. She wiped at her mouth and scooted back against the wall. Her eyes teared up against the thick black smoke and dust that choked the air. The wind tugged at her hair, and she glanced to her right.

The entire wall was gone, exposing the chapel to the raging storm. What kind of weapon could blow through stone like that?

Her head gave a vicious throb, and she lifted her hand to massage the pain away. Vaguely, she registered rain pelting her skin as she pulled away. Her fingers were warm and sticky with blood.

A head injury. Not good.

She blinked a few more times as bright stars moved across her vision. She must not pass out. Even though her ears rang and the wind howled, she could hear screams and the dull ring of steel against steel.

Wren coughed and reached for the nearest beam. How long had she been out? Where was her family? How many were injured or killed? Where was Rowen?

Bile burned the back of her throat as she forced herself to her feet. She swayed and gagged as the wind pushed some of the smoke away, revealing the carnage.

No.

Not nearly enough people had escaped. Too many bodies littered the floor.

A grunt, followed by the clash of swords registered.

Wren jerked and moved farther into the smoke. The fighting was close. Too close. The enemy had made it into the keep. She jerked up the hem of her torn dress and pulled the short dagger from her thigh sheath, painfully aware that she needed something more substantial.

She pushed a wet strand of her hair from her face and once again pressed against the remains of the wall behind her. The smoke wasn't ideal, but at least it gave her cover, and, thanks to the wall, no one would be sneaking up on her from behind. A man bellowed to her left, and her fingers tightened on the hilt of her blade. She held perfectly still when she registered the silhouette of a warrior creeping in her direction. She didn't think he'd noticed her yet.

You have the element of surprise. Strike hard and fast.

He moved within striking distance, and the smoke dissipated some. Wren sagged against the wall, her eyes widening, dagger held to her chest.

"Rowen?" she gasped.

Her betrothed scanned her from head to toe, his eyes wild and far away, his bloody sword in hand. He motioned to keep silent before he took her right hand and led her through the smoke. She struggled to keep her steps quiet, but it was almost impossible. They passed through an arched doorway, and Rowen pressed her against the wall, his attention focused on his right.

"What—" Wren coughed, struggling to find her voice through the smoke. Her throat hurt so much; trying to speak was like having shards of shell stuck in her lungs.

He turned back to her, his face hovering above Wren's. He'd clearly taken a beating. Both his eyes were black, his lip was split and swollen, and dried blood covered the left side of his neck.

"Are you okay?" she asked, but he was just staring at her. "Rowen?"

"I thought you were dead," he rasped. His body trembled slightly. "I couldn't find you. I couldn't—"

"It's okay," Wren soothed, making sure to keep her voice low. "A blow to the head and bruises. Nothing more."

"You're covered in blood," he whispered.

"Head wounds always bleed more." She swallowed hard. "My family? Your family?"

"They all made it out."

She nodded, her head aching with the motion. "Who attacked? The Verlantians?"

"Yes." Rowen's expression darkened. "They broke the treaty. We've paid the tithe all these years, and yet, they still stabbed us in the back."

"We can talk about this later," Wren said, her own gaze straying back toward the ruined dais. "The blockade?"

"It's gone up. My father is down with the navy now." His jaw tightened. "They never should have been able to get this close."

44

Wren froze. Not unless someone led the enemy through the coral reefs. "A traitor," she breathed.

"It seems logical."

She'd deal with that bit of information later. "Is Britta safe?" she asked. Her younger sister was the only heir to the throne.

"Near your parents," Rowen said, pushing back to pull a bow and quiver from his shoulder. He held it out to her. "Can you run and shoot?"

"I have to." Wren knelt and sliced off the bottom of her dress so it wouldn't slow her down. "How bad is it?"

"Much of the battle has moved to the keep already. We need to get out while we still can."

"Rot it." No one had ever breached the Lorne Keep before.

"You ready?" Rowen asked gruffly.

"Where you go, I go," she said resolutely, standing.

He swooped down and gave her a quick bruising kiss before pulling away. "I've got your back."

A dark smile lifted Wren's lips. "Let's go hunting."

CHAPTER FIVE

WREN

Grim determination strengthened Wren as she ran through the wreckage, cutting down anyone that got in her way as she rushed toward her family. She stumbled only once as her comrades fell beneath the enemy's swords.

The Verlantian soldiers, with their pointed ears and black, gilded helmets which obscured much of their faces, fought anonymously and constantly, never seeming to expend much effort in their slaughter. It was as if they were inhuman. Perhaps they were. The dark elves were always the monsters no one wanted to speak about.

She had never seen a Verlantian before, and it struck her as odd how beautiful they were. Even covered in the enemy's regalia and the gore of her people, somehow they were ethereal and alluring.

Wren hated them.

Pretty monsters were all they were.

They were ruthlessly, hopelessly efficient. They were entirely impersonal. The crowd in the chapel were merely victims to be conquered.

She blocked out the cries of her people and focused on the

weapons in her hands. Wren was not useless, nor were her father's outnumbered warriors as they fought with everything they had to combat the pointed eared monsters invading. The people of the Dragon Isles had always been accused of being savages. Today they accepted the title with relish. They screamed as they landed blow after blow, fighting despite the wounds they sustained. Their war calls spurred Wren on, her blood boiling as she began loosing arrows left, right, and center with Rowen at her back.

Dark satisfaction filled her when she never missed her mark. More than a few Verlantian soldiers fell—or at least let out a cry of pain—when her arrows struck true. The vicious part of herself almost wished she had more time to take out all the bloody monsters as she reached the throne room.

Screams and the ring of metal against metal echoed around the stone room.

Her gaze snapped to the dais where her parents fought off a few soldiers.

Fear trickled down Wren's spine.

Britta wasn't with them.

Heart pounding, she scanned the room, chest heaving with rising panic. Where was her sister?

Calm down. They would have secured the heir above all else.

An arrow whistled through the air, and she ducked. It embedded in the scarred wooden door behind her. Rowen grabbed her from behind and wheeled her around.

"Found Britta," he breathed. "The table."

Her attention honed in on a table strewn with wedding gifts. One of the wrapped boxes had fallen to the floor, exposing its contents of delicate silver candlesticks and jeweled goblets for all the battle to see. A gift from the south, going by the craftsmanship. A little hand snuck out from beneath the tablecloth and pulled back one of the silver candlesticks.

Good girl. Britta knew to secure a weapon no matter what.

The little girl peeked out once again, her eyes widening in terror.

Wren had to get her out.

She edged toward the table, cursing as more elves filed into the room. They'd almost doubled in number. They were everywhere. Ceaseless, never-ending. Wren began to absorb the enormity of the situation she was in. It was grave. Likely, everyone she loved would not make it out of this situation alive.

Don't think that way. You will get out with Britta. You have to.

Wren gritted her teeth and soldiered on, fighting her way to her little sister. She cursed as an elf caught her upper arm with his blade and she dropped her arrow. Rowen took out the solider as she curled her hand over the seeping wound and made her way toward Britta. Her little sister gaped at the carnage and Wren was struck by how small and quivering Britta was. She wasn't even seven years old. Her wide green eyes were currently taking in horrors she should never have to see at such a young age. Tears coursed down her face as Wren and Rowen finally cleared a path to Britta. Wren threw herself beneath the table and scrambled beneath the tablecloth. Her little sister cried out and scuttled away.

"It's okay, Britta," Wren whispered. "It's just your sissy. Don't be afraid."

Britta slapped her hands over her ears and began to rock.

She was about to have an episode.

Wren set her bow down and wiped her bloody hands on her dress before she slowly scooted toward her sister. She held her hands out and smiled encouragingly.

"Come here, I have you."

Carefully, she reached out and touched Britta's scraped knee. Her sister flinched and stopped rocking.

"That's it, little girl," Wren crooned. "It's just me."

Britta's bottom lip wobbled, and she threw herself into Wren's arms. She clutched her sister to her chest and tried not to cry as Britta shook uncontrollably. "Hush, little one," she murmured, urging Britta to turn her head against Wren's chest and calm down—perhaps it would work this time. "It's all right. We will get out of here. Just focus on your breathing."

"We need to move," Rowen grunted, his silhouette just visible from beneath the table.

He was right. They needed to move. Someone would soon discover them.

She lifted the tablecloth and scanned the ruinous throne room. It was absolute chaos. Rowen fought in front of them, keeping the soldier's attention on him, not on who hid just behind him. In this moment, Wren had never been prouder of her to-be-husband. He grunted as an elf landed a blow against his side and she had to look away. Rowen was giving her this time to map a path of escape for them, not worry over him.

Her gaze latched onto a familiar head of hair. Anneke.

Her mum's dark hair had fallen out of its jeweled net, flying wildly about her face as she slashed around her with her favorite double blades. A surge of pride went through Wren at

49

the sight of her mother giving as good as she got; even now, with an adult daughter, the woman was still in the prime of her life. Wren had never, not once in all her nineteen years, thought of her mum as vulnerable. Even with her scars. Even with her gentle voice and calm nature. She was a force to be reckoned with.

Anneke dispatched her opponent and spun to meet her next attacker, but then an arrow lodged itself in her chest. Her mum's mouth opened in a silent cry before a soldier kicked her to the ground. King Oswin faltered when his wife buckled to the stone floor, watching helplessly as she lay there, struggling to breathe, before he began to fight all the harder.

"Mu—" she began, then snapped her mouth shut as Britta began to lift her head. Wren pressed her sister's face against her chest as she began to cry. Britta didn't need to see her mother like that.

Get up.

An anguished bellow cut through the cacophony for a moment. Her father screamed and roared and took down every Verlantian soldier between himself and Anneke. But it was too late. The life drained from the queen's eyes with every passing second, and between one blink and the next, she was gone entirely.

Wren clutched her sister to her and rocked back and forth, grief threatening to drown her. The sounds of the room dulled until all she could hear was her own heartbeat. They'd killed her mother. Her sweet, kind mum.

Avenge her.

She shook her head and cuddled her sister closer. Her

mum's sacrifice would be for nothing if Wren didn't get Britta out. She had to keep them out of harm's way until they could make their escape.

She locked her grief away. There wasn't time to take in what had happened. Plus, her emotions would make her weak and slow. Wren need to focus on protecting her sister from the enemy and from the heartache of what was taking place. The little one didn't need such horrors in her mind.

Rowen took down his last opponent and glanced in her direction. He'd carved out a small window of escape for them. It was time to leave.

"We're going to run, little one," she murmured into Britta's ear as she scooted out from beneath the table. "Keep your eyes closed."

Her sister's arms tightened around her. "Don't leave me."

"Never," Wren said fiercely as she got to her feet, Britta in her arms. She hardly weighed anything. "Here we go."

Rowen rushed forward and Wren shadowed him, hot on his heels. They weaved through the destruction toward the nearest corridor. The hair at the nape of her neck raised and she glanced to her left, locking gazes with her father. Time stilled as his dark brown eyes seemed to convey all his emotions.

Fear.

Rage.

Pain.

Guilt.

Love.

Love for her. Love for Britta.

The king opened his mouth as if intending to say goodbye, or to tell Wren to look after her sister, but the words he was about to utter became a choke in his throat when a sword erupted through his stomach. He dropped to his knees, and he smiled at her before he crumpled to the floor.

A scream lodged in her throat and tears rushed down her cheeks. Her steps slowed as she stared at her father's body. This couldn't be happening. Not both her mother and her father.

"Move faster, Wren," Rowen commanded.

Her feet felt like they were stuck in mud. She couldn't tear her gaze away.

Her to-be-husband's hand circled her wrist and urged her forward. His fingers squeezed and he insistently pulled her forward. Maybe if she closed her eyes this would all be over. It had to be a nightmare.

"Sissy?" Britta whispered in her ear. "You're crying."

Wren snapped out of her daze, Britta's shaking finally cutting through some of her pain. She swallowed down her sobs and clutched her sister harder to her body. She picked up her speed once again as they entered the smoky chapel that would afford them some cover.

She had to look after Britta. That was her main focus now.

Rowen released her wrist and attacked a solider that appeared from the gloom. The elf didn't even have a chance. Wren didn't even break stride.

A few moments felt like hours as they managed to cross the chapel unimpeded, a path cleared before them as Rowen cut down any threat. He flanked them with wild efficiency. Their escape loomed before them, and a thread of hope wrapped around her heart. They were going to get out. Wren followed her to-be-husband through the thick cloak of smoke and dust toward the exit. Her parents' sacrifices would not be in vain. They could do this. She could do this.

A dark elf appeared on Wren's left, lifting up his sword. Her mind stopped as he swung. This was how it ended. Like a fool she'd left her bow by the table. Wren covered Britta with her body. At such close quarters, she probably would not have been able to fire an arrow in the first place. She moved so that her sister was protected by her body and closed her eyes, surprisingly calm.

There were worse ways to die.

But the gleaming, wicked metal never hit her head.

Wren opened her eyes.

Rowen stood between her and the soldier, having taken the blow. She cried out at the mess of blood. He'd taken the sword squarely in the chest. There was no coming back from this.

"No!" she screamed.

Her to-be-husband shook off the blow as if it was nothing and lurched forward, making quick work of the surprised solider who had sought to dispatch her. Rowen's lips curled into an animalistic snarl as he wrapped an arm over his wound and pushed her forward until the three of them reached the exit.

Rowen stumbled and fell to his knees.

Her legs gave out and Wren collapsed to the floor, letting go of Britta so she could place her hands on her to-be-husband's chest to inspect the damage the Verlantian soldier's sword had done. The blade had just missed Rowen's heart, but he'd lost too much blood. Too much damage had been done to his insides.

Her hands shook as they hovered over his wound. "You're going to be fine," she said, tears dripping down her cheeks. "Just a little bit farther. Can you stand?"

He grabbed her right hand and placed it against his cheek. "My love, you need to leave me."

Wren shook her head. "No, we can do this."

"*Wren.*"

"Don't use that tone with me," she snapped, her bottom lip quivering. "You're not going to die."

He huffed out a wet laugh and then wheezed. "Always so stubborn. Look at me."

She lifted her gaze from his wound to his dear face.

"Go," Rowen heaved, eyes dangerously glassy as his fingers fumbled to find Wren's left hand. She squeezed his fingers far too tightly; her beautiful soulmate, with his dark hair and swimmer's soul and caramel eyes, had been reduced to a brutal, bloody mess. It wasn't right. None of this was right. "Take Britta and—and *go.*"

Wren shook her head miserably. "I cannot leave you. Britta and I—we can carry you. We can—"

"*Go.*"

"Rowen—"

"Blast it, woman, do you want our last words to each other to be our first argument as husband and wife?" he cut in, his dark humor not leaving him even in his final moments. She cried harder, vaguely aware of her sister clinging to her. It only made Wren cry more.

"Almost husband," she hiccupped, trying to joke.

Rowen turned his face and kissed the palm of her right hand. "It may not be legal, but you are the wife of my heart. I will always love you, Wren."

Britta began cry to, the sound crescendoing into a wail. Rowen turned his attention to the little girl and gave her a warm smile.

"It's alright, little sister. I'll see you soon."

Wren sobbed as Britta released her and hugged Rowen. The man's glassy eyes softened, and he squeezed Wren's hand with all the strength he could muster—which wasn't much at all. "I thought I smelled too yucky for hugs, Britta."

Her sister sniffed. "You still smell like fish."

He chuckled which ended up in a pained cough. "It's in my blood I suspect." Wren pulled away as he pressed a kiss to the top of Britta's head. "I need you to be brave, little one, and you need to mind your sister. Can you do that?"

Britta nodded and pulled back; her dress now soaked with blood.

"Good. You be a good little dragon."

Britta pushed back and pressed her face against Wren's side. Wren didn't know how to move on. Her future was dying right in front of her.

"I don't know how to leave," she rasped.

Rowen gave her a soft smile, his pupils blown too wide. "You get up and walk away."

"I don't have the strength."

"You're the strongest person I know. That's why I love you.

Now leave me. Save your sister and yourself."

"This is not goodbye," she insisted, desperate to believe her own empty words. "It isn't. I love you. We shall see each other again, and soon."

"I don't doubt it," Rowen said, clearly lying. He coughed, and it was full of blood, and Wren's resolve faltered. "Go," he muttered again. He let go of Wren's hand.

She hauled Britta back into her arms and she forced herself to her feet though her legs shook. "I'll be back," she murmured.

"I'll be waiting."

Wren blew him a kiss and then turned on her heel, fleeing down the darkening corridor with Britta in her arms. Every step she took seemed to carve another piece of her heart away.

"I'm sorry, sissy," Britta sniffed.

Wren licked her lips and pressed a kiss to the top of her little sister's head. "So am I."

Tonight, she'd lost the love of her life and her parents.

But she'd not lost everything.

She hugged Britta closer to her chest.

She still had her sister.

CHAPTER SIX

WREN

There was no time to comprehend what she had just lost. All Wren knew was that she and Britta had to run, run, run. Away from the noise and the danger. Away from the swords and the steel and the blood.

Away from their parents.

Away from Rowen.

"We can't leave them," Britta cried as they fled the chapel. "We can't leave Mum and Papa and Rowen. If we don't save them, they—"

"We have to get you out," Wren cut in, not meaning to be so harsh with her little sister but finding it impossible to be gentle. Her grief hurt so much. "If we stay, we'll die."

"That isn't true! We can fight—"

Wren clamped her sister's mouth shut, half to stop her words from filling her ears and half to silence their escape across the courtyard. They had to remain as quiet as possible to re-enter the castle unseen and unheard. The hidden underground passages were their only hope of escaping with their lives. Hopefully, all of them hadn't been breached by the enemy.

She pulled in a deep breath before crossing the courtyard. The elves were everywhere. Tense and frightened, Wren kept to the shadows, her heart galloping as the sounds of fighting filled her ears. The storm whipped her torn dress against her bare legs, and Wren squinted as Britta's loose hair flew into her face.

The skies broke open once more and she shivered as heavy rain drops fell from the darkened sky. She grimaced as her feet slipped in mud and Britta's arms tightened around her neck. Wren paused next to the servant's entrance and kicked off her shoes. She wouldn't leave a trail for anyone to follow. Her sister shivered and began to cry softly against Wren's shoulder. She kissed Britta's now-sodden blond head.

"Be brave just for a little while longer," she whispered to her sister before checking inside the entrance. The lanterns were dark, and no one was about.

Now or never.

Wren rushed through the room and down the corridor, sprinting toward the kitchen. They were almost there. Behind them, a banging noise from the courtyard alerted them to the presence of more Verlantian soldiers closing in. Wren ruthlessly shoved down the panic that threatened to drown her. There was no time to waste: a secret entrance to the underground passages through the larder was their best bet for escape.

Get to the larder. Get to the larder. Get to the larder. One more step and then you're there. Just one more, and one more.

It was a bloody miracle that they reached the larder without Britta slipping into one of her fits, or Wren losing her composure. She closed the door behind them and edge through the room. It was well-stocked and heaving with the produce of summer. Her pulse ratcheted up a notch as a series of curses echoed in a nearby corridor.

It was only a matter of time before they would be spotted if Wren didn't move faster.

With strength she didn't possess, she hauled her sister closer and ran to the end of the larder.

"I have to put you down, little dragon," she whispered to Britta. With shaking hands, she put her sister down for just a moment, breathing heavily as she struggled to lower a wooden shelving unit to the floor, pears and apples tumbled across the floor. She winced at the noise and wasted no time in rushing behind the hidden door the shelf revealed.

"Are we going to hide?" Britta asked, watching Wren close the door behind them and barricade it shut with the curious innocence that only a six-year-old could have in the face of danger.

Wren knelt in front of her sister, so their eyes were level with one another and held her sister's tiny hands in her own. "No," she said. "We are not hiding, Britta. We are going to run away."

"To where?"

"Anywhere but here. Anywhere but here will do."

Wren didn't have it in her heart to admit out loud that she did not know where on earth they could go. She helped Britta through and then righted the shelf as best she could. It wouldn't hide the entrance very well but maybe it would give them enough of a head start. Wren squeezed into the gap between the door and the tunnel and closed the door.

Her sister whimpered and Wren picked her back up. Even though her arms screamed it was better this way. Britta hadn't memorized the passageways yet and would only slow their escape.

For several torturous minutes, Wren stumbled through the darkened tunnels, not daring to light any of the torches in the sconces for fear of giving their position away to anyone who might be lurking in the passageways.

Her lungs and legs burned.

Wren slowed and deposited Britta on her feet. She handed her sister the ruined edge of her wedding dress.

"I need just a little break," she panted. "Don't let go of my dress."

"Okay." Britta's voice wobbled.

"You are doing amazing. What a brave warrior you are," Wren encouraged softly as she began to walk forward, ears straining for any noise.

"Your dress is wet and sticky," her sister whined, hysteria coloring her tone.

"Just a bit of water and maybe some dirt." *Probably blood.* "Do you remember what mum used to say? A little bit of dirt never hurt anyone."

"It's ruined," Britta whispered. "Your pretty dress. Papa said it cost a fortune."

Wren bit her bottom lip as it quivered. She didn't want to think about her wedding dress, nor why she was wearing it. If she did, everything that had gone wrong today, and all that she had lost would overwhelm her. She'd be lost.

You are lost.

No, she would not think like that. She would let her and Rowen's last words to each other ring in her head. *They would meet again. Again, and soon. He was not gone.*

The ground began to slope upward, and Wren slowed their pace. If her memory served her right, this tunnel exited on the very fringes of the town surrounding Lorne Keep. She ran her left hand along the uneven surface of the wall and stopped when she felt the edges of a door. Britta bumped into the back of her legs and Wren leaned her left shoulder into the door. It gave way with a groan that was far too loud.

Wren pulled Britta in after her.

"Something is in my hair!" Britta exclaimed. "Is it a spider?"

The very thought made Wren sick. By the tides, she loathed those eight-legged beasties. She closed the door and brushed at the top of her sister's head and flinched when webs caught on her fingers.

Don't think about it. Elves are worse than spiders.

"All done. No spiders," she lied.

They continued up the sloped hallway, as a little bit of light filtered in from another doorway just ahead. Wren held her fingers to her lips as she caught sight of the fear of Britta's face. No explosions or fighting could be heard from the tunnel. Could it be that the fighting hadn't reached the common people? Wren prayed it hadn't.

She took a deep breath to ready herself. Britta emulated the action, clearly deciding that the best thing to do was to directly copy her big sister. It filled Wren's heart with affection, which only served to enunciate the ache in her chest. She gave the little girl a smile and grabbed Britta's hand, trying to ignore how badly her own shook, and approached the small door.

She leaned her ear against it and listened.

Silence.

"Thank the dragons," Wren breathed.

She pulled the door back and stooped to move through it, Britta her silent shadow. Her skin pebbled as her bare feet met the cold slippery cobbles of the street, well more of an alley. They'd made it out, but they weren't safe.

Hand in hand, she and her sister ghosted down the darkened alleys. The hair at the nape of her neck stood on end. It was too quiet. The town seemed like it was empty. Wren tipped her head back to eye the storm. The dark cloud boiled in the sky and the wind howled, turning the world into an odd shade of gray and blue. Since her wedding, it felt like an eternity or mere seconds had passed. How much time had really gone by since they escaped?

Had it been an hour since she'd said her vows? Three?

In fact, the whole ordeal seemed like a dream.

Or a nightmare.

They rounded a corner of the nearest home and the wind and rain blasted her. She clenched her teeth and tried to see through the rain. The typically stormy weather of Lorne was something she was used to, and she welcomed it. It would give her and Britta the cover they needed to flee through the streets, and hopefully wash away their trail.

The faint rumble of a far-off explosion set her on edge.

They couldn't stay in the town. The Verlantians would search the area immediately. Britta wasn't safe there.

"I'm c-cold," Britta chattered.

"I know, my love," Wren said, kneeling to hug her sister. "Soon we'll be nice and warm and safe. Just a little longer. Can you do that for me?"

Britta nodded, her little body shivering.

You need to get her warm.

Her sister was the only true heir to the throne, and so she had to be protected above all else. It would do no good if they escaped only for Britta to catch her death in the elements. Wren wiped the rain out of her eyes and pulled away.

Even if Britta hadn't been heir to the throne, Wren would have considered her sister's life more important than her own, anyway. She was a wee babe, after all. A child. An innocent.

Where can you take her?

An idea hit Wren: Rowen's grandparents.

They were shepherds, just like Alec had been all those years ago. They loved Britta. They would protect her. They would save her. She would not be found living up in the hills with them, hidden from knowledge and sight.

Britta was too small and weak to wade through the moors that separated the edge of the town from the hills, so Wren once more took her in her arms, though her muscles were sore and tired and protested heavily against the previously inconsequential weight of her little sister. She was so tired.

"I can walk," Britta insisted, seemly sensing her sister's struggle. "I can, so—"

"You will fall into a bog, and I shall never see you again," Wren countered, holding her sister closer, and that was that. "I refuse to give you up to the toads," she said lightly.

They crossed the moors in silence, Wren wishing she had a heavy cloak with which to protect herself and Britta from the rain. Her sister began to cry and eventually fell asleep, her warm breath puffing against Wren's neck in a steady rhythm. Poor thing had gone through too much tonight. Her sister would not truly comprehend everything that had happened today for quite some time.

Stars, Wren couldn't even process most of it, but it was clear Britta at least understood that something horrible and unchangeable had occurred. Her parents were gone— whatever *gone* meant to a six-year-old—and they weren't coming back.

Wren began crying, too.

Though she couldn't feel the tears drip down her cheeks, they were there all the same.

She flinched every time a dull explosion rumbled through the air. It was wrong to run from a fight, she felt that in her bones, but family was more important. Their kingdom was more important. If Britta was lost, the isles would forever be in the clasp of the elves.

A mournful cry of a dragon caused her tears to come faster.

It was the sound of death and heartache.

How many had they lost?

Too many.

A dragon swooped above them, and she looked up to catch dark green scales before it disappeared into the storm. Part of her indulged in the idea that it was protecting the princesses of the Dragon Isles, though in truth it was more than likely unsettled by the commotion—or being ridden by warriors responding to the Verlantian soldiers.

Her chest moved up and down with her heavy breathing as she moved toward the forest, a little home nestled at its edge. A hill rose to the right of the home, giving it shelter from the weather. Once she got Britta settled, Wren would climb the hill and call for Aurora.

With whatever energy she had left, she had to defend the kingdom—to lead the navy in her father's stead. It was all she could do.

All *anyone* could do.

A face appeared in one of the windows and the cottage door flew open.

"Is that—oh my! Wren! Britta!" Rowen's grandmother, Aileen, cried from the open doorway. "You'll both catch your death. Come inside!"

Wren finally staggered to their cottage and Aileen slammed the door closed, making sure to secure it. Hope and worry warred on her face as she spun to face them. She reached for a blanket and threw it over Britta's back.

"What has happened?" Aileen demanded.

"Invasion."

"Where are your parents?"

"Dead," Wren bit out, unable to soften her words. "All dead. Verlanti—they attacked us. At the wedding. Oh, Granny, I am so glad the two of you were not there." At this, Rowen's grandfather Cal appeared beside his wife, his lined and weathered face pale with concern. It had been too much to expect the two of them to traverse the bad weather to reach the castle for the wedding. Wren and Rowen had always intended to fly upon Aurora's back to visit them after the feast and celebrate privately, together. Their old age had saved their lives.

"My grandson. Where is he?" the old man said, though it was clear from the look on his face that he knew exactly what had become of Rowen.

"He fought to get us out," was all Wren choke out.

Britta roused and began to cry again.

Aileen dropped the shawl she held and covered her mouth with her hands, her eyes filling with tears. But she did not say anything—did not cry out in grief and despair or yell at Wren for not doing more to save her precious grandson. Instead, she picked up the shawl and wrapped it around Wren's shivering shoulders.

"Let's get you warmed up," Aileen rasped. "Cal, would you heat up some water? The wee one is far too cold."

Cal and Aileen busied themselves with finding blankets and clean clothes for Britta and putting soup on the hob to heat up. The couple seemed to understand that it was imperative to keep the small girl in good spirits. Well, as good as her spirits could be, given the circumstances. They made tea but Wren couldn't drink it. The thought of consuming anything made her want to vomit.

"You must both stay here," Aileen said, as she tested the soup before pouring it out into four wooden bowls for everyone. Wren took hers with a wordless nod of thanks and set the bowl on the floor as Britta huddled into her right side, finally warming up. "We will all be safe here. If everyone is...if our family is gone as you said, then not a single Verlantian soldier will know that Cal and I exist. They will not know to look for you here."

"Aye, and we'll fight off anyone who thinks it's wise to knock upon our door," Cal chimed in, groaning as he sat in his chair, his gaze trained out the window, a bow resting across his lap. He ruffled Britta's hair, though she did not react. "We'll fight them off, won't we, lass?" he said. "We are all fighters. Nobody will harm us here."

At this, Britta finally seemed to brighten, and she began devouring her soup in earnest. The idea that all four of them would be together, in this little house she loved to visit so much with Wren and Rowen seemed to cheer her up. It was warm here, and there was food and laughter to be had.

Britta nodded; color high in her pale cheeks. "Fighters. We will not let them in."

Wren's heart melted at the interaction between Britta and Cal. Rowen's grandparents would take good care of her. Her sister would be happy here...after she processed her grief.

She peered to her left at Aileen, the older woman's gaze already upon her. She frowned and shook her head as she read whatever expression was on Wren's face.

"No," Aileen insisted, her sharp mind missing nothing. "No. Don't you dare go back out there, Wren. You must stay here. You must—"

"I must protect this kingdom," Wren said. "That is what I must do."

Britta slowly put her bowl down and wrapped her arms around Wren's waist. "Don't go!" She shook as her little hands clutched Wren's wedding dress as if she possessed the strength to keep Wren from leaving. "Don't go like everyone else. Stay here. I don't want you to go."

She lifted her sister's face and pulled Britta into her lap. "You know I must, little dragon. Father would never forgive me if I did not do everything in my power to defend his little girl, and his kingdom."

"You're also his little girl," Cal said, gruffly. "Wren, King Oswin would not want this for you. Stay here."

"Do you have any good stories?" Wren asked, changing the subject. Aileen nodded and pulled a book from the trunk that lay against the rear wall of the room. "Would you read us one?"

Aileen began reading and Wren rocked her sister, slowly carding her fingers through her black curling hair.

"I love you," Britta said, her sleepy eyes gazing up at Wren.

"I love you, too." Her sister sighed and snuggled closer, falling asleep almost immediately. "Where should I lay her down?"

Aileen pushed to her feet. "Our room."

Wren managed to stand and moved into the couple's room. She placed her sister's small form beneath the pulled back covers as Aileen stoked the fire in the room. Wren dropped a kiss on top of Britta's curls and closed her eyes.

This might be the last time you see her.

"I love you more than you will ever know." She gulped back her tears. "Some types of love can fade, change, or betray you. But not a sissy's love. That's forever. I'll come back for you, little dragon."

She opened her eyes and pulled the blankets up to Britta's chin and faced Aileen.

The older woman held out a change of clothes.

Wren took them gratefully and then grimaced. Despite how ruined her dress was, there was no way she'd be able to get out of it. "Would you help me?" she asked, presenting her back to the older woman.

Aileen tutted softy. "The knots are so tangled. It's going to take a while."

"Cut me out of it," she said woodenly.

"If you want me to." Aileen retreated and then pulled the top of the dress away from Wren's back. "Here we go."

She squeezed her eyes shut as the garment was cut from her body. It fell to the floor, and she stepped out of the ruined gown and quickly dressed in the new leathers. They were a little loose but better than her previous outfit. Aileen picked up the remains of Wren's soiled dress and held it out.

"Burn it," Wren whispered. "Or turn it into rags. I don't care." She strode to the older woman and kissed her cheek. "Care for Britta for me." With one last glance at her sister, she left the room and Aileen began to hum a lullaby.

Cal stood at Wren's entrance and approached her with an antique looking bow, a quiver full of arrows, and a flask.

He held out the drink and she took a slug of the whiskey, her throat burning. Cal took the flask back and had a drink too before handing over the weapons.

"I don't want you leaving this house, but if you must, you'll be outfitted like a queen."

Wren pulled the bowstring back, the tension almost perfect. She lowered the bow and ran her hand over the smooth wood. "Is this Aileen's?"

"No, lass. It was my mothers." Cal gave her a smile. "She was a fierce woman who had more courage than a thousand men. May her bow serve you well this night." He pulled her into a gruff hug. "May the winds be with you."

"And with you." Wren pulled away and opened the door. "I'll be back."

"I'll be waiting, lass."

She stepped into the storm and exhaled heavily as Cal shut the door behind her.

Time to avenge her family.

CHAPTER SEVEN

WREN

With every step she took toward the cliffs, Wren had to force herself not to look back at the ever-shrinking sight of Rowen's grandparents' house. If she looked at it, she would rush back to Britta—to warmth and safety—and then all would be lost.

Don't look back.

She did not look back, and the ragged black stone cliffs came closer and closer into view.

Turn your grief into rage. Fight for what you've lost. Protect those left.

Her guilt and pain stoked the ember of rage in her belly and Wren wiped away any lingering tears from her eyes. There would be a time to mourn. Today was not that day. Today, she'd wage war against her people's enemies and *win*.

The chilly air whipped her fiery red hair around her face as she approached the very edge of the cliffs. She closed her eyes and savored the howling wind that seemed as angry as she was. Wren would not be defeated. The elves would pay for what they'd done.

She opened her eyes and surveyed the battle below through the smoke and fog. Waterfalls tumbled down the sides of the immense black cliffs that formed the barrier of an enormous crescent shaped bay. The gusts from the storm crashed against the falling water, pushing the spray into a thousand water droplets that disappeared into the air. Ships bobbed in the angry sea below, the flash of cannons penetrating the fog.

Her lips curled.

How had the Verlantian ships made it into the bay? Such a thing should not have been possible. The reefs and their cannons to the north were their final defense—for the elves to make it this far south did not bode well for Lorne. Ships with the orange and black flags of the enemy spread out as far as she could see. Her heart sunk.

A full-scale invasion.

The shriek of dragons along with the low boom of the cannons filled her ringing ears.

Do something.

She would stop the invasion here and now. For her dead mother. Her dead father. Her beloved Rowen and, most importantly, for Britta.

You will not fail.

Wren moved with purpose along the edge of the cliffs until she came to a weathered set of steep steps that were carved into the side of the cliff. Only the most prestigious of Dragon Riders were even aware they existed. It was a precipitous decline. She grimaced as her bare feet scraped against the wet porous stone. Only once she entered the first cavern did her heartbeat slow. Her family had prepared Wren for this. There was no need to be afraid.

She exhaled heavily and strode through the cavern until she

arrived at the second staircase that was exposed to the elements. Rain fell from the sky, explosions rattled the stone beneath her feet, and the storm and battle raged in her ears. Her borrowed clothes chaffed at her skin, but it was better than her wedding dress. The garment would have made things more perilous than they already were. She picked up her speed, becoming surer footed, her quiver and bow together on her back.

On more than one step, her feet slipped from under her, and, for sickening moments, she truly believed she was going to fall to her doom before managing to do anything at all. But then her instincts kicked in, fingers grappling at sharp rocks and knees bracing her weight beneath her, and she managed to steady herself. But not without injury.

Wren hissed as she lifted up her left hand, inspecting the bloody gash across her palm. Just one more thing to blame the elves for.

By the time she reached the bottom of the cliff, her entire body trembled from the sheer exertion required to have descended such a narrow, slippery staircase. As she glanced up at the sheer height of the cliffs, she decided she didn't want to do that again any time soon. It was a bloody miracle she'd made it at all.

The ocean thundered against the rocks below, dousing Wren with sea spray. She backed away from its hungry waves to the hidden cave behind the stairs. The stone beneath her feet was smooth as she edged farther inside the teardrop shaped cave. She blinked hard to adjust her eyes to the darkness and made sure she stayed on the thin ledge of stone that surrounded the writing pool of water in the middle. Another spray of seawater pummeled her face, finding its way into her mouth. Wren spat it back out, though the tang of salt and brine within the water somewhat reinvigorated her. It took her longer than expected to locate a horn made of shell hanging from a leather cord in a small alcove. It was a conch shell, with beautifully curved spirals that tapered to a fine point along with three holes. It had weathered many battles and yet somehow remained in pristine condition. Her stiff fingers curled around the horn and she cradled it to her chest. She'd been told never to use it unless under the gravest of conditions—and there was never, nor would there be, a graver condition than now.

She brought it to her lips, placed her fingers over the holes, and began to play her dragon song.

The folktales told in Lorne said that the sound emitted from the horn was different depending on who blew on it. Wren had never quite believed this; she had heard other Dragon Riders use it before and decided it sounded very much the same as when she used it.

She blew on the horn until there was no air left in her lungs, and then she took a deep breath and blew again. She did not stop until the cave walls began to rumble. Her song echoed in the cavern and Wren prayed that it was enough. Her fingers tightened on the shell when a familiar hum reached her ears.

Aurora emerged from the pool of water.

"Oh, am I glad to see you," Wren told her dragon.

She placed the shell back into the alcove and rushed to the creature's side. Her dragon whistled and laid her head on the rock shelf of the cave. Wren dropped to her knees and hugged

Aurora's neck fiercely. In the swirling, stormy weather, the dragon was barely visible to the eye, even with Aurora standing right next to her. Her pearly scales took on the color of everything around her, making Wren feel as if the creature beside her was scarcely real.

"It's time to fight, my love. Are you ready?" she asked the dragon, placing a kiss on her snout. Wren pulled back and ran her hand gently over Aurora's brow. "We must be brave."

Her dragon gave a soft whistle and bumped her nose against Wren's chest. She hugged the beastie and allowed herself one moment of comfort. Dragons were sensitive to human emotion. Aurora always knew when something was wrong.

"They're all gone," she whispered the awful words out loud. Aurora whined and puffed a hot breath against Wren's stomach. "It's just Britta, you and me now." She inhaled deeply and released her dragon, steeling herself for what was to come.

Wren stood and rolled her neck. It was time to go. She whistled softly and Aurora perked up and pressed her side closer to the rock. She reached out to her dragon's frill as she climbed onto the beastie's back. Water soaked through Wren's pants as she settled between two spines of Aurora's crest, and for the first time all evening, she felt more like herself.

She stroked a hand along Aurora's sleek side. "Let's go," she commanded with a sharp whistle. Wren took a deep breath before the dragon dove beneath the water. She closed her eyes and held on tight as the tide threatened to tear her from Aurora. It was over as soon as it began.

The beastie broke the surface and jumped onto a tall rock jutting from the ocean. Wren shook the water from her hair and opened her eyes. "To the skies!" she cried.

Aurora's wings snapped out from her sides. Wren's stomach lurched as the dragon caught a draft of wind and launched into the sky. Her dragon hurtled through the air at such a sickening speed that euphoria filled Wren. She'd always loved the thrill of flying. Adrenaline shot through her as they approached the warring soldiers. Her father had trained Wren for this eventuality all of her life, but this was the first real battle she'd ever seen, let alone engaged in.

You will not fail now. You're made of sturdier stuff.

Wren urged the white-scaled dragon onward.

They reached the source of the flashes and bangs in good time. This close to the fight, Wren was able to see the shapes of the ships and the people aboard them, but then the blinding rain combined with smoke that grew ever thicker was painful. Her eyes and throat stung painfully. Sensing her discomfort, Aurora ascended high enough to escape the worst of the smoke, allowing Wren to truly see what was going on beneath her.

It was even grimmer than her first assessment.

The Verlantian navy had three times the number of ships as Lorne—and, going by the numbers out on the water, it was clear that just about every ship available to the Lorne navy had gone out to protect the Dragon Isles. There were a scant few out on a distant fishing expedition, but Wren knew they would not have made a difference in the grand scheme of things.

It was too much.

Upon the deck of the Verlantian ships, each and every soldier Wren could see were fully kitted out in shining metal breastplates and leather armor, with spears and bows and arrows and swords aplenty at their disposal. In a long-range attack out at sea, the Dragon Isle navy was unmatched. However, in a situation like this, where the Verlantian ships were so close, the soldiers were able to spill out onto the Lorne ships and attack hand-to-hand. The Lorne men aboard did not stand a chance. Their cannons were quickly being rendered useless by Verlantian soldiers getting on deck and destroying them.

Where are all of our Riders?

She swung her head around wildly to try to spot them. Then the sickening sound of a crossbow bolt whistled through the air to her right, and she saw a soldier fall from his airborne mount. The maroon dragon screamed and dove after it's Rider.

Wren gaped, heart in her throat. This wasn't how it was supposed to be.

A Rider flew by her side on her large, sage-colored dragon and screamed. "Get higher, Wren!"

Layra. Her commander.

Another bolt whistled through the air and Layra rolled with her mount and avoided the projectile. Wren nudged Aurora with the heels of her bare feet and her dragon soared upward as another Rider fell down.

Then another, and another, and another.

It did not seem to matter that the air was full of smoke and rain and fog; wherever the Verlantian soldiers aimed, a Lorne Rider fell from the sky. How did they see so well? She could hardly see the ships from the sky. Aurora circled the battle as Wren tried to work out whom or what to attack first. Most of the dragons were simply not fast enough to prevent the bolts from hitting *them*, either. The terrifying sound of one such creature screaming for its life tore at Wren's soul, before it fell in a heavy thump of wings and tail and teeth onto the prow of a Verlantian ship.

The enemy soldiers did not seem to care that the ship was quickly taking on water and would surely sink as a result of the fallen dragon: in a matter of moments, another ship had approached and settled side-by-side with it, and the soldiers deftly jumped aboard before the very deck below their feet sank into the stormy sea.

They were too organized.

They are going to win.

"Princess Wren?" someone screamed to her left. Wren and Aurora both turned at the sound of the shout. It was Jed, the captain of the navy, and his emerald-green behemoth of a dragon Sett. Wren had known the pair of them since she was a small girl, and she trusted them with her life. He always knew what to do.

"What's the plan?" she shouted over to him, knowing that the man was not going to insist that she leave the battle immediately.

He gave her a once-over and a grim smile. "It's good to see you alive, Princess." He pointed toward the Verlantian ship that had saved the soldiers from the sinking one.

"If we can take down that ship, then we can at least get some damage done before we're finished," he said. "Give our people a chance to flee."

Wren didn't like hearing that at all—that their defeat was imminent and inevitable. In truth, she had known that from the moment the Verlantians attacked her wedding. All she could pray for was to do some damage and hope to save as many people from the fray as possible.

She nodded. "Understood. What do you want me to do?"

"Aurora is faster than any other dragon we have under our control," Jed replied. "Act as decoy, so the rest of the Riders can avoid the crossbow bolts and coordinate an attack on the ship. Can you do that?"

"It's done." Wren could do nothing but growl ferociously. Beneath her, Aurora rumbled out her own response. "What use is the fastest dragon in the isles if we can't run circles around the Verlantian filth?"

Jed smiled, but it was more of a baring of teeth, pleased with her answer. With a nod, he turned from Wren and began moving the rest of the Riders into an attacking formation along with Layra. Wren took a deep breath, then patted Aurora.

"Let's do this, girl," Wren whistled, in the tongue of the dragons. Her voice was barely audible over the rush of the wind around her, but she knew Aurora understood. With the barest of nudges from Wren, the dragon spearheaded a sickening descent toward the Verlantian ship, Wren clinging to her mount for dear life.

Breathe, just breathe.

She knew, in all likelihood, that this would be the last day of her life. Her day. All she could do was protect Britta and slay as many of the enemy soliders as possible before the end.

"Let's do this!" she roared, just as Aurora careened out of the dive moments before she would have crashed through the deck of the Verlantian ship. Soldiers yelled and scattered with fright, and Wren was gratified to see that the enemy was so courageous when faced with the fearsome jaws of a dragon hurtling straight toward them.

They scrambled to aim a wickedly huge crossbow at the pair of them, clearly perturbed that they had not seen them in the first place. That was what Aurora did best: sneak attacks. Blindingly fast and almost impossible to see, her prey didn't know they were dead until they were.

We can do this.

Aurora climbed back up into the sky, her wings pumping hard. All they had to do was follow the years of training the two of them had undertaken together.

The first bolt fired was easily dodged. The second and third crossed paths in order to try to catch Aurora in the middle, but she dodged them, too. There wasn't enough time to fly out of range. Wren whistled.

With wordless agreement, Aurora snapped her wings closed and dove for the waves. Wren braced herself, pulled in a deep breath, and closed her eyes against the sting of the sea. They cut through the water smoothly. She opened her eyes and held on as Aurora swam beneath two enemy ships, the water bloodied and full of sharks. Aurora banged the bilge with her skull.

Even beneath the waves, Wren heard the cries of surprised and fearful soldiers in reaction to the tumbling of the ship. But then a cannonball came hurtling through the water toward them, and Wren pressed heels to her dragon, just barely managed to direct Aurora back out of the ocean before the deadly weapon could hit her tail.

That was too close!

She gasped for air as the soldiers scrambled to redirect their crossbows. "Higher!" she commanded.

Aurora's response was a mere click of her tongue, as if telling Wren not to worry.

The two of them repeated this series of actions three more times, Aurora diving down toward the deck of the ship only to swiftly back out at the last second, then going underwater to dislodge the soldiers and prevent them from firing crossbow bolts at the other dragons in the sky. Finally, Jed and Layra managed to lead a coordinated attack against the ship with four other Dragon Riders.

It was with sickening satisfaction that Wren and Aurora flew up higher to watch the carnage of the ship being torn apart by six fearsome beasts, the Verlanti soldiers helpless to resist. But the satisfaction of watching quickly dissipated. With six dragons all together, they made far too easy a target for crossbow bolts, and it wasn't long before a dozen were being fired through the air.

Wren scanned the smoke and fog to try and catch sight of Jed, but when she located the naval captain, her heart sank. He'd been shot through the heart with a well-aimed spear. And with no captain, Wren knew it was only a matter of time before the rest of the navy fell. This was a suicide mission.

Don't think like that. As long as one Rider is fighting, there is hope.

Once again, she shored up her nerves before directing Aurora down, down, down, toward one of the largest Verlantian ships. But they did not pull out of the dive this time;

instead, Aurora landed directly on the deck of the ship, the wooden boards groaning dangerously beneath her claws. Wren wasted no time yanking her bow from her back and loosing a slew of arrows, screaming alongside Aurora's roars as together they felled one soldier after another after another.

"If I am going down," she bellowed, hair flailing wildly around her face, "then I am taking you all with me!"

She meant every word of it.

CHAPTER EIGHT

ARRIK

A flash of red in the stormy sky caught Arrik's attention, but he knew better than to let it distract him. He focused back on the battle. It was a deep-blue massacre on the seas, where the only light to be seen was either a flash of white when a cannonball was loosed or the ugly orange of explosives going off.

"Commander, to your—"

Arrik did not need to hear the rest of his soldier's warning. For before his comrade finished his sentence, he swung his heavy axe around and caught his would-be attacker square in the forehead. The Lorne soldier had no helmet upon his head; the poor sod never stood a chance.

He stared down at the slain solider and felt nothing. Logically, he should have felt something. Guilt, fear, satisfaction. Arrik turned away from the man and scanned the battle.

Verlanti had been planning their invasion for a long, long time. Having to stand and listen to the 'negotiations' his father and his council pretended to go along with during peace talks with Lorne had been, at the very least, tragic. The country had been doomed from the start: how had King Oswin ever imagined he could keep his tiny kingdom full of black diamonds and impossibly valuable dragons safe from Arrik's covetous, war-happy father?

Part of him admired Oswin's determination, but the other part said that the Lorne king had been a fool. No one won against Verlanti.

What your father wants, he gets.

Now the King of the Dragon Isles was no more, as was his queen, and soon the heir to the throne would be in the grasp of the elves.

All Arrik had to do was wipe their navy clean off the map first.

He squinted as he spied the flash of red in the sky once more. It was getting closer now, closer, closer, and then, in one fell swoop, it disappeared back into the smog and smoke and clouds.

"A Rider," he murmured, before turning back to the far more pressing matter of securing their victory. One lone Rider could be dealt with later.

He braced himself against the railing of the Lorne ship he and his men had commandeered and wiped the rain from his eyes. Verlanti didn't necessarily need any more ships, but it was senseless to destroy an otherwise high-quality vessel when its occupants could just be tossed into the sea.

The Dragon Isles people were like rats. They could survive almost anything.

His father's motto was to take no prisoners.

Arrik had lived his life by those words. He'd made a career

out of it.

Prisoners made things complicated. Prisoners made things messy. Unless someone was the literal heir to the throne, there was little point in taking them hostage. Verlanti had enough slaves to last eons.

"Commander!" another one of his men shouted. "Dragons!"

Arrik pushed his wet braid from his face and tilted his face toward the sky. "Why were they not shut down upon impact?" he demanded. The Riders were supposed to have already been dealt with. "What are the crossbows for, if not to shoot down dragons?" It pained him to take down the dragons, but he had to do what was necessary.

The soldier pointed at something in the sky.

Another flash of red.

"That Rider kept the crew of the ship distracted," Shane called from the bow. "The dragon is too fast; every bolt thrown into the sky misses them."

Impressive.

Maybe he needed to rethink the policy of taking prisoners. A skilled Rider and dragon would be an asset. Learning the dragon's language, as well as controlling them, wouldn't be easy without an ambassador of some sort.

"*The Vengeance* is burning!" one of his men shouted, his voice barely carrying over the chaos of sounds.

Arrik gritted his teeth and glared at one of his burning ships. *The Vengeance* contained double the number of soldiers as their other ships. He'd already taken far more losses than anticipated. Verlanti would win, yes, but the losses were heavier than his father would accept.

He would not go unscathed for this.

But there was nothing to be done about it now. He'd dispatch their dragons and the Riders as swiftly as possible, then obliterate the rest of the Lorne navy.

Though it had cost them one of his larger ships and a considerable number of men, the dragons all being in one location for their attack was now to Arrik's advantage. He caught Shane's eye and, via hand signals, passed a quick series of orders along.

His second nodded and sent along the message.

All crossbows were to be aimed at the ship of dragons.

Arrik held his hand high and then dropped it, and a dozen bolts were sent flying simultaneously, sharply whistling through the air.

There was a certain amount of sadness as he watched the dragons try—and fail—to escape the deadly metal bolts by flying upward, only to be pierced in the wing, the chest, or the leg before inevitably crashing down into the sea. They were majestic beasts without greed, deception, or ambition. They didn't deserve their fate.

May the waters receive you.

A piercing shriek cut the air, and his attention was drawn back to that flash of red in the sky. It was almost as if the beast could vanish in thin air. The only way he could discern the dragon's location was when he caught sight of its Rider's blazing red hair.

"Shoot it down!" he bellowed.

He watched as the dragon and its rider came hurtling down at a frightening speed and, instead of diving back up, crashed onto the deck of the ship next to Arrik's. The dragon was smaller than most of its kin, and now, observing it against the wooden planks of a ship, he realized that its scales were an impossibly beautiful, pearlescent white, that seemed to reflect almost any color of its environment.

A stunning creature.

His gaze moved to the Rider.

All sounds ceased.

It was a woman.

Emotion rushed to the surface for the first time.

Her wild mane of red hair whipped around her in a frenzy as she released arrow after arrow. Not a single one flew false. Something about this took Arrik firmly aback. Female warriors were uncommon in his land and looked down upon. He should have loathed the sight of her, but there was something frightening and exciting about the woman. She seemed to be as untamed as the beast she rode upon.

"Bring her down!" his second commanded.

Movement caught his eye, and he pulled out a short sword from his belt with his left hand when he spotted two Lorne soldiers climbing aboard. Arrik attacked, each movement made with brutal efficiency until he was the only one standing.

His gaze once again sought the fierce beauty.

It was a pity she was fighting on the wrong side.

There was a spirit to her—a savagery—that he wanted to experience, tame. His gut clenched as she fought off his men, slowly losing ground. Arrik cursed himself and wiped more rainwater from his eyes. Savage beauty or not, she was the enemy. There was no room for compromise.

The Rider and her dragon managed to take out another half-dozen of his soldiers when a bolt grazed her shoulder, causing her to drop her bow. She had no other weapons, and her dragon could only claw and bite so many soldiers at once. The beast took to the air.

"Don't let her escape!" Arrik commanded, numbness starting to invade his senses once again. They couldn't allow her to get out of range. Even so, he found himself hoping that they'd make a clean getaway.

The pair was the stuff of legends. They deserved to live.

Several different crossbows aimed at the dragon and its ferocious rider.

Impassively, he watched as the bolts went whistling through the air, chasing the near-invisible creature as it tried its damnedest to get away.

Three.

Two.

One.

One of the bolts hit true.

The creature screamed in agony and crumpled, plummeting from the sky.

A flicker of guilt and sadness moved through Arrik as the dragon and Rider hit the tumultuous sea with a crash that should have been deafening but was instead swallowed by the sound of the storm all around them.

He stared at the waves for a moment, willing them to break the surface.

They didn't.

More deaths to be laid at his feet.

Arrik locked his feelings away. His thoughts were dangerous. He only had one purpose. Bring the isles to their knees. To succeed, he needed to become the beast his father championed. A conqueror without mercy.

Nobody was spared in war.

CHAPTER NINE

WREN

She screamed as Aurora shrieked and then plummeted toward the ocean.

This was it.

The thrashing unforgiving sea rushed toward them and Wren closed her eyes.

The impact *hurt*.

She clung to Aurora as they tumbled in the dark water. Wren opened her eyes, trying to discern which way was up and pressed her heels gently into her dragon's side.

Aurora didn't respond.

No.

Wren used her dragon's frill to heave herself over Aurora's head. She spun, pushing her tangled hair out of her face as she reached for her dragon's snout. Aurora's eyes were wide and glassy; nothing remained behind them.

This isn't happening.

They sank deeper in the water, but she couldn't believe her eyes. How could Aurora be gone? Heat burned at the back of her eyes and the tears she shed were swallowed by the sea. Wren hugged her dragon's face and closed her eyes. And for one horrible moment, she thought about simply sinking to the bottom of the sea with her dragon. It would be so easy. It was quiet here.

Think of Britta.

Even if she wanted to sink into oblivion, her sister needed protection. If anything, Wren had to survive for the heir of Lorne. The enemy could never get their hands on her.

She forced her eyes open and pressed a kiss between Aurora's eyes.

I love you.

It took all her strength to unwrap her arms from her dragon. Wren's lungs began to burn as Aurora sank deeper and deeper below.

Goodbye, my friend. You will always be in my heart.

Wren kicked her legs and started to focus on the waters around her. It was a bloody mess of ship debris, bodies, blood, and sharks. She slowed her ascent so as not to attract the attention of the predators feasting around her. The waves fought against Wren as she tried to make it to the surface unscathed.

If Rowen were here, he'd have made it to the surface already.

He always swam like a fish. The stormy sea would have been no problem for him.

Her body ached as she neared the surface. She caught movement from the corner of her eye and faced it. A sleek shark darted toward her, and she pulled back her fist and rammed it in the nose just before it took a bite of her arm.

The beastie shot away like a wounded pup.

Wren mustered some more energy from her tired body and

broke through the surface. She wheezed a desperate, life-saving breath of air into her lungs. Her chest heaved as she treaded water, frantically looking left and right to try and get to grips with her surroundings. A wave temporarily knocked her back beneath the surface, and, for a moment, Wren panicked. But then she remembered her training, forced herself to calm down, and resurfaced once more.

Just work out where you are. You can do that.

The trajectory of Wren and Aurora's descent into the water had been diagonal, which meant Wren now found herself out of the sphere of the battle. It was to her left, still deafening in her ears, but with the way the current was pulling her, all she had to do was let the sea continue to carry her farther away to remain safe.

To her right, through the fog, Wren thought some of the gray mass seemed more solid than the rest.

Move, this is what your father trained you for. Work though the fatigue.

She inhaled deep and swam toward the solidness with slow firm strokes. The fins slicing through the water made her want to speed up, but she kept her pace measured so she wouldn't drown, nor draw the sharks attention. It took her far longer than it usually would have to reach an outcrop of black, polished, volcanic rocks. She heaved a sigh of relief at the sight of them. She'd made it.

Clawing her way out of the water just enough that the current could not so easily carry her away, she felt around until she was reasonably sure she had good purchase on the rock to keep her above the waves.

She held on and stared at the massacre in the bay.

All at once, Wren broke.

She began to wail.

The storm answered, screaming right back at her. Lorne—and by extension, the entire Dragon Isles—had suffered a heavy loss. Wren had no doubt she was not the only one crying right now. But there was no comfort to be had in this collective sadness, so she merely sobbed harder.

She was in so much pain. Mental, psychological, and emotional, yes, from the insurmountable losses she had amassed today, but also physical. Her muscles ached from having carried Britta for so long and clinging to her dragon. She was bleeding. Every inch of her felt bruised.

Her eyelids lowered and her teeth began to chatter.

Her body was shutting down.

She'd experienced it twice in her life before when she'd pushed herself too hard.

She hauled herself higher out of the water and rested her cheek against the stone. Her body had nothing more to offer. Wren had used every ounce of energy up and now she'd pay for it. A low chuckle escaped her at the thought of falling asleep and drowning after everything she'd survived. It was nothing short of a miracle.

Wren closed her eyes.

Just ten minutes. She needed a small break before she hauled her carcass back to the island.

She woke up with seawater in her mouth.

Wren sputtered and tried to reorient herself as she clung to her rock. The tide had risen considerably. How long had she slept? She clambered further up the rock with a groan and sat down, her feet still in the water. The nap was supposed to help, but if anything, she hurt more than before. Shivers worked through her body and Wren wrapped her arms around herself, tucking her fingertip into her armpits.

It was bloody cold, no—freezing.

The blanket of true night covered Lorne properly now, though since it was midsummer, that wasn't saying a lot. The worst of the storm had abated, but dark and swirling clouds still covered the sky, obscuring the fact that at this time of year, the horizon never quite got dark.

She craned her neck and blinked slowly as she noticed the large black sand beach not far behind her. How had she missed that?

"Storms are debilitating, even for the most experienced sailors," her father's voice echoed in her mind.

She examined the waves and the tide. The tide was still coming in so at least she had that working for her. It would still be rough. The waves were choppy, dark, and angry. Perhaps a dragon was around?

Wren cupped her hands around her mouth and whistled.

No answering shriek.

She licked her lips and began humming as loud as she could. Perhaps that would help.

Still no reply.

Hanging her head, she stared at her toes. The dragons always answered. *Always.* They couldn't all be gone?

Think, Wren. They're afraid. They would not venture out from their nest so soon.

Her teeth chattered harder, and she swallowed stiffly. She needed to get back into the water or she'd die here. Wren waited until the next wave rushed toward the shore before she slipped into the water, riding the wave as far as she could. She kicked slowly, treading the water before the next one pushed her closer to the shore. Her feet finally touched the sandy bottom. Clumsily, she made her way forward, only to trip on a rock covered in coral.

She crashed to her hands and knees, spraying water everywhere. Gritting her teeth, Wren crawled through the shallows until she reached dry sand. She was lucky; in half an hour, she would have been rushed back out with the sea, and everything would have been lost. Which meant she'd been out for hours not minutes.

Catching her breath, Wren sat up to inspect her foot. The top was scraped, bloody, and crusted with black sand but not horrible. Even through the dull evening light, she could see that her skin was mottled with large purple and black bruises. Her leathers were torn and bloody but nothing needed stitches. That was something at least.

She abandoned her examination and blankly stared at the sea.

Keep moving. Keep your mind busy.

Where exactly was she?

Wren craned her neck and studied her surroundings, head pounding. A shaft of moonlight broke through the clouds and illuminated the cliff face. The distinctive three points above marked it as the small cove just north of the castle. Which meant that there was a secret underwater tunnel that fed back into the passageways beneath the castle.

She groaned, thinking about getting back into the water or climbing more stairs, but there wasn't a choice. This beach was too exposed. She needed to get to safety and recoup.

Steeling herself for the bite of the water once more, along with the strain on her muscles, she staggered to her feet and stumbled down the beach to the south. Taking a deep breath, she walked against the tide, legs almost buckling against the pull of it. She clung to the cliff face and tried not to scream. Could nothing be easy?

Letting go would be easy.

"Stop it," she growled out loud. "You're no longer living for yourself."

Britta needed her big sister.

And you need her. She's your only family now.

Though Wren had always loved the water, it was terrifying now to dive into its murky depths and reach out, blind, until she felt the telltale curve of the underwater archway that signaled the beginning of the secret passageway—something nobody could possibly find unless they knew it to be there already.

She counted backward from thirty as she swam through the tunnel, grateful for the fact that the punishing current of the bay did not quite reach inside. When she got to number nine, which felt more like she'd been holding her breath for two minutes rather than twenty-one seconds, given her current state of duress, she stretched out a hand until it hit the edge of what could only be a stair hewn into the rock itself.

She clawed her way out of the water and blindly groped the wall with her right hand for the curved railing that she knew to be carved into the stone. Her fingers brushed over it and Wren sighed in relief. It was slippery but it was better than nothing. Falling from the stone staircase in complete darkness below was horrifying.

It was a matter of pure will to stand up on her shaking legs.

"You're okay," she whispered softly, blinking repeatedly as if she could clear the darkness away from her vision. "Just take one step at a time."

One shaky step, then another, and another.

She climbed and climbed and climbed.

Wren cursed.

She cried.

Finally, she sang.

Her voice echoed softly around her in the cavern. She was literally surrounded by stone now, inside the cliff. Someone could hear her, but Wren couldn't stop until she finished. The last note hung in the air as she used her foot to feel for the next step. Nothing.

She knelt and swiped her left hand across the floor. A smile crossed her face. She'd made it. Wren knew this passageway by heart. It was flat, narrow, and led straight back to Lorne Castle.

Almost there. Just a little farther.

She limped down the hallway, running her hands along each wall. The air warmed and she hesitated. The castle was right above. Ordinarily, she would have known where she was going by the noise of footsteps and chatter above her head.

But everything was unusually quiet.

She was surprised by this—she had been sure the Verlanti soldiers would be celebrating their win by now, feasting in the great hall on all the food that should have been served after her wedding. The Dragon Isles were not known for their fancy, fashionable foods, but they sure knew how to cook things right.

Her belly growled at the thought of food, and she slapped a hand over it.

A peal of laughter threatened to escape her, and she clamped her lips firmly shut. It would be ironic for her growling stomach to give her away to her enemies.

She squashed her mirth, even as her belly clenched painfully again. There was no way to avoid the keep, so it wouldn't hurt grabbing some food on her way out.

Wren held her hands out in front of her as she walked until a wooden door stopped her. She paused, heart racing and waited for an incredibly long time, her ear to the door as she listened for signs of life on the other side. Her shredded leather's dripped onto the floor beneath her feet and her shivering grew worse. Either the soldiers were experts at staying silent or no one was around. It was an option to keep hiding. If she did not get warm, then hypothermia would set in. Hell, she was probably hypothermic already.

Wren opened the secret door that led to a fake fireplace in one of the smaller studies. She stooped low and stepped over the unburned logs in the hearth. The stone floor was overlain with carpet, which felt lustrous beneath her bare, battered feet. She reveled in the feeling of the lush, deep-crimson material between her toes and was tempted to simply lay there and fall sleep.

Stop it. That's the cold talking.

She had to stay alert and moving. Finding dry clothes was good. Hot food, even better.

Wren picked up a fire poker and tiptoed to the opened door. Never go anywhere without a weapon. She peered down the hallway. Not a soul. Time to move. She made her way down the passageway, flinching at each little sound. When she reached the courtyard, she swallowed and gasped and skidded to a stop.

The stones were covered in blood, dark and ominous in the murky moonlight. This she had expected. What Wren *hadn't* expected was the complete and utter lack of bodies. Where were her people? Had the elves killed everyone? It wasn't possible. They were cretins and brutes, but they wouldn't do something like that. Strategically, it was stupid. And if she'd learned anything from tonight, the Verlantians weren't unintelligent.

The wind blew from the southeast bringing with it the tang of iron and smoke. She spotted the plume of smoke crawling up into the sky from the southern bay.

Horror filled her.

Were they burning the bodies? That they would not give the grieving families of Lorne a chance to bury their dead was nothing short of blasphemy. The many men who had given their lives today deserved a true send-off, not the one the Verlantian soldiers were giving them.

Rage and helplessness filled her, and she found herself crossing the empty courtyard, headed toward the chapel. Her mind screamed at her to run, but she couldn't stop. She needed to see if they'd taken her parents and Rowen. Another dangerously hopeful part of herself wondered if Rowen would step from the shadows and wrap his arms around her.

Wren could not stifle the dry sob her throat emitted. *Stop it. He is gone, Wren. You know this.*

Her fingers tightened around the fire poker as she eyed the bailey. It was empty. Not even the echo of a footstep could be heard around her. What had taken place in her absence?

The wooden doors that led into the grand hall were chained closed and were unbroken. She frowned and then realization dawned. They'd locked the people in before they attacked. Disgusted, she limped around the side of the building to the left-hand corner of the courtyard, knowing that there was a secret entrance from there into the great hall and chapel.

The castle really was full of a ridiculous number of secret passages.

Wren was thankful for the countless hours she'd spent memorizing them with her father. And for exploring them with Rowen, believing them to be their own personal gaming grounds for hide and seek. The memory of those secret passages truly had been put to good use.

The entrance to this particular passageway was a trapdoor made to look suspiciously like the cobblestones that covered the courtyard, nearly impossible to spot, even if one knew it was there. Wincing at the strain in her arms, Wren swung herself down into the passageway before closing the door behind her. The tunnel was pitch-black, but she knew where she was going.

A few short steps forward and some more to the right, and she reached another door. This one, she knew, opened behind the tapestry that hung wide and proud on the southern wall.

Her hand shook as she turned the doorknob and swung it inward, a cool waft of air hitting her face as she did so. The chapel had always been colder than anywhere else in the castle, not to mention the east wall was completely missing now. Feeling her way around the tapestry, she clung to the fabric, and, when she reached its singed edge, she forced herself to pop her head around to view what remained of the once-beautiful place.

That was when she realized she was not alone.

In the very center of the chapel stood a man.

He stared at the spot where Wren had said her vows. Her heart twinged.

Stop thinking about it.

This room, again, had been cleared of bodies, only serving to fuel her rage. But Wren was too tired and upset to do anything about it; perhaps if the man had not been in the room, she would have kicked something in her despair, for all the good that would have done. Instead, she continued to observe her enemy.

He wasn't wearing helmet. That was unusual.

He was huge, all tight muscles and long, braided, silvery-white hair pinned messily back. His pointed ears gave him away for what he was: a Verlanti soldier. What was he doing in this desolate place? Was he here to gloat over the lives he'd taken and ruined?

Her fingers squeezed the fire poker as she eyed his weapons. A sword hung at each of his hips, along with several daggers strapped to his thighs and upper arms. A bow and quiver hung over his bare back. The man was dangerous. She could tell that much. Only an assassin carried that many weapons. Perhaps he was sent in last to clean up the mess?

Bile burned the back of her throat and Wren was happy that she hadn't eaten anything yet.

The elf rolled his neck and prowled toward the edge of the room, the wind ruffling his silvery hair. The way he held himself was like that of a...mountain cat—sleek and powerful. He leaned over the edge and if she thought she had a chance, Wren would have sprinted across the room and shoved him off the cliff.

But she held her place.

Her attention returned to the engraving on his vambraces that covered his forearms. They were intricate, *expensive* even. Something told Wren that this man was no mere foot-soldier. He was important, of that she had no doubt.

He dropped his right hand and flexed his fingers. An alien sensation moved through her as she stared at him. He could strangle her with one hand. But even with his back to her, standing on the edge of a four-hundred-foot drop, he looked completely comfortable.

He's not on guard.

He glanced to the right, giving her a glimpse of his profile as he clenched his jaw. High cheekbones, slender nose, and a dimple in his cheek. Wren blinked. It didn't seem right that her enemy had dimples. Dimples were too cute for the predator who stood casually in front of her.

The elf ran his right hand over his face and sighed, shoulders slumping as if he was upset about something.

What did he have to be upset about? He stood in *her* home painted in her *kin's* blood. Wren's anger burned hot.

Out of the corner of her eye, she saw a bloodied sword abandoned in a corner. Without thinking, she snuck over to it on silent feet and switched the fire poker to her left hand. Wren picked up the sword before she could shake some sense into herself. She indulged a terrible desire to creep up on the man and cut him down where he stood.

This is for my family.

Without sound, she closed the distance between them in a few scant seconds.

You should have been on your guard.

She stabbed him, but it glanced off a rib.

The soldier growled and spun toward her, knocking the sword from her hand. She stumbled back, clinging to the fire poker. He rushed her, his face contorted from the initial pain in his side before he removed the blade from his flesh and tossed Wren to the ground. No energy was wasted in his movement; he was lithe and careful and very, very calculated. He dropped to his knees and his huge hands found her throat, and, though she scratched and scrabbled at them and kicked the man in the stomach to try and shake him off, he simply would not budge.

On another day—when Wren was not exhausted, nor injured, nor overburdened with grief—she would have been able to find a way to squirrel away from the man. She could have outsmarted him and landed a crippling blow. Or, at the very least, managed to get away. She had no doubt she was faster than him. As her vision grew dark, she found herself focusing on the man's face, committing his features to memory to take with her to the grave.

Impossibly light, reflective blue eyes, as if they were made of crystal. High cheekbones. Longer eyelashes than she'd ever seen on a man. A strong jaw and regal nose. His face looked too handsome—too heroic—to match the savagery splashed across his features. Even the snarl on his face looked elegant.

In the last second before she plunged into darkness for good, Wren thought she saw a flicker of recognition cross the man's face, and she imagined that his hands might've loosened just a little from her throat. But then her vision went entirely, and all of her thoughts—of the man who was killing her, of her parents, of Rowen, of Britta—faded away, and then there was nothing.

CHAPTER TEN

ARRIK

This was exactly why he hated female warriors.

It was wrong to hurt a woman and yet she'd been the one to draw first blood.

Arrik sighed and released her throat. Her breaths were steady, but she wouldn't be out for long. He'd only held her down long enough to get her to pass out, so he didn't do any permanent damage on accident.

His father would call him weak. Maybe, he was.

What was she doing up here?

He'd specifically chosen this spot to gain some peace. After his men swept the keep one last time, they had taken every last morsel of food, wine, and ale from the castle and carried it down to the beach. Arrik had stayed behind to watch them from above as they ate, drank, and celebrated their win while the bodies of the fallen burned to ash as was proper.

Many of his men still hated that Arrik gave their enemy's bodies the same respect. It didn't seem right to leave the fallen warriors behind to rot. They were soldiers following orders just like he and his men were. They fought valiantly and deserved a warrior's send off and proper burial.

He leaned back, still straddling the woman. Pain lanced up his side, and Arrik winced and cupped his left hand over the wound. She'd come at him like a wraith. He noticed her presence a split second before she so foolishly chose to stab him. Did she know her chances of gutting him were slim from the back? There were too many bones in the way.

He pushed to his feet and stood and growled as heat and pain radiated from his wound. While she hadn't killed him, his wound still hurt. Arrik cursed and strode toward the tapestry hanging on the southern wall and tore a section from along the bottom before holding it against his bleeding injury.

Facing the woman, he glared at her. Any other man would have died for deigning to attack him. And yet, he hadn't killed her and that was a problem.

He didn't take prisoners.

The dark elves didn't take prisoners.

Arrik had made a name for himself by being a cold, brutal monster. He couldn't make exceptions to his rule. That's how people got killed.

He tossed away the soiled rag and yanked another long strip from the bottom of tapestry. From the corner of his eye, he could still see her flaming red hair. It was clear from the way she moved that she was exhausted and lacked the strength to counter-attack while he almost lazily removed the sword from his side. Nimbly, he wrapped the torn tapestry around his waist, over the seeping wound, and knotted it below his naval. He hadn't even gotten a good look at her face before she passed out.

In all honesty, he hadn't really noticed anything but her wild mane. The other rule he abided by was not to allow himself to see the people he conquered. Too many faces already haunted his sleep each night. She was merely a faceless, desperate Lorne citizen.

Look at her.

Arrik lifted his head and fully faced her once again. She was the one bright spot amongst the destruction in the room. He frowned at her. Why was he so drawn to her? What the devil was this? He prided himself on control. It was a skill he had to learn at a very young age. His father's court was a depraved place where only those with an unflinching mask or a sadistic streak a league wide could survive.

Steps echoed in the corridor across from him, but he didn't move from his spot. The man's gait was distinctive.

His second stepped into the room, his attention moving straight to the unconscious woman on the floor. Shane's upturned hazel eyes narrowed and then turned to Arrik, missing nothing. His black brows lifted in surprise.

"She wounded you?" he asked, leaning a shoulder against the wall. "And yet she still lives?"

Arrik didn't have an answer for Shane.

His second pushed away from the wall and approached the woman. He paused at her side and cross his arms. "What obscene hair." A pause. "I like it."

For some reason, that caused Arrik's hackles to raise. He moved to the woman's left side and stared down at her as well. Her face was turned toward Shane, like she didn't want to look at Arrik. Some of her hair covered her eyes and cheek so he couldn't see her face.

"It's nothing like the women of our court, no?" Arrik asked.

Shane shook his head. "While I appreciate the finer things in life, there are times that I'm tempted to join the wild side." He sighed. "But alas, her fate has already been decided. She spilled royal blood and so she must pay with her own."

"A moment," Arrik commanded, something in the back of his mind bothering him. He knelt, looming over her now almost-peaceful form, and took in her appearance properly for the first time.

Of course, his eyes strayed first to her intensely red hair, which was wet and knotted from the storm outside but unmistakably a shade he had seen just once in his life before— earlier that very day, upon the head of the warrior he'd ordered to be shot from the sky.

It couldn't be.

He ran his fingers through the woman's hair until he picked out a stray pansy from within a ruined braid. But he knew it had to be. Nobody had hair *that* red.

Only her.

"My lord?" his second asked.

"Did you find the heir?" Arrik asked quietly, pushing the woman's hair from her pale, cheeks. He gently turned her face toward him so he could get a good look at her. Freckles dusted the tops of her cheeks and nose. Long lashes and a pert, full mouth.

"There has been no sign of her. My men are now scouring

the outlying moors."

Arrik hummed and took in the rest of her appearance. Her clothing was too big for her as if she'd changed in haste. Had she thrown on the clothes to join the battle or because she was trying to disguise who she was?

He reached from the hem of her wet soiled shirt and lifted it until he could see her belly button. Shane cursed when Arrik pushed down the right side of her trousers, revealing a jagged scar.

A shark bite.

Princess Wren.

By the stars, he'd almost killed the heir to Lorne.

"How in the blazes did she come upon you?" his second questioned. "Surely, they would have hidden her away?"

Arrik traced the scar gently and then pulled down her shirt. He was a barbarian not a lecher. "I have a feeling no one can control this woman."

"Which is a problem. Your father doesn't like wild women."

He chuckled darkly. "Oh, he does, but only to break them." Like he'd done to Arrik's mother. The heir's eyes began to rove beneath her lids. She'd be waking soon, and he needed to be ready. Soon their battle of wills would begin, and he'd be the victor. It was the only way...for the both of them. "Call your men back. We'll need them I suspect."

Shane nodded and strode away, disappearing the same way he came.

Arrik stared hard at the woman who would make the king of Verlanti the most powerful man in the western hemisphere.

Nothing would be out of his father's grasp. Not much was known about the royal family of the Dragon Isles. Oswin had kept his kin deliberately private, which almost anyone in Verlanti took to mean that he was hiding any number of secrets. Illegitimate children were the most obvious of these secrets. It was common knowledge that the former king of the isle had one daughter, but her appearance and age were a mystery. It was only through a very, clever spy that they were able to discern that she was of age, had red hair, and had a scar on her right hip from where a shark bit her.

His attention moved to her bare arms. No markings. Legally, she had not been married.

Wren had lost her family, her future husband, and her dragon in one fell swoop.

He recalled how she'd recklessly dove from the sky time after time on her mount. She flew like she didn't care how it all ended. That was a problem. A person with nothing to lose was dangerous.

Arrik gave her another once-over, taking in the lean and compact muscles of her arms and her legs. Even beneath the ill-fitting clothes, he could tell she was strong. The young woman was in prime fighting shape, and given the way she'd so fearlessly attacked Arrik...

She was no mere princess who spun thread, sang songs, and read all day. Wren fought fiercely for her people. He would have to tread carefully, or he'd find another sword in his back.

"It's fortunate for me that you didn't die when I had you shot from the sky," he murmured. "You should have remained hidden," Arrik told her unconscious form.

Several sets of footsteps approached and he stood as Shane and his men filed into the room. Arrik's hard mask slipped into place as he strode from the chapel.

"Bring her to me when she wakes," he commanded. "We have things to discuss."

CHAPTER ELEVEN

WREN

"She's waking up."

Wren groaned as someone seized her arms and dragged her across the floor, her shins bumping painfully against the debris of the chapel. Her eyes snapped open. She lifted her head and glanced up at the brutes on either side of her. The elven warriors were both extremely tall and were almost mirror images of each other except one had long shiny black hair and the other orange curly hair and a short beard.

She struggled to get her feet beneath her, drawing the attention of the redhead. He smirked at her and shook his head.

"Lass, you're going nowhere. Save your energy."

Baring her teeth at him, she struggled harder, although much to her embarrassment, their grips didn't loosen in the slightest. Her breaths drew short as they exited the chapel and entered the grand hall. A lump rose in her aching throat at the destruction. The furniture was broken, the decorations destroyed, and red splatters covered the gray stone floor.

Wren's attention moved to the bottom of the dais where she's seen her parents last. Their bodies were gone but she couldn't get the images of them dying out of her mind. Her bottom lip wobbled, and she sucked it into her mouth to keep from crying. She wouldn't let the enemy see her grief.

The warriors stopped before the dais and hauled Wren to her feet. She swayed, not taking her gaze from the stones where she'd lost her parents. They were gone.

"Kneel before your lord," the dark-haired elf to her right demanded.

Wren tore her gaze from the stones and glared up at the elf. His dark eyes narrowed as she held his gaze and stood a little taller. She would never kneel for the Verlanti.

She grunted when he kicked the back of her knee, causing her to fall. Her palms slapped against the floor as she caught herself. Her heart pounded and she glanced over her right shoulder. Wren gathered the saliva in her mouth and spit at him. It landed on his dirt-smeared boot and he took one step toward her.

"Enough," a deep voice commanded.

A shiver ran through her body at the power in the one world alone. A small smile lifted her lips as she stared down the dark-haired elf. He clenched his jaw and retreated.

"Coward," she rasped, pain flaring in her neck.

"Silence!"

"Or what?" she muttered.

A hand grabbed the hair at the back of her head and pulled. She winced, hating that she dismissed the redhead. Her gaze locked onto the man sitting atop the dais.

On her father's throne.

The same man she'd tried to kill.

Rage filled her and she tried to move forward, only to be

yanked back by her hair by the redhead. She clawed at his arm, and he cursed but didn't release her hair. The other dark elf stepped in, securing her arms behind her back. Wren glared mutinously at the warrior sitting on her father's throne.

"How dare you sit there!" she spat.

He arched a silver brow and leaned back as if to get more comfortable. "What is it to you? The man who previously held this position was weak."

"My father was not weak. You're half the man he was."

A glint entered his ice blue eyes. "That was easier than I expected. Welcome, Princess."

She frowned. What was he getting at? "What of it?"

"I would have thought your people would have hidden you away from me."

Dread crept into her chest. "What do you mean?"

"I'm just surprised that your family allowed their only heir to wander about the keep. Especially, one helpless when it comes to battle."

She schooled her expression. Heir? They thought she was the heir? For once in her life, she was so bloody thankful for her parent's paranoia. They had shielded Britta from the world. Anyone outside Lorne Keep believed that there was only one princess.

Wren held her head high and eyed the bandage tied around his bare stomach. She slowly lifted her eyes to his face and smirked. "Not too helpless it seems," she quipped.

He didn't rise to her bait but the hands holding her arms back tightened painfully. Someone didn't like her attitude. She gritted her teeth and glanced up at the dark-haired elf. He glared at her.

"Watch your tone," he growled. "You're speaking to your betters."

Her betters? Her upper lip curled. "Did you not hear your master? I'm a princess, how dare you think to command me."

"You're nothing but isle filth," he retorted. "Speak to my prince again like that and you'll not like the consequences."

Prince?

Things started to fall into place and the air seemed to thin. There was only one Verlantian prince that led the elven army.

The beast. A warmonger without a conscience or morals.

The king's bastard born child.

Her focus snapped to the man lounging on the throne. This was all *his* fault. He killed her family.

"I'll kill you," she shrieked, trying to dislodge the soldiers holding her in place.

"Feisty one," the redhead grunted as he wrapped her hair around his fist and yanked, causing her body to bow.

The prince stood and walked down the stairs, looming over Wren. He cocked his head as he watched her struggle. "You have two choices, my lady."

Wren strained toward him, ignoring the pain in her body. "Let me go."

"All in good time," he murmured. His gaze seemed to pierce her as he observed her. "I have been tasked with bringing you back to the king of Verlanti. You will be wed to him."

"Never," she hissed.

"I'm not finished," he said softly. "I am giving you a choice. Death or marriage."

Don't be rash.

Wren wanted to die rather than marry the depraved elf king, but her death would be senseless. It would solve nothing. She panted, her pulse pounding in her ears. She already knew what her answer was.

"I'll marry your king," Wren answered with calmness she didn't know she possessed. She'd play their games until a route of escape made itself known. This was an opportunity. Spies did not survive in the Verlantian court, but Wren was being invited into their intimate circle. If she kept her head down, she could tear them apart from the inside and reclaim the Dragon Isles. "I'll see you dead first."

A glint of interest entered the prince's gaze and he smiled. He reminded her of a shark. Predatory and intelligent. "Come and get me, little dragon. I love a good challenge."

She launched herself at him and pain exploded in her shoulders. Spots crossed her vision a moment before everything went dark.

CHAPTER TWELVE

ARRIK

"It's done," Shane said softly.

Arrik gazed at the unconscious princess laid out on his bed in the small cabin of his ship. She was a bloody mess. There wasn't part of her body that wasn't covered in bruises and cuts. Their healer had done his best to clean her up, but she was still a disaster.

"You know I didn't dislocate her shoulder on purpose?" his second asked.

Arrik glanced to his left at Shane and nodded. His second was many things but an abuser of women wasn't one of them. "She did it to herself."

Shane grunted and crossed his arms. "I didn't expect her to launch herself at you. I'm not really sure how she was able to get to her feet in the first place. It happened so quickly." A pause. "You'll have to watch your back with this one."

Everyone was always out to get Arrik. The moment his father had shone any favor toward him, a target had been painted on his back. "She won't be my problem for long."

His second snorted. "I think our journey back to Verlanti will seem longer with her aboard."

Arrik agreed but not for the reasons Shane thought. There

was something compelling and alluring about the woman. She posed a challenge and that excited him. Plus, there had been a glint in her eyes that spoke to his soul. She was unabashedly wild where Arrik had to remain calm. They were opposites. She was the light and he the darkness.

He sighed and rolled his neck, his attention flicking to the windows to his left. Half his navy would stay in the isles while Arrik returned to the capital with the heir and then he'd return.

"Hopefully, she heals quickly," Shane commented lowly.

Arrik winced and frowned at the unconscious princess. The king of Verlanti was a man of picky tastes. He collected stunning trinkets in all forms, but women were his favorite. If the heir didn't hold up to his standard, Arrik didn't want to think about what the king would do with her once he'd legally claimed her land.

Why do you care?

He couldn't afford to. Each time he did, it ended in death.

Arrik turned his back on her and strode for the door. "Take her to the brig."

"Do you want me to question her when she wakes? Another royal is a problem," Shane called.

Arrik paused in the doorway and glanced at his second over his shoulder. "I'll do it. There are always illegitimate children running around when it comes to the monarchy. If our princess doesn't give us what we want, we'll tear the isles apart looking for the source of the rumor."

CHAPTER THIRTEEN

WREN

Wren's head was filled with fire and rain and smoke and fog. Water swirled all around her, throwing her this way and that, and she discovered she could not breathe. She forgot what it felt like to be *able* to breathe. Then, somewhere far off in the distance, she heard a voice.

An achingly familiar voice.

"Go!" Rowen called to her. "Take Britta and go!"

But Britta is not with me.

Confused, she frowned and tried to shake off the fatigue.

She is...with Rowen's grandparents. And I am...

Wren woke with a jolt that shook her to her very core. Everything around her was moving in an uneven motion that meant only one thing—she was on a ship. Blurrily, she tried to make sense of her surroundings.

"What hap—" she began to say, only to gag when the ship hurled over a particularly large wave. It was this roiling feeling of seasickness that clearly awoke her from unconsciousness, for though she was comfortable fighting on a ship and sailing out across the sea in the worst of conditions, being trapped in a confined space upon the waves plagued her with the worst kind of nausea.

Bile burned the back of her throat as she finally figured out where she was.

It was barely a room with height enough to stand. Her stomach lurched again, and she tried to crawl forward. Wren blanched when she discovered her wrists were shackled, chaining her to the damp wooden wall.

"Blast it," she managed to spit out, then immediately regretted it. Despite all her training to the contrary—and in no thanks due to the terrible condition of her body—Wren could not stop herself from vomiting the moment she opened her mouth. Tears stung her eyes as she heaved over the edge of the narrow bunk again and again. Even when her stomach had nothing left to throw up, she could not stop retching, until her mouth tasted of bile and she wished for nothing more than a hearty gulp of water—or wine—to wash it away.

She slumped in her chains. They barely gave her the space to sit, let alone lie down, so she placed her cheek against the wooden wall of the ship, trying to ignore the stench of her own vomit. The wall of the ship was cold, and it helped settle her stomach, despite the rocking all around her.

She swallowed hard and breathed slowly to keep from puking.

Focus on nothing, Nothing at all. You are nothing. All of this is nothing.

Wren closed her eyes and drifted off to sleep.

The second time she woke was slower and gentler than the first. It was as if her broken body was easing her back into the impossible task of consciousness, for which she was grateful.

She became aware of the fact she no longer felt so seasick, and that the tumbling of the ship had settled.

Which meant they were well past the Dragon Isles.

Fear and a thread of excitement assaulted her.

She'd never been away from her home.

Don't get so excited. You're a prisoner.

Her skin prickled. Someone was watching her.

She opened her eyes.

"*You!*" she hissed through gritted teeth, though she was so dehydrated and her throat so hoarse that it came out as barely a whisper. Crouched in front of her was the Verlanti warrior she had tried to kill back in the chapel, who had wrapped his hands around her throat and—

The one she'd made a deal with.

A rush of memories of the last however many hours flooded Wren's brain in one confusing, overwhelming swoop.

He's a prince. He was supposed to kill me, yet here I am. A prisoner, not dead.

Wren didn't know which one she preferred.

Her focus moved to her bare legs and the long black shirt that covered her to her knees. Someone had undressed her. She swallowed hard and steeled herself before meeting the prince's gaze again.

"Did you undress me?"

"No."

"Did your men?"

"A healer."

"You didn't kill me." A statement.

The man neither smiled nor frowned nor gave away any

other sign of emotion as he stared at her. His ice blue eyes darted from Wren's to her hair and back again. "Yes," he finally said, so softly she barely heard him over the quiet roar of the sea. "It is me. You did not expect to still be alive, did you, Princess?"

She held his gaze and rubbed at her left wrist, her shackles clattering. "Your kind aren't known to keep their word." He didn't react to her barb. Not easily ruffled. That was good to know. Wren cocked her head and kept silent. She watched his eyes go to her hair again, as if he found it impossible not to stare at it. Why did this strange Verlantian warrior keep looking at her hair? Hadn't he seen red hair before?

Maybe he has a fetish.

She glared at him, feeling exposed and angry.

"Are you in shock?" he asked. "It would not surprise me if you were. You've been though much."

Wren did not know how to answer that—nor if she *should.* For of course she was in shock, but that was not why she hadn't answered the man's question. She had far too much to process and work out to do what he wanted. And besides...she peered through the darkness to try and grasp the lines of the man's face; she was dealing with the Beast of the Barbarians. Wren had heard of his interrogation techniques during her training. He was known for his brutality. She had to tread carefully. He thought she was the heir and that would keep her safe.

At least for now.

As if reading her mind, the man's gaze fell to her chest, though not with the lecherous look in his eyes she had become accustomed to from some of the less savory traders who occasionally came to Lorne.

It was assessing.

"You agreed to a treaty between our two nations through marriage, but I have a feeling it's not as simple as that. Are you going to be difficult?"

She stayed silent. Her shoulders ached and she rolled her left one. They'd put her shoulder back into place. That was a good sign at least.

Unless they want you to be healthy when they start the torture.

He sighed before standing up and stretching his huge arms up and behind his head. Wren heard one of his shoulders pop, and the man sighed in satisfaction. "Ah, I've been trying to work out that knot in my shoulder since I ordered you to be shot from the sky."

She stiffened. *Aurora.*

The prince glanced in her direction, and he gave her the barest hints of a smile. "Yes, that was me. You truly were a sight to behold. I did not know Oswin had trained his daughter to be so fierce. You risked much by flying with the warriors. You could have died."

Wren was disgusted by the compliment. Every word that came out of the man's mouth felt manipulative and soaked in poison. The prince seemed to like twisting words to get his way. She could see why he'd received the reputation of being a serpent. He could make anyone his pawn, but not her. She'd win. He just didn't know it yet. She had to keep calm.

He killed your family.

She battled back her rage, barely keeping herself from trying

123

to tear his face off.

"Have you forgotten how to speak? Should I remind you?" the man asked, his hand lingering over the pommel of a dagger in a move that was clearly meant to be frightening. And Wren *was* frightened; she was not so foolish as to not admit to that. The Verlantian prince was tall and broad and fierce, with his sharply handsome face and even sharper mind, she was in danger if she didn't play her cards right.

Get yourself together.

"I don't see why I should waste my words on you," Wren uttered, hating how difficult it was to get the words out. They were cracked and hoarse and barely audible. By the tides, she needed some water. She licked her lips.

The prince moved his hand from his dagger to a waterskin hanging from his hip, and deftly opened the lid with a thumb. He knelt to place it against Wren's lips. She was tempted to turn her face and refuse the precious liquid that began pouring out, but that would have been stupid. She was too weak and too thirsty to resist. Her tongue lapped at the water, her throat gulping it down as if she might never taste such sweetness ever again.

Far too soon, he pulled the waterskin away and stoppered it. Wren could not prevent the flash of disappointment that crossed her face as he did so, which only caused him to smirk. He waved the receptacle in front of her. "Answer my questions, and maybe you'll get more."

"What do you want from me?" What more could he take?

"Many things."

How delightfully vague.

"Looks like we're off to an excellent start. Where is your sister?"

Wren blinked slowly. She was under the impression that the prince thought there was only one princess. "I don't know what you mean."

"Come now," he rumbled softly. "Let's not lie to each other. Our spy revealed that there was only *one* princess but no monarch would only have one child."

"My father was faithful to my mother," she replied honestly.

The prince laughed. "King Oswin was much too clever for that. The Dragon Isles needed a secure line. One child is too much of a risk. So I'll ask you again, where is your sister?"

Lie.

She glared at him, wishing every ill fate upon him that she could think of. Clearly, he'd received more information after she'd been knocked unconscious.

"Dead," she whispered. The enemy had to believe that Britta was not alive. It was the only way to protect her people and her sister. Still, the lie stung Wren's tongue. After witnessing everyone else she had ever loved die in front of her eyes, the mere *idea* of her little sister being dead was like an arrow to the heart.

Use the emotion. Make him believe you.

The man set his clear-as-glass eyes upon hers. "How did she die?"

"We were escaping the castle," Wren replied, finding the lie easier to tell now that her head was full of the ghosts of her loved ones. "There's a network of tunnels hidden beneath the castle which leads out into the town and to the beaches. I'd suggest you check them out if we hadn't already clearly left the Dragon Isles."

He did not respond to her suggestion of incompetence on his part; he merely waited for her to elaborate on her story.

Wren looked away, not needing to feign the stinging in her eyes. "I tried to carry her through the darkness—she was so afraid—but the journey was long and the passageway narrow. I grew tired. She had to walk the final few turns toward the shore. But then she..." Wren let out a sob, and it wasn't false even though her story was. Her grief wasn't far from the surface. "The st-stairs to the beach cut into the cliffside," she continued between tears, "they're so steep. I can barely manage them. And my sister—she—she couldn't. By the time I knew what was happening, it was too late."

A silence spread between the two of them. If Wren wasn't so distraught, she'd have been impressed with her tale; even to her ears, it rang true.

For the sake of my sister, this is what happened to her.

Unable to wipe the tears that fell from her eyes, Wren cried unabashedly in front of the elf.

Eventually, through the dull light of the hanging lantern, the man shifted slightly. "And her body? Where is it?"

"Beneath the waves with my *dragon*," Wren fired back immediately; grief turned to rage in an instant. "Where you intended me to be. I hate you."

"This is war. Lives are lost on either side."

"This wasn't war—this was a massacre."

"Yet lives are lost all the same," the callous prince said, standing up as he did so.

126

She jerked against the chains, her fingers itching to claw at his handsome face. He deserved to feel all the pain he'd wrought on her.

He watched her seethe at him for several long moments, and she almost imagined he was searching for something in her face. A hint that she'd been lying, perhaps, or something else entirely.

"You better get that under control, Princess, or you'll find your stay in Verlanti very uncomfortable. As I told you before, life can be easy or difficult. It's your right to choose which path you walk, but you and your people will suffer if you choose the wrong way."

"I hope you burn in hell."

He chuckled darkly. "I already am. Any other venomous words for me?"

She snapped her mouth shut and turned her face away from him. She would not speak another word to the savage, heartless man.

"So, it's going to be that way. So be it. I love a good challenge."

The prince gave her a sharp nod, and swiftly left the dank cell, his steps thundering up the wooden stairs to her right. For a while, she did nothing but look at the staircase. What would become of her now? Was she going to be left to rot in here? Would she be thrown mercilessly overboard to die by the hand of the sea? Or was she to be brought back to Verlanti, where she would be tortured within an inch of her life to give up all of Lorne's secrets?

Stop. Think. What did the prince offer you?

Wren rubbed her temples and tried to remember her hazy conversation she'd had with him in the great hall. He'd offered her marriage to his father.

You're going to be another bride to the man with a hundred wives.

She bent over and retched again. Wren panted and wrapped her arms around her middle, hugging herself. Her mum had told her stories of what the highborn elves were like. They treated their wives as expendable trophies.

"I have to get out of here," she murmured, moving her gaze from the stairs to the wooden planks on her left, imagining a circular window there overlooking the horizon. There was clearly going to be no opportunity for her to escape while still aboard the ship. And if that was the case...

Wren had to prepare to fight for her life and run the moment she set foot in Verlanti.

CHAPTER FOURTEEN

WREN

She marked the time by how often she received meals. The men who brought her sustenance also brought her a bucket in which to relieve herself; if she couldn't wait between meals, she guessed she'd be forced to piss in the very clothes she wore and then sit in a pile of filth. She was determined not to reduce herself to such a humiliation, though the time between meals often varied wildly, she resolutely held in all of her bodily functions until the next guard opened her door.

Even when they gave her food, Wren was not let out of her shackles. They fed her morsels by hand and fully expected her to eat in such a way. If Wren had not been so intent on building her strength back up to be ready to fight, then she would have refused any and all such undignified meals.

Her wounds healed on the outside.

Inside, she bled and mourned.

Days blurred together.

Nightmares plagued her.

The Verlantian prince with the haughty face and searching eyes had not once returned. Though Wren had never cared to listen to the many rumors brought to the Lorne Court about its neighboring nations, she *did* know that the Verlantian king was not shy about having shared his bed throughout the years.

A bard had passed through Lorne once, equipped with a lute and a jaunty little song about how the number of the king's bastards was in the double digits. Wren had dismissed the song back when she'd heard it; now, it was the closest thing to truth she had to cling to. The illegitimate prince who served as the king's war dog was only spoken about in whispers. He was rumored to be cold and merciless. His name was Erik, or possibly Aron, Wren had never cared enough to know for sure. She'd never imagined that he'd enter her life. The beast from the horror stories had captured her.

She held her hands up and stared at the manacles around her wrists.

Wren still couldn't fathom the situation. The isles had fallen to Verlanti. She'd gone over and over it in her mind. The elves shouldn't have been able to make it passed Lorne's defenses. Only a few trusted commanders knew their ways through the corals, rough waters, and traps.

Someone had betrayed them. But who? That was the question that plagued her night and day. Did that same person know about Britta? There were too many unknowns.

Her attention moved to the dirt that covered her hands and arms. When was the last time she'd been clean? It could have been days or weeks or months since she had been captured, and she would never have known. All that existed for her right now was her mind, her mealtimes, and the sound of the sea. Although...

Wren took a heavy sniff and grimaced. She smelled horrible

but at least none of her wounds had festered. The stiff healer visited her every so often to make sure she was healthy and alive. The willowy man was a mystery. He never spoke a word to her during his visits. His sage green eyes were hard but not unkind.

She exhaled and tried to breathe through her mouth. Her person wasn't the only thing that stank. No one had cleaned up her vomit and her privy bucket wasn't emptied as often as it should have been. All in all, it was disgusting, but it could have been worse. No men had tried to accost her and no one had tortured her for information. They did however give her the bare minimum allotments of food and water. It was clear they wanted her weak. Her chances of immediate escape were slim. She needed to build up her strength and gather information despite how much she wanted to get away from her captors.

She closed her eyes and another unknown amount of time passed as Wren went over her sums in her mind. She'd always hated arithmetic but her mum had been a stickler when it came to learning her sums. Wren smiled and one tear tickled down her cheek. Her mum would be proud to know her daughter was keeping to her studies even in a prison.

Her eyes popped open as she heard something that broke the monotony of her confinement.

A horn.

That was new.

Her brows furrowed as the horn sounded again.

There was only one reason for that.

The ship must have reached the shores of Verlanti.

Despite her grand idea of escape, Wren's heart sank. What

horrors awaited her? She pulled her knees to her chest and leaned her head against them.

You must be brave. You need to survive.

Wren swallowed and steeled herself for whatever was to come. Her mum hadn't raised her to roll over. She was a fighter. If the Verlantians hoped to find her worn down and defeated, they were going to be sorely mistaken. When the king came for her, he wouldn't find a pliable maiden. They would not break her.

She was her mother's daughter.

Steps thumped against the ceiling from above.

Wren lifted her head regally and tensed all her muscles, ready like a cat to spring into action. Part of her wanted the person who came through those doors to be the prince. She didn't want to lose her chance for vengeance. He'd taken everything from her. She intended to do the same to him.

The warrior loped down the stairs, a grin on his face. She squinted at him as he paused in front of her. The man was vaguely familiar. He worried his red mustache and it clicked. He was the elf that had yanked her hair.

"Time to get up," he said cheerily.

She blinked slowly at him but didn't move.

He sighed heavily. "You're going to be difficult, aren't you?"

"Depends if you're planning on touching me again," she rasped. Her voice was rusty from disuse.

"I'm not planning on dragging you by your hair." He pulled a vial from a pouch at his waist and wiggled it at her. "I'll drug you. It's your choice."

Being at the complete mercy of her enemies was terrifying.

She uncurled her legs and set them on the floor, making sure to avoid the dried vomit. The redhead eyed her warily as he approached, and she held her hands out. He leaned closer and she eyed his ear. It would be so easy just to bite it off. As if he could hear her thoughts, his amber gaze snapped to her face.

"I know it's difficult for women but keep your mouth to yourself."

She snorted before she could help herself. The elf grinned and unshackled her wrists. She rubbed at them; the feeling odd after wearing the shackles for so long. He took a step backward but held out his hand.

"I can do that myself," she retorted, swatting his hand away and pulling herself up as tall as she could. Her legs shook but she managed to keep her chin up. She was a bloody princess. In Verlanti that meant being haughty and cold. It was better she put it into practice now.

"Suit yourself." He gestured to the stairs. "You first, my lady."

My lady. What rubbish. She looked and smelled worse than a vagrant.

Her body quaked as she made it up the first set of stairs. Wren walked through a room full of goods. Stolen goods from Lorne. She swallowed over the lump in her throat and marched through the treasures of her people to the second staircase.

She used the wall for support and blinked furiously as the sun beamed down on her as she made it to the top deck. Wren inhaled the salty breeze and shielded her eyes from the morning sun. Her skin prickled and she knew she was being watched. She stiffened and lowered her hand. What seemed like the entire crew stood at attention. Their focus? Her.

Every single one of the soldiers' eyes were on her, their gazes crawling up and down her skin from her head to her toes. They lingered on the torn, filthy fabric of the giant black shirt she'd woken up in. Standing, it stopped just above her knees and she blushed, feeling exposed and humiliated. She had never been in such a compromising position in front of other people before—especially not men from a foreign country, with their pointed ears and cruel faces.

You're a princess.

The redheaded warrior wrapped a hand around her left bicep and propelled her through the men to a pile of crates waiting to be brought off the ship. She shivered but straightened her spine.

Do not let them get to you. You are powerful.

He released her and she leaned against a crate. Something sharp dug into her spine. Wren schooled her expression. It felt like a loose nail. It was possible she'd never get another chance like this again. In a split second, she wiggled her hands behind her and began to work furiously and as inconspicuously as possible to remove the nail from the wood. It took several twists and turns, but she managed to pull the nail free.

With nowhere else for it to go, she slipped it into the waistband of what remained of her underclothes, hiding the motion by pulling down the hem of the black shirt, pretending that she felt embarrassed by her state of undress. The soldiers laughed at her, but it did not matter.

She had a weapon.

"Commander," the redhead called.

Wren lifted her head as the prince strode in their direction, all power and lithe. Her breath hitched and she clenched the fabric of her shirt between her fingers. Dressed all in black, he made an even more intimidating figure, somehow, than how he'd looked in the chapel, bare-chested wearing only pauldrons and vambraces. It served to accentuate the sharp lines of his face, which were not softened even by the scruff growing along his jawline—the result of however many days or weeks they had spent at sea.

A monster wasn't allowed to be attractive. Or was that the point?

The prince stopped and eyed the soldier.

"I've retrieved the prisoner as you asked," the redhead said.

She kept her head held high as the prince peered in her direction. She stared down The Beast of Verlanti who had tried to kill and then imprisoned her. He held Wren's gaze strong for a moment, before dismissing her.

He turned his back to her and spoke in low tone with the redhead. Her fingers itched for the nail. The arrogant man thought him safe with his back to her. What a fool. She could easily take his life.

Patience.

Killing him would only lead to her death or permanent imprisonment. Neither would help Lorne. Her gaze moved to the sprawling white city beyond the docks and emotion swelled in her chest. She'd never actually been away from Lorne before. In fact, her very first trip to visit the southern islands of Neamh and Meith had been due to take place that summer, two weeks after her wedding. It felt only proper to do it then, her father had said. She had a dragon now, and was in the prime of her life, and she would be married to a fine man in the navy.

Now, that would never happen.

Wren held back what felt like the millionth sob. She had no idea when she had become such a crybaby, but now it felt like tears were a welcome friend of hers. The elven capital Wyrn was absolutely stunning. It was so different from home. The isles hosted small stone homes or buildings with thatched or moss-covered slate roofs. Wyrn was comprised of interlocked bone-white buildings with terracotta and cerulean roofs, and cobbled streets. A thick dark green forest crouched at the edges of the city.

"Welcome to our kingdom, Princess Wren."

She stiffened and looked at the prince when a couple of his men sniggered. Had she been gaping like a country bumpkin? Or was it because he'd sneered princess? Either way, it didn't matter.

The prince gestured to the castle just west of the docks. "Upon reaching the palace, you are to meet the High King Soren. A great honor indeed. I fully expect you to cooperate or things will," a weighted pause, "go badly for you," he finished, his voice much softer than before.

It was chilling.

The commander's words, alongside his tall, well-built, and ruthlessly efficient crew truly did frighten Wren. The Verlantians were a cruel people, and now she was caught in their web.

Don't show fear.

She kept her mask in place and forced herself to focus on the feel of the cool nail twisted beneath her shirt.

You can defend yourself. You're not helpless.

"You will be afforded the privilege not to be gagged or bound on our way there. If you trespass upon my generosity, customs be burned. I'll treat you like a common piece of trash."

It was with great difficulty that she held her tongue.

He nodded and once again dismissed her, walking across the ship ramp to the dock.

The redhead smiled at her then mockingly sketched a bow. "My lady, if you please."

She arched a brow at him and walked off the ship on wobbling legs. It was embarrassing how weak she'd become in captivity. Regardless of how she was half-starved, sore and filthy, she kept her head held high. Men could take many things, but they couldn't take your spirit if you didn't let them.

Barefooted, Wren trudged along a grandly built harbor twice the size of Lorne's, then up, up, up an elaborately paved path that led through a small grove of oak trees. It continued to climb until Wren was struggling to breathe, and then, when she thought she might pass out from malnutrition, the group came across perhaps the largest building she had ever seen.

The Verlantian Palace was immense and not like Lorne Keep. The palace was not built upon many levels, for one, instead spreading itself out like a yawning cat in all directions for what felt like forever.

Three towns could fit in that building.

She hated it but Wren had to admit it was impressive.

The stonework did not seem to have any lines that suggested the building had been made with anything but one singular piece of carved, smooth white rock.

It looked like magic had been wrought upon it, though Wren knew that was impossible. Perhaps the palace had been built back in the day when dragons might've roamed farther from the isles, and the rare ones which blew fire from their lungs could have been used to reinforce the building and turn it into such a seamless, beautiful thing. It screamed wealth. How many kingdoms had the elves raided to afford such a place? How many lives had been lost for such luxury and greed?

It was a stunning landmark for a cruel people.

She huffed out a breath as she was directed up a set of steep white stairs that lead to the entrance of the palace. Wren kept her head down and focused on not passing out. Her head spun and she slipped. A hand clamped around her forearm, halting her from dashing her brains out on the marble stairs.

She lifted her head and gasped. The prince stared impassively down at her. Wren tore her arm out of his grasp, almost losing her balance again.

"Don't be stupid."

"Don't touch me," she countered as she righted herself and continued up the steps.

He sprinted up the remaining stairs, leaving her behind with his guards.

The steps weren't the worst of it.

Their cruelty was only further reinforced when Wren was paraded through the palace toward what could only be the throne room. She tried not to tug at her soiled black shirt that exposed too much of her legs.

Her face flushed with indignation, though she forced herself to calm down. There was nothing she could do about the situation she was in, aside from keeping cool and taking the first opportunity she was given to attack. Who cared if she was humiliated in front of all these people she did not know? They did not care about her, and she did not care about them. Their opinion of her meant nothing.

So why was her heart beating so quickly? Why, with every pair of eyes laughing and sneering in her direction, did she feel even more like she wanted to crawl inside herself and never return?

Only you have the power to let others shame you.

With her mother's words ringing in her ears, Wren conducted herself as a bloody queen. She'd bring no reproach on Lorne. Cruel laughs and stares would not take her dignity.

A pair of ornately carved doors opened and she was led across a marble floor polished to a high shine to stand in front of a tall, gilded chair. She looked up to find what was potentially one of the most beautiful—and most frightening—faces she had ever seen carefully regarding her.

The High King of Verlanti. Soren.

Even sitting down, Wren could tell that the man was willowy and tall: taller than almost any man she'd ever seen in her life. His white-blond hair tumbled over his shoulders all the way down to his waist and was delicately braided with all manner of jewels, spindle-like gold jewelry, and silver pins. His eyes were framed by lashes of black and blue and silver, accentuating the crystalline color of his irises.

Crystal.

Like father like son.

Wren glanced over at the commander dressed all in black before she could stop herself. The resemblance was uncanny: the same eyes, the same high cheekbones, the same pale hair. The main differences that Wren could see between the two men was that one was slender whereas the other was broad, and that the king clearly preferred fine silks and gems to leather and armor.

It was surprising however to find the prince of a nation in the frontlines of an invasion. Leading it, in fact. Was it because he was illegitimate? The fact that Wren herself had been treated like Oswin's daughter by blood did not mean that other kings felt the same way about their own children who were still theirs by blood but born out of wedlock to another woman that was not their queen.

She kept her thoughts to herself.

Someone pushed her from behind and she fell unceremoniously to the floor. The resulting crash echoed all around the throne room, and she grunted when her knees cracked against stone. Pain radiated up her thighs, but she didn't cry. Wren panted through it and then gritted her teeth. She knelt for no man.

Though she was just as likely to be thrown to the floor again, Wren stumbled back to her feet. She held her back straight and lifted her head, peering through her red locks at the highborn courtiers tittering around her. They were dangerous, glittering creatures but what they didn't know was that the king had let the fox into the henhouse.

Lifting her chin, she pushed her hair from her face and locked gazes with the king. She lazily arched a brow at him, daring him to do something about her impertinence. Unexpectedly, the man laughed uproariously. The dark elf appeared at her side and tried to push her back down to her knees but she struggled against him.

"Oh, you truly are a fiery one," King Soren commented, his words drenched in aristocracy. "I rather like that. I had heard the Dragon Isles were full of high-spirited people. How exciting." He laughed again and some of the highborn lords and ladies followed suit.

He wouldn't be too delighted when he found a nail in his gut on their wedding night. Her lips lifted and she smile for the first time since her wedding ceremony.

"Just look at her," someone whispered to Wren's left, followed by the giggling of some women of the court.

She forced herself to ignore the women. But that comment seemed to open the entire floor to other goading insults and jokes, and then, all Wren could see was red in front of her eyes as she was filled with an insurmountable rage she was struggling to keep back.

The only thing she noticed through her anger was the prince who watched her like a hawk, his hand unmistakably hovering over his sword as if anticipating an attack. Only he truly knew how dangerous she was. She would risk life and limb to get in just one shot against her enemies. At least he wasn't underestimating her. He knew what he was dealing with.

King Soren sobered and brushed a lock of hair from his handsome face. "I must give my condolences to you for the tragedy that befell your family," the king said, his lofty voice clear and true and easy to hear, even over the ruckus of the room. The smile on his face was anything but sincere. "I am truly sorry they had to die, especially your little sister." The smirk curled into something wicked. "The court could have used some fresh meat."

Her stomach dropped. Children were to be protected. Just how bad was this den of depravity?

"I am told she would have been welcomed."

The king smacked his lips and Wren broke.

They could make fun of *her* all they wanted. King Soren could even pretend to care that she lost her family. But he would not talk about Wren's sister like that—like she would have been some toy for the Verlantian Court to play with and dispose of at their whim.

"You sick cretin!" Wren exploded, in a voice louder than any she had used since the night she had lost everything. She launched herself forward, too fast for the guards behind her to react, and revealed the nail she'd taken from the ship. Wren raised it above her head, ready to jump at the king—his eyes widened with genuine surprise—before a black blur tackled her to the floor in one fell swoop.

His huge arms wrapped around her, and she knew she couldn't break from his arms, but she did not stop screaming obscenities at Soren. The king had quickly taken up laughing at her flailing, useless words, his previous surprise completely overwritten on his face by mirth. The rest of the court, which had been stunned into silence by Wren's sudden, violent outburst, now joined his laughter, until it was all Wren could hear.

"It seems our prisoner princess needs to be taught some

lessons," Soren said, extending his hands out to the entire court as if welcoming their opinions. Everyone yelled in agreement.

King Soren's eyes grew as cold as beads of glass. "I do hope you enjoy some of Verlanti's hospitality."

Wren knew she would not like what this 'hospitality' was.

CHAPTER FIFTEEN

WREN

"*Ah!*" Wren cried, though the sound of her voice was drowned out by the splash of water that followed her as she was tossed into a cell, landing on her hands and knees. The icy water licked at her skin and she spat out salty water.

Seawater?

She frowned as she righted herself and tried to take in her dimly lit surroundings. The guards who'd led Wren into the dungeon slammed the cell door shut and turned their backs on her without a word. One glanced over his shoulder and even through the darkness she spied the smirk of satisfaction on his face before he walked away.

"You would not be smiling if you faced me on the battlefront like real men, you cowards!" she roared after them. But her threat—and its resultant booming echoes—fell on deaf ears. The guards were gone, and Wren was once more alone.

Now that Wren was fired up from her altercation with King Soren, she reasoned there was little point in wasting time crying. She leaned back on her heels, the seawater lapping at her thighs. Wren was no stranger to water and underground tunnels; if she could make sense of this prison, perhaps she could find a way out that the Verlantians would not anticipate.

She staggered to her feet and almost slipped on the mossy cobblestones beneath her soles. Squinting, Wren glanced around. Behind her was a stone wall with a heavy iron grille door set within it—the exit through which the guards had left. On Wren's right and left, heavy metal grilles separated her from the adjacent cells. She thought she could spy another prisoner a couple of cells down, but in the dim light she could not be sure. It could just as easily have been a sack or a pile of mud.

What was right in front of her intrigued Wren most, for the front of her cell was open, as was the front of *every* cell she could see. Instead of a wall, or an iron grille, a canal ran along the far edge of her prison a mere six feet from where she stood. The dark, murky water caused goosebumps to raise along her arms. Something about the canal set her on edge.

Wren set it aside and tiptoed over to the edge when the stone floor abruptly stopped and met water. She could hold her breath for five minutes. If she were careful, maybe she could escape that way. Her lips pursed, and a shiver of foreboding worked through her. The water was nothing like the clear ocean that surrounded the isles. Wren could see nothing through the murky liquid. What lurked beneath the surface? It couldn't be anything good. Wren was quite sure she didn't want to find out what that was. She had no doubt that she'd find out soon enough.

You have no one to blame but yourself.

Wren kicked at the water and sighed heavily. The plan was to remain calm and collected but there was something about the depraved lord and the rest of his court that got to her. He oozed corruption. There was nothing she could do about it now.

She crouched down to get a closer look at the water. She held a hand just above its glassy surface, toying with the idea of tracing a line along the very top of it. But, just as she was about to, she withdrew her hand, deciding that it was better not to risk such folly. Whatever was hiding in the water wasn't something to be trifled with.

A clap in the darkness startled her so badly, she nearly fell into the water. Instead, she fell backward onto her hands and feet and crawled until her back was against the stone wall of the prison cell, the water lapping on her toes.

"A wise choice," a singsong voice called, seemingly to float upon the air. "Beasts and demons lurk in those waters. Demons and beasts. But which one is which?"

Deciding that the voice had come from her left, Wren clambered back to her feet and approached the bars on that side of her cell and peered into the darkness. The lump she'd thought could just as easily be a sack as a person was indeed a man. Or, rather, as Wren's eyes adjusted to the light, he was a boy. He seemed a little younger than she was.

He turned his grubby face toward her. She gave him a once-over in the dim light. He wore a tunic over a loose shirt and leggings, with a feather cap resolutely sitting upon his head. The feather was all but destroyed, but clearly the boy had found some importance in wearing it even in this deepest of dungeons.

A bard, perhaps?

What had he done to be tossed into the dungeon? A small

smile curled her lips as she entertained the idea that he'd been imprisoned for creating the song about the High King's many ill-begotten sons. Then she sobered; locking someone up for such a thing seemed more than cruel. It was barbaric.

"What is your name?" she asked the boy, curious despite herself. Her voice echoed around her like a mighty chorus, and she cringed.

The boy's tilted eyes flashed in the darkness. "Oh, this and that," he replied quite easily. "Sometimes I am one thing, and sometimes I am another. Why do you have but one name? How silly!"

Wren shook her head, confused. "I am not quite sure what you mean. Who are you?"

"To some, I am nobody. To some, I am a lie. To others, I am the only one who matters."

"How long have you been here?" she tried again.

"A moment, a lifetime. Does it truly matter? Time does not exist in this place."

"I do not have time for this." Wren sighed impatiently, turning from the boy to stare sightlessly at the water. Clearly, the boy had been trapped for a long time. He'd lost his mind. He began to recite a riddle that made absolutely no sense and she cursed her bad luck. His prattling would drive her insane. Perhaps that was what the elf king wanted?

The boy's voice rose. "Beware the water."

She glanced in his direction. "Why?"

"Danger," he whispered. "And death."

For two days the boy truly did only speak in riddles—going by the dry, tasteless meals they were brought at random intervals, Wren could only guess how much time had passed—she still did not risk touching the water. Instead, she found that she had not yet exhausted her ability to physically grieve for her family.

"So much for being too angry to cry," Wren sniffed, not caring if the mad bard could hear her or not. He'd heard plenty of her tears over the past two days, anyway. At first, when it had become apparent that all Wren was going to think about was her family, she had tried to focus on Britta. For Britta was still alive and safe, of that Wren had to firmly believe in.

Rowen's grandparents will look after her. You know that things will be bad for her for a while—will likely never be the same again—but Britta will recover. She can grow up and be happy. Even if you never reach her side again, even if she never ascends the throne...she will be all right.

But this train of thought caused Wren to inevitably replay the moment her mother and papa had died over and over and over again, until there was nothing but the sound of their final screams in her head and she had to hold her hands over her ears in a desperate attempt to keep them out.

"Hearing voices in your head?" the boy asked from two cells over. "In that direction madness lies!"

Wren ignored him. She knew, in fact, that his words were at least in part true. If she kept mulling over the ghosts of her past then she would go mad, and then what use would she be to anyone?

Rowen would not act like this.

Her heart stung as his image raced through her head, first

smiling and delighted and so full of love Wren could have burst, and then...covered in blood, his lungs struggling as he told her to go save her sister. To save herself.

He would know what to do. He would not lose hope. He would sit and think on the matter for barely a second and then he'd be up and ready for action. *That's how he is.*

Wren gulped.

How he was.

Rowen wasn't rash. You cannot lash out again. You must think your every action through. No more mistakes.

Her tears dried and Wren vowed not to cry again. It helped no one. Dwelling on the past and stewing in her emotions would only serve to weaken her.

On the third day, when two guards brought food to the two of them for part of the time—which Wren took to mean nighttime, though she could have been wrong—a third man also entered the prison, and he did not seem like a guard. He held within his arms a large bucket, which sloshed loudly as he moved. It was clearly heavy; even with his muscled arms, his legs still bowed slightly beneath the weight of the bucket.

She watched as he entered the cell to her right and approached the water, though he kept at least two feet from the edge of it. *Just what is he doing?* she wondered, glancing at the boy for a moment to see what he thought of this. He wasn't even watching; clearly this third man was constantly part of his dungeon routine that he was bored by it. Just how long had he been down here?

She turned her attention back to the man with the bucket.

Wrinkling his nose, the man stuck his hand in the container

and pulled out something thick and wet, though Wren could not see what it was. Then he tossed the *thing* in the water and repeated the action over and over until the bucket was halfway empty. Then he dumped the rest of the contents in one go and turned to leave the cell.

He paused by the grille that separated them, the grin spreading on his face entirely unpleasant. "That was the prisoner who lived in your cell before you," he sneered. "Just in case you were getting any ideas of escaping."

Her stomach bottomed out.

And with that horrific remark, he was gone, disappearing alongside the two guards who had given Wren and the boy their dinner.

"Watch the water," the boy said when they were alone once more. "Watch the water and despair. Despair!"

And, so, Wren did, thoroughly discomfited by the boy's ominous statement and the knowledge of what had been thrown into the liquid darkness that contained something clearly unknown and dangerous. Then, before her very eyes, the water began to froth and bubble, as if it was a boiling pot upon a fire. But the water was not heating up: it was being churned up by something.

A school of little fish.

It took Wren a few seconds to discern the shape of them, but when she did, she backed away instinctively, though she was several feet away from the water to begin with. The fish were small, but they had huge, incredibly sharp teeth and made quick work of the former prisoner who had been thrown in the water for them to consume. It took barely a minute for them to eat everything, the sound of their jaws snapping in disappointment echoing all throughout the dungeon when it became clear there was no more food to be had.

And then the fish dissipated, swimming back deeper into the water until Wren could no longer see them. The water grew still once more.

Out of sight, but not out of mind.

She was sincerely glad she had not touched the water once over the past three days. She had no doubt the fish had an incredibly keen sense of smell and movement. One stray slip into the water, and Wren might not make it back out alive.

Wren's head was left full of snapping jaws, prisoners turned into chum, and the faces of those she had lost, as she wondered how many days she was supposed to put up with the torment she had found herself in. Surely, the High King had no use of her stuck in here forever? She lowered herself to the left rear corner of the cell and leaned her head against the wall, eyelids heavy. Perhaps the king thought to break her? He would not be successful. She closed her eyes. Tomorrow, she'd begin training again. It was time to stop playing the prey and become the predator.

When she awoke, she was not sure why.

Exhaustion plagued her and the aches in her bones complained as she shifted on the hard stone, ready to go back to sleep. She could not have been asleep for longer than a couple of hours. Her eyelids closed, but something kept her from falling back asleep.

Something was wrong.

She opened her eyes and froze as realization dawned.

Water lapped at her ankles.

Wren jerked to her feet in an instant, looking down at the water that was filling her cell. It rose with the tide every day, but this was the highest it had been. Even now, as she watched it, the water climbed farther and farther inside, until after a minute, it was around her calves. Her mind flashed back to the man-eating fish. She needed to get out of the water *now*.

"What do we do?" she called to the bard.

"Climb, climb, climb!"

She glanced in his direction. It was almost completely impossible to see him in the darkness of deep night, but she tracked the sound of his movements and realized he was higher up than her.

"High, up high, as if it were the sky," the boy sang at her, his shadow clinging to the metal grate of the cell walls. "Fish do not fly, do they? That would be a sight to see!"

Wren did not need to hear the riddle twice. Without another thought, she scrambled up the bars on her left, climbing up and up until she was out of the water. But it wasn't high enough; in five minutes the water reached her toes, so she climbed even higher.

"Do they mean for us to die?" she fired at the boy. "What is this madness?"

"I'd make a good corpse if I am dead," was all the boy said, in lieu of a real answer.

He had been through this before and he was still alive. But not completely sane. Had night after night like this driven him into madness?

She could believe it.

Already, her muscles were beginning to ache with the effort of clinging to the bars. There was nowhere for her to lean her weight against, so the only thing that was keeping her out of the water was pure strength. Which wasn't great, considering the terrible, insubstantial meals the guards had been feeding her, and the previous injuries she had sustained in battle.

Yet, clinging onto the bars was all Wren could do. If she fell into the water, she would be dead.

"How long does it last?" she barked. Silence. "How long does this last?" she demanded louder. Silence answered her once more. The little rascal chose now to be quiet?

Wren glared in his direction, listening to the silence. Well, not complete silence. Her eyes rounded. The blasted boy was snoring. She couldn't believe it. How the devil was he sleeping?

"You're mad," she grumbled.

After what felt like forever but could, in fact, have been mere minutes—time passed as slow as a glacier—Wren's eyes began to grow heavy, and she jolted herself awake several times. Panic and sheer adrenaline were the only things stopping her from falling to her doom. But it was getting harder and harder to keep herself up, and, with every passing minute, she felt her fingers and her toes and her knees trying to give way. The metal bit into her fingers and toes, cutting off the blood circulation.

You're going to fall.

It was inevitable.

Wren hung on for as long as she could. Her fingers cramped as her foot slipped. She crashed, spraying water everywhere.

Water covered her face and she jerked upward, breaking the surface. She screamed as the water lapped at her neck with her sitting there. Wren scrambled to her feet, the canal water at her midthigh. Her muscles quivered as she tried and failed to climb the bloody cell wall again.

Panic swirled in her gut. How long did she have until the fish attacked?

She glanced at the canal as a spine broke through the surface of the water.

What the devil was that?

That is no small fish.

Wren clung to the bars when yellow, catlike eyes gleamed at her from beneath the small waves that her fall into the water had created. Her jaw dropped.

Is that...?

Wren could scarcely comprehend it. In a dungeon, in Verlanti? It seemed impossible.

But it wasn't.

Swimming in front of Wren was a water dragon.

CHAPTER SIXTEEN

ARRIK

His father was up to something.

The Verlantian navy had suffered heavy casualties during the battle near the Lorne capital. The king was a prideful man who took any mishap to be a personal affront to him. It was never *his* fault, but he always found someone to blame and punish. That was usually Arrik.

Or it had been, until he'd stopped making mistakes the king could trace back to him.

They'd lost too many ships for Arrik to sweep under the rug and his father hadn't said a bloody thing about the losses. Something wasn't right and it made him uneasy. His father was a mercurial creature but he had a pattern of behavior that Arrik had figured out years prior. The fact that it was changing now unsettled him.

"Brother!"

Arrik scowled in the dark and slowly turned around. It was better he faced his second eldest brother Cathal than try to outrun him, lest he find a knife in his face. In all truth, Arrik was older than Cathal and Ares, but the king had his birth date changed. No one knew Arrik was really the first born and if he wanted to keep living, it would stay that way.

Cathal sauntered up to him, a woman clinging to each of his arms. He smiled maliciously, flashing crooked teeth. Arrik rested his left hand on the pommel of his sword and braced himself. Dealing with his brother was like trying to dance with a viper. Dumb and extremely hazardous for one's health.

"Brother," he greeted, barely keeping the sarcasm from his voice. His half-brothers had never acted like true family. Cathal had sent a minimum of five assassins after Arrik throughout the years. He'd learned a few tricks. His brothers liked to rile him and cause mischief, so he did the exact opposite. He'd learned to master his control and never attacked outright. Arrik learned how to pull the strings from the shadows.

"I heard you visited your mother's grave today," his brother commented.

"I did." He knew where this was going. The rat.

"Did you know," Cathal continued conversationally, glancing at each of the women hanging on him, "That our precious Arrik's mother killed herself on this day five years ago?" The woman with sable skin and black hair glanced at Arrik in sympathy but stayed silent when Cathal chuckled. "She lived life in luxury with everything a person could want. My father even buried her in the family tombs despite her disgrace."

Arrik kept his temper in check even though he wanted to punch the drunken smirk off his older brother's face. The fool didn't know what he was talking about. Arrik's mother had been a duchess and had refused the king's advances as she was a married woman. Plus, his mum hated Soren. They'd grown up around each other as children and he'd proved himself to be bully with a god complex that enjoyed hurting others. She managed to rebuff him as a young woman, but he hadn't taken kindly to it the second time. The king had her husband killed, seized their lands, and then made Arrik's mum one of his many wives. Soren found special pleasure in tormenting her. One such time led to the creation of Arrik. She used to say he was the only good thing to come out of the cursed palace.

"Why would anyone want to leave this place?" the other woman slurred, her green eyes glassy.

"Why indeed?" Cathal said with a smirk. "The tarte had everything."

Arrik tensed and a strong hand gripped his left shoulder. He glanced at Shane, not surprised at all that his friend had snuck up on him. He moved like a wraith.

"My prince," Shane murmured with a bow. "I believe the rest of your company eagerly awaits your arrival in your chambers."

"Perfect!" Cathal grinned and plowed forward.

Arrik and Shane stepped aside as the prince and his entourage weaved past them with a fit of giggles and whispers. He stared after his brother and spat on the ground once he'd disappeared into the building. The lanterns wavered in the light breeze, their shadows dancing on the cobbles of the path.

"You need to get that under control," Shane said softly.

He tipped his head back and peered through the trees to a small patch of visible sky. Stars glimmered above. "He spoke of my mother."

Shane sucked in a sharp breath. "That sod."

"I could have killed him."

"Arrik," his friend growled. "Control your words. The walls have ears."

Shane was right. One misstep and everything they'd built in the last few years would be ruined. He needed to do better.

For his mum.

For those abused by the royals.

CHAPTER SEVENTEEN

WREN

It couldn't be, and yet...there was no doubt about it: there was a water dragon lurking just outside her cell. The dragons never lived this far north. It was too cold. The thermals from the underwater volcanos around Lorne made it the perfect home for dragons. What in the blazes was one doing her? In a dungeon. Facing the Princess of the Dragon Isles.

In the near-pitch-darkness, the dragon seemed to glow faintly in the water in an enthralling, luminous manner. Wren knew some dragons lit up like that to attract prey into the deepest depths of the sea; for Wren to witness it first-hand was nothing short of astounding.

Going by what she could see of its head and face, she knew the dragon was bigger than Aurora, though it seemed just as sleek as her. The spines that protruded from the water were tall and thin, however, making the dragon perhaps more suited to water-dwelling than sky-flying.

From the neon blue light the dragon emitted, Wren concluded that its scales were a rich blue-black, like spilled oil. The beast's spines flared, and she held her ground at the sign of aggression. At the first sign of weakness, the creature would attack.

She exhaled slowly and tried to calm her racing heart. The dragon rumbled softly, its gaze focused completely on her. Wren was staring death in the face. She was unable to tear her eyes away from the feline gaze of the beast. It hissed and bared its long, pointed teeth. Dark humor seized her and she had to stifle her laughter. After everything that had happened, it would be ironic if the creature killed her.

In some ways, Wren found it fitting. Almost welcome, in a twisted kind of way. To be so far away from home, a prisoner no less, but to die under circumstances the people of Lorne were accustomed to, was far preferable than any other method—tiny fish with razor teeth included.

You're not going to die today. At least not without a fight.

Not while she still had a kingdom to save and a sister to protect.

What would her mother have told her to do? How could she work the situation in her favor? The dragon was different from those of the isles. Did it communicate in the same way?

Wren gave a small chirrup, but the beast didn't respond in kind.

She frowned, worry churning in her gut. Did the Verlantians know that the dragon was in their dungeon? Was it put there to eat her?

Regardless, Wren was a daughter of the isles, and she wouldn't idly sit by while there was the smallest hope of the dragon helping her.

She swallowed hard, opened her mouth, and began to sing. Her dragon song started off softly, just testing the waters. The

FROST KAY

beast didn't attack, but neither did it retreat.

Her lips trembled in nervousness, causing her hums to vibrate off-key. The dragon shifted in front of her, a low growl emitting from its throat.

Come on, Wren. You can do this. Think of everything your mother taught you.

Her mother. Her mother had taught her everything she knew about dragons, even though the woman had not been a native of the Dragon Isles. She had loved the creatures as fiercely as Wren had and ensured her daughter knew everything there was to know about communicating and befriending the beasts. And yet she had been sure to instill in Wren a reverence and a fear of the creatures.

Dragons were not to be trifled with. Even the naval officers of Lorne did not escape injuries and death at the hands of the dragons.

They weren't pets. They were partners.

Emotion saturated her song, and added depth to her humming and power to her voice where, before, there had been none. Her pitch leveled out, and, though the dragon growled louder when she paused to consider what to say or sing, Wren's resolve stood firm.

In the end, she sang a sorrowful, haunting tune that her mother taught her when she was but a small child. It was for calming the most tempestuous of hearts, her mother had said. Wren had never understood, back then, why a song to tame a dragon sounded so sad, but it was only in losing almost everything that she finally understood it: there was, indeed, a calm that came with accepting grief and pain, then accepting that it did not rule a person's life.

Wren's loss was a part of her now, yes. That would never change.

But it did not have to define her.

All she had to do was accept it—to not hate herself for crying when it was all she wanted to do—and then her sadness was merely an emotion she felt. It would not be the end of her. It would not be all she felt until the end of time.

The dragon's spines lowered, it ceased its rumbling, and stilled. She could have sworn she could see a similar sadness in its golden eyes reflected back at her. It was possible she was seeing things, but animals had souls. And the dragon in front of her? Well, it had suffered. Wren could sense it as she continued to sing.

For the dragon was still a dragon, and an unknown one at that. She had no rapport with it. It had no reason to trust her, nor her trust it. It wasn't like it had been with Aurora—an immediate connection, almost love at first sight. Wren had been there when Aurora hatched when she was a child. They had grown and evolved together. There was not a single moment when they had not trusted each other with their lives.

This time was different. One wrong move, and Wren would be dead.

So, she kept on singing like her life depended on it, because it did. She kept on singing even when her throat grew raw, and her voice became raspy and hoarse. As long as the dragon remained, Wren would not let up an inch.

The beast stayed at the mouth of Wren's cell, never moving and never making a noise until, finally, the water around

Wren's knees began to recede with the tide. The dragon made a motion to move backward, just an inch, then one more. As it moved backward, its luminescence grew duller, as if it was tied to the pull of the water.

Ten minutes later, the creature had disappeared with the tide.

Wren stood there, heart in her throat. What had just happened? Had she imagined the whole encounter?

"Beautiful voice you have," the bard commented, breaking the spell.

She blinked, realizing she'd hardly been aware of her surroundings. Wren glanced toward his cell as he climbed down the bars to the wet cobbles of the floor. She stared at his silhouette. How long had the musician been awake? Or had he been faking it the entire time?

"You had me transfixed as much as the beast."

Wren ignored him, her attention moving to the tide that pulled the water back along with the dragon. The creature's appearance in and of itself had been a telltale giveaway that the water in the dungeon was connected to the sea at large. Which meant there was a way out of here.

Only if the dragon isn't trapped in here with you.

Either way, the beast could be the key. For Wren also noticed that, while it had been present, no fish had dared to try and attack her. There hadn't been a single one of the animals in sight. They were scared of the dragon. If Wren kept close to it, then she need not fear the fish.

This could be her way out.

She dropped to her knees the moment no more water

remained in the cell, though she gasped in pain when she hit the bare stone floor. She had been exhausted before the tide came in, but that was nothing compared to the weariness that washed over her now.

Sleep. She needed just a little rest and then she'd figure out what to do with the dragon.

The sound of heavy footsteps echoed behind the prison door, and then the door was swung open. Two Verlantian warriors stepped into Wren's cell.

Alarm filled her. "What is going on?" she just barely managed to say, but the words were hardly audible due to her previous singing.

The soldiers did not answer. Instead, they roughly dragged Wren to her feet and pulled her from the cell. It was as if they knew what she has just been thinking. As if, somehow, High King Soren had gotten into Wren's head and seen the bare sliver of hope of escape and planned to snuff it out before it could be realized.

She looked over her shoulder at her cell as the door clanged shut. Wren never thought she'd willingly want to return to the dungeon, with its carnivorous fish, deadly dragons, and mad boys who spoke in riddles.

But anything was preferable than dealing with the High King of Verlanti.

CHAPTER EIGHTEEN

ARRIK

Arrik was half-tempted to ignore his father's summons when he received them. He was in no mood to deal with the man's court, much less put up with the king himself. But ever since Arrik had returned from the Dragon Isles, his father had paraded him around like a prize bull, ensuring no man nor woman nor child was left unaware of what Arrik had achieved for Verlanti during the invasion.

He has a reason for doing so.

He grimaced at his reflection and set down his goblet of wine on the dresser as he threw off the plain gray shirt he'd been wearing in his own chambers for something more befitting his father's taste. Well, as much as he could stomach to do: Soren was known for loving everything shiny and opulent. *Like a dragon with a pile of treasure.*

So Arrik slid himself into a silken, black shirt, over which he wore an even darker black tunic that was heavily embroidered with silver, with a double breast of silver buttons running down the front. He did not bother to change the pale leggings he was already wearing, finishing off the look with knee-high, polished leather boots before pulling his braids back with a silver band.

It was as close to the High King's preferred image as Arrik could suffer, yet he knew it would still not be enough. He was the favorite son for now...but he knew that couldn't possibly last. Not while he was considered illegitimate. Not while he could be used to rile up Soren's trueborn sons.

For though the High King adored the wealth Arrik had brought him, through the many nations he'd conquered and shorelines he'd raided, Arrik knew fine and well that only a trueborn son would sit on the throne. Which meant his achievements could only be used to shame and motivate his half-brothers into being half the man the illegitimate prince was.

"As if that will ever happen," Arrik told his reflection, finishing off the goblet of wine he'd been drinking when he'd been going over the reports on what had been taken from Lorne Castle.

Though he was tempted to take his time reaching his father's throne room—not the grand one used to entertain foreign guests, but the smaller, far more intimate one that Soren preferred when talking with his advisers and parasitic court followers—Arrik knew it was wiser not to dally. His father's patience was notoriously thin. No one wanted to be out of his graces.

So, he hastened his step, making his entrance to the hideously gaudy, opulent room only a moment before he would have been considered late.

High King Soren was displeased, nonetheless, looking bored as he picked at his nails. "You have kept me waiting when I have such grand news to share with you, *Son*."

Around the king, his true-blood sons barely smothered their sniggers at this admonition of their half-brother. Arrik knew that his brothers despised him. But he did not care; if they'd brought in even half the amount of treasure and land and fame that Arrik had brought to Verlanti, then they, too, would be preferred by the king. While he'd come to accept that he was a tool, Arrik also knew that he was invaluable to the king at the moment and that gave *him* power.

He passively eyed his brothers in distain. They were just as cruel as their father, and had his taste for shiny and beautiful things. However, they lacked the drive that the king had. Ultimately, the High King's trueborn sons were lazy. They expected things to be handed to them and did not seem to have any clue about how to get those things themselves.

Instead, they languished around the palace at large, as well as around the kingdom of Verlanti, spending their days partaking in petty trifles, drugs, alcohol, and—of course—women.

Of course, Arrik had tried all of these things, too. But what separated him from his brothers was that he knew how to control his impulses. He was *always* in control. And he knew that petty trifles were exactly that—petty trifles. Mere distractions from what was important. Letting oneself be ruled by the flesh was the worst mistake any person could make.

None of them should rule.

The worst part was that Arrik was probably the most qualified son to rule, and yet it would never be. Verlanti would inherit a lazy, spoiled king when Soren died, the last one standing after murdering all of his other brothers.

As if they haven't tried already.

Arrik bowed his head to his father. "Apologies, Your Royal Highness. I was distracted by the bounty reports from Lorne."

At this, the king laughed easily. "Always business with you, Arrik." He cast a sweeping gaze over Arrik's brothers, his eyes narrowing and his lips thinning in what seemed like disapproval. "But I suppose that is why you are the only one who gets things done, isn't it? So devoted. Too bad my *other* sons don't know the meaning of the word."

The tittering from his brothers stopped. Though it was a jibe entirely pointed at their own faults, they would still blame Arrik rather than themselves for it. He kept his mask of polite interest in place.

Children, the lot of them.

"You mustn't forget to relax sometimes," a feminine voice added, all soft and sweet and entirely seductive.

The queen. Astrid. He suppressed a grimace.

Even though Astrid had known Arrik his entire life, and despite the fact she was his stepmother, she was always trying to tempt him into her bed. It disgusted him. The front of adoration she put up toward her husband was exactly that: a front.

The queen was unearthly beautiful, with her long, thick raven hair and deep eyes the color of burnt umber. She did not seem to age which if magic were real, he knew she'd have sold her soul long ago.

She sauntered past him and brushed a finger down his arm before she approached her husband, hips swaying. It still floored Arrik how the queen blatantly flirted with men in front of her husband, let alone one of her husband's sons. Her affairs were unending, but so were the king's, even though he'd collected over a hundred other wives and countless concubines.

I will never do that.

Arrik was many things, but cuckold wasn't one of those. He would never do such an accursed thing as to lie in bed with his father's wife and queen. Even if the woman hadn't been his stepmother and married to his father, but to some other man, he still wouldn't do it. He may not have had many morals in war and battle and many other things but touching another man's wife was wrong.

He'd never cross that line.

"Perhaps I will find time to relax when there *is* time to relax," Arrik said carefully, more than practiced himself in the art of hidden jibes. If his brothers had been snakes, they would have hissed in response. Their barely suppressed rage was almost enough to make him laugh.

Almost.

King Soren seemed thoroughly amused by his quip, as was Astrid, despite the fact Arrik was insulting her own children. She flashed him a dazzling smile, not caring that the entire room of advisers and court-goers in the room could see what she was doing. But they were all under her spell, it seemed. No one would refuse a place in her bed if she asked it of them.

All except Arrik.

He wondered if that was the only reason Astrid kept trying to tempt him: because he always said no.

His attention was drawn elsewhere when the sound of a struggle in the corridor some ways off from the throne room pricked his pointed ears in interest. Soren straightened in his ridiculously decorated, gilded chair before nodding at him.

"You have done well these last few weeks," he said, addressing the room at large. All absent-minded conversations that had previously filled the air stopped, and the attention of each and every single person was on Arrik and the king. "It should come as no surprise to you, my son, that you highly deserve a reward." A pause for dramatic effect. The struggling outside grew louder, and Arrik began to discern voices. One of them sounded female, and Arrik worked out what was happening in an instant.

No. That degenerate.

Arrik pushed down his anger.

His father pointed toward the door. "I need a strong and trustworthy man to rule over Lorne and the rest of the Dragon Isles. After all you have given the kingdom of Verlanti, it seems only fitting that your reward is a kingdom all your own. Bring her in," Soren ordered, his voice booming around the room.

Not one, not two, but four warriors struggled through the doorway with Princess Wren. Arrik smothered a grin at the sight; he highly doubted all four men had been originally sent to get her from her prison cell.

She was soaking wet, still wearing his old, tattered black shirt. Her bare feet scrabbled against the floor as they forced her into the room. The princess glared at all that would look her way. Her time in the dungeons didn't seem to have the effect the king hoped.

The guards tossed her toward Arrik, and he caught her bound hands against his chest. He stared down at the top of her deep red hair, the urge to run his fingers through it pricking him. A disgusting smell caught his attention and his nose wrinkled. It emanated off the princess.

"You stink," he muttered.

Her head slowly lifted, and she bared her teeth. "I'm not here for your pleasure."

He snorted. That was for bloody sure.

Arrik pushed her away and she hovered next to his side. Water dropped from the sodden shirt onto the floor, and he tried not to look at the way the fabric plastered to her curves. His fingers flexed with the need to run them along her waist.

Get it together.

Wren did not look at him, choosing instead to stare blankly ahead. It was difficult to avoid noticing that she was mostly naked beneath the layers of muck and blood that caked into her skin. Some deep, protective instinct within Arrik made him want to remove his shirt and place it around her shivering shoulders, but he knew such weakness would not be tolerated by his father. So, he stood his ground instead, waiting for his father to continue.

"A gift for you, my son," Soren said, clearly pleased with himself. His blue eyes had lit up at the sight of Wren in all her damaged, disgusting glory. *Like a lion with its prey firmly trapped between its paws.* "Secure the cooperation of the Dragon Isles using her. You will be not only their conqueror but their king!"

King.

The word rung in his ears. How had his father known? Arrik's goal had been to survive his father's greed long enough to take his kingdom. By Soren placing him in the ransacked isles, it kept him from sowing anarchy in Verlanti. Blast it all.

Think. Just think. Not everything is ruined.

Lorne contained black diamonds, dragons, a stellar long-range navy, and the trade routes...if the king thought he was tossing his son into a backwater kingdom that he could control through Arrik, he was mistaken. This was just one more step in taking Verlanti from Soren.

The princess wavered at his side, drawing his attention once more. Marriage wasn't ideal. He'd promised himself that he'd never take another bride after the death of his last one. There wasn't anything wrong with the princess. If he was honest, beneath the filth, she was attractive. But he could not think about such a thing now. Soren had a canny way of ferreting out a person's deepest thoughts. The undertaking of dethroning the elf king was no small matter. It would take time, planning, and deviousness.

He cast his gaze back down at the last remaining member of King Oswin's line. For a moment it looked as if Wren was going to keep her eyes forward but then he caught her peeking at him from the corner of her eye. She scowled but smoothed over her expression.

Oh, so that's how the wild princess would play it. She thought to fool him. But as he eyed her regal stance and flaming hair, it was physical proof that she was not broken or tamed. She'd have to do better if she thought to fool Arrik.

But another wife? He barely kept himself from growling.

While it was certainly intriguing, the idea of having this warrior princess belonging to him, he knew it would only end up one way. With her dead. Something stirred within Arrik at the thought—the same feeling that had erupted in him when she fallen from the sky—guilt and sadness. Their marriage would only end up in tragedy but there was no other way.

"Well, what do you think, Arrik?" High King Soren asked expectantly.

Arrik took a second to observe his brothers. Their reactions ranged from anger to amusement. His youngest brother, though, seemed to be very interested in the dragon princess. The wild woman commanded attention even dressed in rags and covered in grime. She held power.

Power that is yours if you take it.

He bowed at the waist to his father. "I humbly accept your generous gift, my lord." He straightened and held his hand out to his betrothed. "Will you accept me, my lady?"

Her deep blue eyes snapped to his face and Arrik could see she wanted to say no. Instead, she clenched her jaw and exhaled heavily, before placing her grimy hands in his. "As my lord says," she grated out.

"There you have it," the king crowed.

The courtiers cheered but Arrik hardly heard any of it as he stared down at his new bride to be. No doubt his life was about to become a whole lot more colorful...

That's if he and his new bride made it out of their wedding night alive and unscathed.

His past brides hadn't been so lucky.

CHAPTER NINETEEN

WREN

This was not part of the plan.

After everything she'd endured, now she had to marry the man who'd destroyed her life. Wren seethed, making her fury clearly apparent on her face. It took every effort on her part not to spit in the man's face as she slowly, very slowly, turned to face him. She'd prepared to marry the elf king but not the monster that stood in front of her. She stared him down, willing him to look away in shame.

But he didn't.

The prince—Arrik, his father had said—merely held Wren's gaze with his cold, glass-like eyes. She could discern nothing from them, nor from his expression. It was as if he was made from stone. Like he was empty inside. Maybe he was.

Her mind flashed back to his hands around her throat. There *had* been something behind Arrik's eyes then, though she was quite certain she did not want to be at the receiving end of that once more. Rowen would have never touched a woman like that. She focused her attention on his chin and tried to breathe passed the pain in her chest at the memory of her betrothed.

"Princess."

She clashed gazes with him, and she swore a glimmer of emotion flashed though his eyes. Wren did not wish to work out what that was, nor did she care. She hated the man who stood in front of her—even more so now that she was going to become his bride, whether she liked it or not.

"What say you?" the elf king asked.

Wren glanced at the monarch who smirked at her from his throne. A shiver ran down her spine at the chilling smile he gave her. There was something about him that was off. It was more than his too pretty exterior; something dark lurked beneath the surface.

She tipped her chin up and prepared herself. Wren needed to insinuate herself in his court but if she came too willingly, her plan would be too obvious. She could do nothing but ensure everyone knew she decidedly did *not* like it.

Her belly churned and bile rose up her gullet with every moment the elf king watched her. She couldn't look at him any longer. Wren cast her gaze around the throne room instead. It was a smaller one than before, but it was still full of High King Soren's retinue. Some of the people lingering by the throne seemed to be advisers or warriors of sorts, judging by their clothes and armor. Others were clearly vain, hedonistic court-goers who had little use aside from looking pretty and predatory. Even as they turned their noses away from Wren—she knew perfectly well that she smelled like something closer to death than life—they delighted in barely keeping their gossip at the level of whispers.

Wren's upper lip curled in disgust at the lot of them. "I would rather die than marry the Beast of Verlanti." It was the truth.

Rowen wasn't even cold in his grave. His ashes had barely left the Dragon Isles upon the wind. She turned back to face Arrik once more, who seemed more amused than anything else at her answer. It only made her hate him more, that he belittled the suffering that he himself had caused.

It was clear Wren's indignant answer was exactly the one the room at large hoped she would give, for all around her was an eruption of laughter and comments made about her, all of them awful. It was then that Wren became aware not just of how she smelled but of her physical state, and she flushed with shame.

But she did not *want* to feel shame.

Even covered in rags and muck and blood, with salt crystallizing in her hair, she was a princess. She spoke in the tongue of dragons and flew upon their backs. The only people in the entire room who could stand on level ground with her were the king, his beautiful, dark-haired queen, and his sons. Even then it was in stature only. They were all degenerates, the beast especially.

High King Soren sighed in exaggerated fashion, as if Wren's answer disappointed him deeply. "Your death could be arranged for you, if that would be preferable to marriage," he said. "But it would be such a waste of human flesh." He turned to his followers. "Wouldn't you agree? Even beneath all that grime and filth, she's worth something."

"My dear," the queen chastised, running her fingers seductively over her husband's arm. "Let's not speculate her worth like a horse."

"Both of us know a horse would fetch more," the king

retorted.

She clenched her jaw but kept silent as the queen pressed her lips together.

The courtiers responded like a pack of dogs on the morning of a hunt, nodding and agreeing with an enthusiasm Wren found positively shameful in its obvious shallowness. The whole thing was despicable and all she wanted was to go home. She hated it more than the dungeon she'd been thrown in, regardless of the fact her companions had been a mad bard, tiny, carnivorous fish, and a deadly dragon.

All three of them are like a walk across a meadow on a sunny day compared to this lot.

Hysterical laughter bubbled from her belly, but she choked it down, wishing she could cover her ears to the sounds of everyone talking and laughing and insulting her.

They cannot hurt you unless you let them. Focus on something positive.

She tuned them out and the wild dragon floated to the forefront of her mind. He was her ticket—the way out. All she had to do was put up with the people of Soren's court a little longer—especially Arrik—then she had no doubt she'd be tossed back into her cell for the evening. And if the dragon showed up again...

Wren might be able to get out.

"Unfortunately," the prince said, his tone bored. "Whether you would rather die or not is inconsequential." He dismissed her and turned his attention to the king. By the tides, she wanted to punch him in the face. "I accept this gift, Father. And I would prefer that the wedding occurred sooner rather than later."

Her stomach bottomed out.

Soren cackled and looked delighted by his son's impatience to be wed. Wren bit down on her bottom lip as hard as she could muster to stop herself from saying something stupid. She'd always thought of herself as being levelheaded but here amongst her enemies, Wren was a danger to herself.

"Then it shall be tomorrow," the king announced, gesturing his hands wide to his adoring audience. "Which means we have much to prepare. Get to work!" He clapped his hands and held one out to his wife. "Would you be so kind as to arrange it, my love?"

"Of course, my lord." The queen rose from the throne and clasped her hands. "My ladies, we have much to do." With that one action, a flurry of motion filled the room as people went off to do whatever it was that needed to be done.

Wren imagined she would not like any of these preparations organized for 'her' wedding one bit. Probably a host of slaves. The thought made her mood sour further. Slavery was barbaric and immoral. No person had the right to own another.

For just a moment, she locked eyes with the queen before the woman exited the room. The queen's soft smile in her direction was completely at odds with everyone else. There was something sympathetic about her face. Something understanding. Something...motherly.

Wren wished, in that instant, that she knew the queen's name. Maybe she'd be a friend and ally.

She was startled out of her thoughts as large hands settled on her waist a moment before she was swept off her feet.

"Time to go, Princess," Arrik said, lifting Wren up and carrying her out of the throne room before she regained the wits to oppose such an undignified exit. Not caring about how much of her body she exposed in doing so, she twisted within his arms and flailed her legs wildly until, finally, Arrik dropped her on the ground.

Her rear smarted but she ignored it as she climbed to her feet. "Don't touch me!" she spat in his face. "How dare you presume to touch me?!"

He merely laughed, before picking her up again and throwing her over his shoulder. "It seems I will not be able to trust you in my chambers," he replied. "Another night in the cell it is, then. I can't have you killing me in my sleep!"

Wren had not meant anything by her outburst aside from getting as far away from Arrik as possible, though it was clear that in attacking him she had ensured that she was returned to the location she actually needed to go.

She wanted to avoid his chambers at all costs. Wren didn't want to think of what that would have meant.

You need another weapon.

She punched him in the back one last time and hung there. She tried not to stare at his arse, but it was right in front of her face. He may have been a vile cretin, and she was loathe to admit it, but he was attractive.

Stop it. Focus on what's important.

Wren was going back to her cell, and that was that. It was what she wanted. If Arrik knew that—if he grew suspicious of the fact she wanted to go back there—then he would no doubt do everything in his power to stop her being in the dungeon.

Then her hopes of escape would be dashed, and she would be buggered.

She kicked her legs and punched him a few more times to keep up the pretense of her distaste all the way down to the underground level of the palace. Wren screamed and cursed, doing just about anything she could think of to make it as difficult as possible for him to carry her.

"You are wild, dragon lass," he said upon their approach to the dungeon. He was barely able to keep hold of Wren as he waited for a guard to open the door. "Are you like this in the bedroom, too?"

Wren swore loudly in response, only to repeat the curse when the prince unceremoniously dropped her upon the cold stone floor of her cell.

"Until tomorrow then, Princess," he said, crystal eyes flashing in the dark, looking down on her, like the inhuman barbarian that he was.

She leapt to her feet as the door clanged shut. Wren slapped a hand against the bars. "I hate you!" she screamed as he walked away.

"The feeling is mutual," he called over his shoulder before ascending the stairway at the end of the hall.

"You shall pay for this!" Her voice echoed around her but he didn't respond.

She puffed out a breath once the last guard disappeared up the steps and she turned, leaning her back against the bars. A twisted sense of enjoyment filled her at needling the man. He deserved to be as disturbed as she was.

And one day he *would* pay for it. But that was for another

time—if Wren survived long enough to give him his comeuppance.

She glanced toward the bard, and found him staring at her. Wren cocked an eyebrow but he stayed silent. *Figures.*

Wren wasted no time in approaching the water's end and eyeing its unknown depths. Was the dragon lurking below? Or were the fish waiting for her?

"What are you looking for?" he asked.

"A way out." She sat down and waited.

"If your way out involves death, then you are staring it in the face! Death with the fishes!"

She did not even glance at him. "If you have nothing useful to say, then I don't wish to hear it. Either tell me your name and speak plainly, or do not speak at all."

"The Princess of Dragons has no manners," the boy replied, jutting out his lip as if he was incredibly offended. But then, he grinned like the fool he was. "I told you: I have many names. But none of them matter."

"Then I guess you should be quiet. I'm thinking."

It followed, of course, that the boy resolutely did exactly the opposite, and Wren was forced to listen to him reciting all manner of riddles and poems and songs until she thought she might be going just as mad as he was.

But eventually what little light had been in the dungeon faded away, and when the water began to shift and creep toward her, Wren knew it was time. Getting to her feet, she rolled her shoulders, arched her back, then climbed up the iron bars of her cell, hoping against hope that the dragon would appear once again.

The boy watched curiously from two cells down. He clambered up the bars, though he kept his eyes on Wren. "You look ready to kill someone," he commented. "What is your target? The fish?"

Wren said nothing. She had to concentrate. There was no guarantee the dragon would even show up. Which meant Wren had to be on the lookout for any kind of sign that it may be lurking beneath the water.

Anything at all.

Time ticked by at a glacial pace. The water rose and rose and rose, and, by the time it reached its full height, Wren's muscles felt close to breaking once more. How had the bard managed it twice a day? She was going to fall into the water when the dragon was not around to keep the fish away. Then she would be chum.

Dark amusement filled her. That was one way to deny the king. Die.

Pale blue luminescent light shimmered beneath the water and she smiled.

It was time.

Wren climbed down into the water as the long, luminous spines of the dragon sliced through the surface as it made its way toward her. It stopped by the edge of her cell, as it had the night before. Then a pair of yellow, narrow pupils emerged from the water to watch her.

She took a deep breath and began to sing.

Wren sang a variation of what she had hummed the night before, still haunting and plaintive but less tragic and more dreamlike. She wanted to entrance the dragon: to make it *need* her to continue singing like its life depended on it. Wren had to get it on her side.

To her left, the boy grew silent, apparently listening intently to her song.

She ignored him once again.

All her attention was on the dragon.

Wren hummed and sang for what felt like hours, throat already sore from the night before, but whenever she paused to see if it had been enough, the dragon shifted, unsettling the water by growling softly, large spines lifting up along its back.

A male then.

She had not done enough yet. He did not trust her.

It has to be tonight.

Her panic rose when the water began to recede, and, in the space of a few minutes, the dragon stared her down one last time before disappearing beneath the waves.

"Blast it all!" Wren cried, slapping her palms against the stone floor. "Come back."

Only the echoes of her own voice answered Wren. She'd failed.

There was no escaping her fate now.

Tomorrow, she'd marry the enemy.

CHAPTER TWENTY

Arrik

It was ironic that the safest place for his betrothed was a man-eating fish infested cell.

Arrik entered his bed chamber. It was a huge rectangle room with a massive four poster bed on the left bracketed by two side tables and a large gilded mirror. To the right sat a set of chairs that bracketed the fireplace and his weapons. It was sparse, but it was the way he liked it. It wasn't as if he really stayed here.

The far end of the room was open to the outdoors, only supported by large marble columns. Sheer white curtains hung from the ceiling that gave the impression of privacy. It was a farce. Arrik never could sleep a wink in the room. It was too exposed.

He passed through the room and pushed through the gauzy curtains, entering the courtyard filled with leafy plants. Arrik shoved them aside until he reached the heated bathing pool in the middle. Shane and Ronan stood beside the pool waiting for him.

Ronan—the normally jovial redhead—stared at him with pity. Arrik held his hand up before his friend could utter a word.

"There's nothing to be done about it."

Shane scowled and crossed his arms. "Another wife?"

Arrik glared at his second in command. "How could I refuse? Soren had already made up his mind. He knew I did not wish to wed again which is exactly why he made the announcement in public."

"Do you think he knows what we're up to?" Shane asked.

"It's hard to know." Arrik pushed his braids back from his face. "I've done all that he's asked of me. He's arrogant enough to believe that I worship the ground he walks on but intelligent enough to know that I could also pose a threat if not checked."

"The wild lass from Lorne is how he plans to control you," his second supplied.

Ronan snorted. "That's if she lives long enough." Arrik shot a glare at his friend. Ronan scowled and held his hands up. "Everyone was thinking it, but I just said it out loud. She has a target painted on her back now and she doesn't even know it."

Shane snorted. "That woman knows she's deep in the enemy's lair. She's not stupid, but she is a liability. I wouldn't put it past her to try and kill you, Arrik."

That made him smile. He liked a woman with a feisty spirit. His smile disappeared. But would it be enough to help her survive? He doubted it. "The king has granted me power whether he intended to do so or not. The isles control trade, the diamonds, and dragons."

"The people won't take kindly to your rulership," Shane advised.

"True, but if I were to return with the heir...it may work to our favor."

Ronan scrubbed a hand over his beard. "Hypothetically, that could work, but only if she's not assassinated. At this moment, she could have someone coming for her."

"I placed trustworthy men over her," Arrik replied. "No one will get to her this night, but she will need constant protection."

"Invisible protection," Shane added. "Any special treatment toward her will be noticed and stir more trouble. You can't show her any favor."

Arrik chuckled. "When have I ever fallen for a woman? I have one goal."

Shane studied him and nodded. "Then we are agreed. I will arrange for invisible protectors to follow the girl. No one will know they are there." He strode to Arrik's side and clasped his shoulder. "I know you don't want this, but it is in our favor."

He nodded as his second disappeared through the plants.

Ronan pulled a flask from his vest and held it out to him. "Shall we celebrate your last night as an unmarried man?"

Arrik took it from him and uncapped the spirits. "To my fourth marriage. May it not end in blood and guilt."

CHAPTER TWENTY-ONE

WREN

There was far too little time between the dragon disappearing into the dark water and several Verlantian warriors returning to the prison to collect Wren the next morning.

For her wedding.

For her doom.

"My lady, it's time to get ready for your lucky day," the largest of them announced, his booming voice echoing off all the walls of the prison. To her left, the mad boy awoke from his sleep and waited with curious eyes for the drama that was undoubtedly about to unfold.

Wren merely stared at the four men—four because two hadn't been enough to get her to the throne room the previous day—and made no effort whatsoever to move. She was even more exhausted than the night before, her voice all but gone after singing tirelessly to the dragon for hours.

And all for nothing.

When the Verlanti warriors approached her, she rose and stood her ground. She would become the bride to the Beast of the Barbarians but she wouldn't make it easy.

"Don't make this more difficult than it already is," one of the guards insisted, irritation plain as day on his face. "The wedding is going to happen, whether you like it or not."

"In what world would I like it to happen?" Wren bit back, snarling and jerking away from the man's touch when he reached out for her. She took a step back and then another, forcing the soldiers to come farther into the cell.

"You should be honored to wed Prince Arrik!" another of the guards spat out, his green eyes snapping with anger. "You're just a wild bit of tarte. You don't deserve him."

How ridiculous. He was a monster who invaded neighboring kingdoms and laid waste to all that he saw. "I was under the impression that he was ill-begotten," she quipped. "Surely, his station is lower than mine…"

The guard grunted and stepped closer.

Wren shifted just a little bit farther back, and then a little bit farther back again, until all four guards were in the cell with her.

"Let's get this over with," the green-eyed elf growled before coming at her. Wren kicked out, knocking him out of her path in order to avoid the other guards. His eyes widened as he slipped on the slimy stones. In one agonizingly slow second, Wren could do nothing but watch—alongside the other guards, and the boy two cells over—when he lost his footing and fell into the water.

Oh no.

The water bubbled immediately, and though Wren waited for the man to erupt from the surface to scream at her in outrage, he never did.

The water grew silent, and the man was gone.

By the tides.

Wren retreated from the edge of the water, seeing with her own eyes just how quickly the carnivorous fish had reappeared once the dragon had gone, and the rapid work they made of living flesh. Nausea rolled in her stomach.

That was not a bucket of chum. It was a whole living, breathing man. He did not even have a chance to defend himself.

Perhaps it was because of this, or perhaps it was because the small amount of exertion required to send the guard to his doom had tired Wren out, but she did not fight the other three guards when they took hold of her and silently led her out of the prison.

She shook and glanced over her shoulder at her abandoned cell. What had she done? Wren hadn't meant for anyone to die.

The guards seemed shaken by what they had just witnessed; there were no jibes or comments thrown her way regarding Wren's state of undress as they walked up several sets of stairs to a handsomely varnished, hardwood corridor. She stumbled, feeling off-kilter.

They made a left turn, then, a little farther along, another left, before entering through a door that led them to the right. After that, Wren lost count of the twists and turns the journey took her. The Verlantian Palace was truly a labyrinth.

Finally, the guards came upon a door which lay open in wait for them. They tossed her inside as if they could hardly bear to touch her, then slammed the door shut behind her without another word. She slipped on the stone floor and caught herself against the left wall.

Wren winced against the sunlight streaming in through

huge, floor-to-ceiling windows, which were surrounded on all sides by all manner of plants. Then, once she got used to that, her eyes became dazzled by torches set within sconces burning in impossible colors. Emerald green. Sapphire blue. Deep, deep red, like Wren's own hair. The flames made the room seem to glitter and pulse, which felt bizarre and entirely unreal to her.

What is this place?

Dizzy from the lack of food and sleep, she took a staggering step or two into the opulent room; it took all the strength from within her not to collapse to her knees and pass out. A man had died, and no one had batted an eye.

It was at this point that two hard-looking women approached her, their arms thick with muscles.

"Who are you?" she asked.

They ignored her and ushered her farther into the room. She yelped as they stripped her down and hauled her to a bathtub set in the center of the room. Wren hissed as the hot water covered her skin. She considered struggling but wanted to enjoy her bath. It had been weeks since she'd bathed properly. And honestly, she was bone tired. Perhaps this one small luxury of basking in steaming hot water would enable her to get through the horrible day to come.

She settled into the tub and wrapped her arms around her legs. The servants began pouring water over her hair and Wren closed her eyes. The last time she'd bathed, her mother had helped. Tears burned at the back of her eyes, but she blinked them back.

Opening her eyes, she took in the room once more, scanning the huge selection of plants and trees that filled the air with the pleasant smell of crisp herbs and plant life. They were largely tropical and so entirely unfamiliar to her, and their shiny, thick leaves reflected all the different-colored flames in an entirely hypnotic way.

A gilded cage.

Once more stricken by how heartbreakingly beautiful her prison was, Wren thought about how, back in Lorne, she would not have been able to imagine such an absurd, alien place like Verlanti. Its people loved shiny, colorful, and resplendent things, but they were just as cruel as the fish swimming in their dungeons who would eat anything dead or alive in a second.

"Filthy," one of the women grunted.

Wren glanced at the elven servant with black hair streaked with silver and shrugged. "I wasn't really given a chance to bathe." She settled back in as the two women scrubbed and washed her skin with unforgiving relentlessness. "You don't have to be so rough."

They ignored her.

She glared over her shoulder when one of them yanked her hair so hard it felt like they'd torn some out. "That hurt," she growled.

They stayed silent and continued scrubbing. The water around her quickly turned pink, dried blood and scabs alike sloughing off her skin until Wren was bleeding anew.

Hardly an appropriate look for a wedding.

She snatched her arms away from the women and held them protectively against her chest when her patience finally snapped.

"That is enough," she told them, her voice coming out as a

raspy whisper belonging to a woman three times her age. "I will not abide by this."

"As neither you should," came a voice from the door, surprising both Wren and the old women.

The queen, dressed in soft swathes of pearlescent fabric that seemed to both hide and reveal her figure all at once, stepped into the bathing room. She looked nothing short of a goddess, with an angelic smile and kind, wise eyes.

Entirely unlike everyone else in her godforsaken country.

The queen smiled at Wren, all perfect white teeth and disarming charm. "That's enough, ladies. I shall take it from here. My soon-to-be daughter-in-law deserves a gentler hand."

The two women nodded and exited the room without another word. For a moment, the queen simply stood by the door, inspecting Wren in the bathtub with polite interest.

Acutely self-conscious, Wren moved to cover herself even more, but then the queen laughed and closed the distance between them. She knelt down, gently pulling Wren's right hand free so that she could wash it. "My name is Astrid," the queen said with a soft smile. "I imagine you're scared and confused and more than a little bit angry right now."

Wren did not trust herself to speak—she doubted she knew what to say in the first place—so she merely nodded. Was this a trick?

Queen Astrid scrubbed soft circles against her hand, carefully clearing all the dirt and blood from beneath Wren's fingernails, only stopping once her skin was pale and white again before moving onto Wren's left hand.

It was the kindest touch Wren had felt in what seemed like

forever, and though this queen was very much her enemy in the same way that Arrik and High King Soren were, Wren could not find it in herself to hate Astrid.

"Thank you," she rasped.

"Think nothing of it, my dear. We're family." Astrid smiled. "Well, soon to be family."

Wren wisely kept her mouth shut. Her family had died in the isles. The elves were not any relation of hers.

After a few more minutes of cleaning, the queen rose to her feet. "All right," she said, allowing a demure servant Wren had not even noticed was standing behind a tall, spiky plant to hand her a towel. "Time you got out of there, Princess Wren. Let's get you dressed."

Wren had never thought of herself as meek, but that was exactly how she felt as she shakily got out of the tub and allowed Astrid to wrap her in the towel. It was soft as sin— nothing like the rough-spun cloth with which she dried herself back in Lorne Castle. A wave of tiredness washed over her once she was wrapped firmly in the towel, and she let out a yawn.

Astrid merely laughed. "Not the reaction I would hope to see on the day of your wedding! But I guess even I would be tired if I went through everything you have been through." A pause. Astrid squeezed Wren's hands. "But you just have to get through today, and then you will be sleeping in a real bed. A soft bed. Then you can recover from all your woes and sleep at will. It's not so bad here. You'll find your place. We all do."

Wren, once again, said nothing. Just having to get through today seemed like the hardest trial of her life so far, which was saying something. It was only when the servant presented

Wren with the dress she was to wear for the ceremony that she finally spoke aloud.

"I—I cannot wear that!" she objected. The dress was everything her own gown for her marriage to Rowen had not been: all gauze and sheer material, with a low back and plunging neckline.

And it was black.

All the more skin for the Verlanti Court to ogle.

It was obscene. No self-respecting woman of the Dragon Isles would ever wear something that revealing outside of her own chambers, and even then, the nightwear was, in all likelihood, less scandalous than this. They really expected her to wear that to the wedding?

"You are too modest for someone so beautiful," Queen Astrid said, and though Wren looked for the jest or insult behind her words, she could find none. "You will look truly a sight in this dress. I have not a doubt about it. Don't be shy, dearest. I chose it for you. My stepson seems to prefer black, and your hair will set it off perfectly."

Wren didn't care what the prince liked or disliked. Plus, Astrid's compliments were not enough to convince Wren to unwrap the towel from around her body to put on the ridiculous dress. She merely stared at the fabric, wishing it would disappear.

"I hoped you would not be difficult about this." The queen released a sigh and smiled. "It's no matter." She moved to the door and opened it.

Wren's heart thumped hard as the prince entered the bathing room like he the owned the place. She clenched the towel tighter to her body as he scanned her from head to toe, his expression revealing nothing. He dismissed her and stared out the windows.

"My darling," the queen purred, placing a hand on his forearm. "Why did you not knock? You know I wouldn't keep you from your bride. Do you wish to speak with your betrothed?"

Arrik shrugged her off. "I was waiting for *my beloved* to get dressed. If she takes much longer, we will be late."

What a terrible shame if that happened.

Wren edged backward until she had immersed herself in the plants. It afforded her more cover than the bloody towel at least. The prince arched a brow at her but said nothing. She glared at him, hating how uneasy and naked he made her feel. Rowen had never even seen her so undressed. It seemed wrong for Arrik to see her this way.

The queen chuckled and waved her hand at Wren. "No need to hide, my dear. He's not going to eat you."

"Are you so sure?" she retorted. "There have been rumors of his appetites."

"Let's hope some of them are right," the queen tittered, causing the prince to frown. "Now, stop hiding."

Wren swallowed hard and slowly emerged from behind the plant, watching Arrik carefully all the while. He did not have to dress up in the same gauzy, barely-there material that was expected of her. Instead, he wore a finely embroidered silk tunic in black and gold over what looked like soft and supple doeskin leggings and knee-high leather boots polished to a high shine. A sword belt cinched in his waist, adorned with a clearly ceremonial rapier and several daggers of various lengths.

With his hair perfectly braided back, and several tiny, golden chains adorning his pointed ears, she had to admit that Arrik was just a little bit handsome.

More than a little bit, the wretch.

It was ironic that under such beauty lay a beast. Beauty could not overwrite the atrocities he'd committed. His looks wouldn't sway Wren. She knew what he was.

Arrik watched Wren watching him, a spark of interest in his eyes, then let out a chuckle before heading for the door. "Get dressed," he ordered. "Or don't. I don't care what you wear to the wedding. I'll marry you without any clothes on if that's the way you wish it. Though I imagine..." He turned his head and raised his eyebrows suggestively at Wren. "I imagine you do not want that."

She didn't doubt it for one second that he would follow through. The only thing more humiliating than the wedding would be if she had to go to said wedding *naked*. She reminded herself, not for the first time, that since she had not been able to flee the night before, she truly had no choice but to go through with the wedding. Wren had to cooperate—however tenuous that cooperation was—for the sake of Lorne.

For Britta.

How could she ever return home if she was kept as a prisoner in a dungeon? At least as Arrik's wife she might make it back to the Dragon Isles.

Not might, will.

And even if he *was* the king, the people of Lorne would hold no trust in him. They would want him gone. Perhaps this was the best thing Wren could really hope for: return to Lorne with her new, murderous husband, then stage a coup against him. The Dragon Isles would not be so unprepared against a second attack from Verlanti. They would take their navy out onto the open sea to protect the bay, and everyone would be safe.

"Very well," she responded and the prince shut the door as he left.

She sagged a little as the queen handed the gown to the servant and they both helped her dress.

Astrid took Wren's hand and pulled her in front of a full-length mirror that was as wide as five people. "Look," she said gently, adjusting the ties on the shoulders of Wren's dress until they were perfect. "You're beautiful. You're a princess. This is not the kind of clothing you are used to, but you are undoubtedly still you. There is no shame in wearing beautiful things. They are simply another version of armor."

What an interesting and cryptic comment.

Wren's eyes widened at her words as the servant and Queen Astrid both began drying and adorning her hair with jewels. It was nothing like her wedding to Rowen and for that, she was thankful. It would have destroyed what was left of her heart to go through this farce if it had. Even as she looked into the mirror, she hardly recognized the woman staring back at her.

You can do this.

Astrid was right; every pretty thing they were putting on Wren was armor, to make her look every inch the perfect Verlantian bride. And that was what she needed to be until such a time that she could put real armor back on and fight the way she was used to.

When they had finished getting her ready, the queen touched Wren's shoulder and smiled reassuringly. "Things are not as bad as they seem. I'm here for you and you're not alone. You're a princess. So, keep your chin up high, even though you feel like you're crumbling inside. Trust me. I know how you feel. Can you do that?"

Wren stared at Astrid through the mirror.

For the first time, Wren wondered how this gentle and kind woman became queen to none other than Soren, who seemed the exact opposite of her. She seemed genuine, but was it all a game? Being queen amongst a hundred wives wasn't for the faint of heart. Was Astrid as kind as she seemed? Maybe not, but perhaps—just perhaps—Wren had found a friend-in-arms.

"Everything about today feels wrong," she admitted.

"I know." Astrid hugged her, sympathy on her face. "This isn't how I imagine I'd gain my first daughter in law either. We'll brave it together, I suppose."

"Was your marriage arranged?" Wren whispered.

"It was and it wasn't." The queen smiled, and it was sharp. "In our world, women are left powerless. I chose power, not love."

"Mine was stolen from me." She hated Arrik for it.

"Stop complaining and start fighting."

"I am."

Astrid shook her head. "Causing scenes and challenging Soren gets you nothing. Find a new way." The queen hugged her once again. "Such heavy topics for a wedding day. My advice to you is survive today with grace and take what you want tomorrow. Just know that you're not alone."

Wren managed the barest of smiles for Astrid. "I can do that."

And she could...for a while. She simply didn't know for how long before the wrongness of the day seeped into her soul and cracked her brand-new armor.

CHAPTER TWENTY-TWO

WREN

The wedding was awful. It was everything Wren's wedding to Rowen was not. With Rowen, there had been love. Spoken consent. A crowd of people who adored both parties getting married, who wished for nothing but the best for them.

Every single member of the Verlantian audience knew this wedding for exactly what it was: another moment for the glorious Prince Arrik to conquer. A chance for Verlanti to further humiliate a foreign princess, and, in so doing, solidify their own hold of her kingdom.

Despite what Wren had told herself earlier about how she could use this wedding to her advantage, it had been all she could do not to run away the moment she'd spied the aisle. But Queen Astrid had linked their arms together, preventing her from escaping the impending doom of marrying the prince.

Wren wanted to crawl inside herself and die as she walked down the aisle lined with courtiers. She observed the room. It was a ballroom of some sort filled with fresh flowers and plants. Lanterns hung from the walls and ceilings, casting soft light throughout the grand chamber. Her steps slowed as she reached the dais on which the prince and king stood. The queen led her up the three steps, placed a kiss to her cheek and took her place at her husband's side.

King Soren sat on his throne and the queen perched on the arm. He waved his hand and an ancient elf approached clad in dark purple robes. Wren's heart threatened to burst out of her chest as he began the ceremony.

The vows were spoken in the Elvish tongue, with King Soren overseeing them from his ostentatious throne. Thank the tides that Wren's mother had insisted on her learning the Elvish tongue. She'd hadn't been as studious as she should have been, but she could understand a bit of what the pompous windbag was waxing on about. The words were complicated and antiquated, and, before long, she gave up trying to keep up with what was being said.

Arrik locked gazes with her and she wanted to look away. There was too much intensity in his eyes. He spoke his vows with so much sincerity that if she had not known him for all the evil he had committed, she would have believed the truth of his words. But she *did* know him—in all the ways that mattered—so she took his show of affection as simply another way for him to degrade her.

When it was her turn to recite the vows, her throat closed up and the air seemed to leave the room. She'd resigned herself to marriage with the prince but looking too compliant was an issue. Her hands shook and Wren couldn't force the vows out. It was too soon after Rowen's death.

Arrik's fingers tightened against hers and she trembled. The king repeated the vows, but she kept silent. Her tongue felt too heavy to utter the words. The prince stared down at her stone-faced and she flinched when he ran his thumb over the top of her knuckles. It was a small caress but it jolted her very bones. Was he trying to calm her? Be encouraging? The pit of her stomach soured as Soren laughed and continued on, taking Wren's silence for compliance.

It made her sick.

Arrik placed a quill in her right hand and helped her sign a marriage document. The quill scratched against the paper, setting her teeth on edge. She stared at the binding document as the prince signed it. It was done. She was married to the man who annihilated her family.

She scanned the room full of courtiers. Not one of them batted an eye.

How could they see the wedding—this marriage—as good and true and legal when she had not given consent? Never mind the fact she was already married.

Not true. You were never bound. You were not sealed with your markings or documents.

Wren swallowed the tears that found their way into her throat. She'd never been Rowen's wife and she never would.

When the ceremony finally concluded, the room erupted into a cacophony of noise. The king moved purposely toward Wren, and Arrik immediately moved out of the king's path. The way his eyes roved over her body was not the way a father-in-law should ever look at his new daughter-in-law.

Soren grinned at her and brushed a lock of her hair from her cheek. "As is custom," he said, getting so close to Wren that her skin crawled. He towered over her, his blond hair full of golden beads and gem pins that glittered. "The High King gets the first kiss from the bride."

Wren was speechless. There was no way she could get out of it; of that, she had no doubt. Soren's hand pressed against the small of her back, and he wasted no time in capturing her mouth and kissing her. Wren stayed stiff and lifeless, pressing her lips together. A shudder of disgust went through her body when his tongue touched her bottom lip.

Not even kissing on the cheek, but on the mouth!

Everything about the king felt slimy and wrong. He was a snake if ever there was one.

"My turn," the prince said, his tone somewhat bored.

Wren gasped as Arrik pulled her away from the king and into his arm. Soren chuckled behind her. "Enjoy your new wife. I did."

Repulsed, she lifted her left hand to wipe her mouth when the prince caught her wrist. She glared at him and then frowned when he gave her almost an imperceptible shake of his head. What the devil?

He moved closer, his thighs pressing against the gauzy fabric of her black dress, and lifted his hand to her face. Arrik ran his thumb over her bottom and then top lip. Her eyes widened. It wasn't a caress. He was wiping away the king's kiss. Her breath stuttered as he dropped her left hand and cupped the other side of her face. The prince drew closer so that they were breathing the same air. She stared into his ice-colored eyes that seemed to have grown warmer despite his impassive expression.

"Don't think," he whispered. "And don't bite me."

Wren's pulse thundered in her ears as he pressed his lips to her own but made no other move. They gazed at each other, and he gently pulled her to his chest. She splayed her hands across his torso as the kiss went on, but never progressed further than lips pressed against lips. There was no passion, no desire.

He pulled back slowly and she stared at the column of his throat as he straightened. Bawdy cheers filled the air but she didn't focus on them. She'd seen something in his gaze and the way he'd kissed her...the prince wasn't a decent man, so perhaps he wanted her cooperation as much as she wanted to escape. If that was the case, then maybe they could come to some sort of agreement. They could be allies.

Keep your friends close, and your enemies closer.

She yanked her hands from his person and wiped them on her dress, causing the king to laugh raucously at her reaction. It was clear as day to anyone watching that all this was a farce meant purely to entertain. Even if the prince could be swayed to be an uneasy ally, she would never forgive him for what he did. He'd murdered her family.

"Let the celebrations begin!" the king announced.

The doors burst open, and servants filed into the room, carrying golden trays of food. The elvish highborn moved to the low tables and reclined against the pillows on the floor as the food was placed on the tables. It was just as opulent and over-the-top as the Verlantian people were.

Arrik led her to a table on the dais and she woodenly sat

down as the king, queen, the princes and their consorts began to eat from the table. A servant approached Wren and poured wine in the goblet.

"Thank you," she murmured, trying to catch the girl's eye.

The servant froze for a moment and quickly backed away.

Wren frowned and then glanced back at the table. The eldest prince who sported silver beads in his jet-black hair smirked at her, and her stomach bottomed out when she realized everyone else was snickering.

"They are not to be spoken to," Arrik murmured.

And they called those from the isles barbarians.

She ignored her new husband and focused on the food. Wren couldn't even begin to name half of what was on the table, and though she had previously been starving, she found she had no appetite for such unknown things. The bright colors and shiny appearances of most of the food made her think of poison, so she reached for her goblet of wine and swirled it around as the royal family feasted and gossiped. Wren listened, storing little bits of information. Who knew what would be useful? The queen tried to goad her into eating, but she politely refused. Today wasn't a day for feasting and celebrating.

Time dragged by and the evening deepened.

The music changed and the elves began to dance.

Wren had always loved to dance. Her mum used to say that it was in her bones. But not this day. Though she got away with not eating, she couldn't escape the dancing.

The king and his sons all led her through their dances. Some with veiled threats, others with lurid offers and promises. Then she was passed amongst the highborn. Much to her chagrin, not all of the elves were horrible. In fact, she'd met an older elf, who, under different circumstances, she'd have liked to have played chess with. He was witty and smart.

Then again, it could have been an act.

Once again, Wren was yanked into the arms of her husband, who pulled her through a series of intricate moves effortlessly. She stumbled and he caught her. Humiliated, she jerked away and he hauled her against his body. His left arm wrapped around her waist and she squeaked when he lifted her until her toes brushed the tops of his boots.

"Put me down," she gritted out.

"No, you're dragging this out for both of us," he muttered.

"What?" she gasped, outraged.

He ignored her and they whirled around the room until King Soren cut in, taking over for the next dance. The music slowed and she shifted away from the elf king as he leaned down to whisper in her ear.

"Welcome to my family."

"I am not part of your family." She'd never be.

"You are bound to my son, thus making you my daughter."

"Do you kiss all your daughters?" she quipped. "I've been told that is frowned upon in all parts of the world."

He chuckled. She glanced up at the king, his shrewd blue eyes already watching her. His gaze moved from her face down to her chest and lingered, before moving back to her face. She blushed which seemed to amuse him.

Chin up. You're a princess. You can do this. Just look him in the eye and hold your ground. He will not get the better of you.

"Is it wrong to appreciate beauty?" he mused.

"No, but coveting what is not yours is a sin, is it not?"

His fingers tightened on hers as he spun them around, her dress flaring. "Everything is mine to give and to take. Remember that." He smiled and it was anything but friendly. "I've always loved wild things, especially breaking them." Soren leaned closer. "That is something both Arrik and I share."

With that parting remark, he passed her off to his youngest trueborn son, Kalles. Kalles shared the same blond hair and high cheekbones, but his eyes were a cerulean blue instead of glass and crystal.

He was a peacock that spoke entirely about himself, but at least his hands hadn't wandered once. Five sons had sat at the royal table, including Arrik. They all resembled the king in some manner but what bothered Wren the most was that amongst the crowd, she'd seen more than one man or woman who could have been a sibling to the princes.

Base-born children to be sure. Just how many children had the king sired? Wren didn't want to know.

"I can't imagine this is what you wanted to be doing today," Kalles murmured, pulling Wren closer so that he could speak directly into her ear. "It is not right to do something like this to someone of your status. It is humiliating."

She blinked at him. What did he expect her to say? Was the man's intention to lull Wren into trusting him, only to stab her in the back later on? She had seen all of Arrik's brothers laughing when her marriage was announced. But perhaps that had been the show, instead, for the king. Wren had no idea what to believe.

She knew it was perfectly possible that Queen Astrid had been attempting something similar earlier—to get into Wren's good graces merely to use Wren to her own advantage. But just as Wren considered breaking away from Kalles, the man slipped a stiletto down the front of her dress; it rested in her corset, cushioned by her breast.

Wren gasped and managed to mask her surprise. "What are you up to?" she growled. Anyone who looked closely would be able to see the top of the hilt.

"Mischief of course. Keep it or throw it away. I don't care." Kalles pulled a smile. "Arrik's brides never survive very long."

Brides? "What do you mean?"

He nodded toward a group of nobles looking their way. "Do you really think they're all interested in you—the wild princess raised with dragons? You're amusing to be sure, but you're part of a larger game. They are betting on how long you'll live."

Ice trickled down her spine.

Kalles spun them as she caught sight of Arrik moving in their direction, his silver hair a beacon in the crowd.

"Why would they do such a thing?" she asked urgently.

"It's the secret the court holds close to its chest." A dramatic pause. "He's been married three times. All of his wives died on their wedding night."

Wren's heart plummeted into her stomach. "All—all of them?"

Kalles nodded. "All of them. Get out of here while you still can." He dropped her hand and tapped the top of the stiletto, pressing it deeper into her corset. "Use this if you must. Goodbye, princess. It's been a gas knowing you."

She stumbled back from the prince and ducked her head. Wren did not need to hear his warning a second time.

Before Arrik could reach her side, she fled the celebration, weaving this way and that, between the crowd, making it hard for anyone to follow. She bolted out into the corridor, throwing off the absurd heeled shoes she had been forced to wear, then ran on silent feet down one corridor and then another and then another.

Eventually, Wren realized she was following her nose. Before long, she reached a kitchen three times as large as the one in Lorne Castle. There was something savory and delicious and entirely unlike the smells of the food at the feast emanating from the fire, so Wren kept on walking until she reached the fire itself. She needed to think. Her belly growled. And she needed to eat.

"You—Princess," a woman—one of the cooks—said upon recognizing Wren. She bowed her head. "What can I do for you?"

"If I could have some of what's in that pot, it would be more appreciated than you know," Wren said, pointing toward the pot in question that contained the delicious smells. "Please."

The cook blanched. "No thanks is needed." She retrieved a wooden stool for Wren to sit on and placed it next to a long table in the middle of the room covered with herbs. The cook ladled out a bowlful of what turned out to be chicken and rabbit stew. She set food before Wren and went back to her work. Wren could not believe her luck. Then the woman gave her a plate with several slices of thickly buttered bread that was still warm from the oven.

"Thank the tides," she whispered.

She sat there in silence for several minutes, reveling in the warmth of the bowl between her fingers and the delicious taste of the stew that passed her lips. It reminded Wren of home, which was bittersweet because her home was now in the hands of her enemies. The servants cast nervous glances in her direction. It was clear she was not supposed to be here but it gave her time to think.

Kalles had given her a weapon. Even now it dug into her breastbone. What was the meaning of it? She didn't trust him as far as she could throw him. Was he setting her up? It was a possibility. Wren's mother had told her the elves were partial to hiring assassins. They didn't like to get their hands dirty.

Was this Kalles' plan? Did he expect her to kill his half-brother? Arrik certainly had garnered the attention of his father. Were his other sons jealous?

She finished her soup and then rubbed her temples.

No one in this bloody palace seems trustworthy. They are all vipers. Truly, it seems as if the mad bard in the dungeons is the only one who speaks any sense around here.

She chuckled and ignored the looks tossed her way. The poor servants probably thought she'd lost her mind. Her laughter faded as she stared down at her wedding dress. She ran her fingers over the black fabric. Wren wore her husband's colors.

Husband.

She was well and truly married to a monster. What had happened to the prince's former wives? Had he killed them all? If he came at her, she'd strike him down. She would not become his next victim.

Wren chuckled at the thought, which caused the cook to furrow her brow in concern for her. "Is everything... Will you be all right?" the woman asked.

Wren waved her away. "I will be. I swear. Thank you for the food—it is the only true kindness I have seen in this land."

Wren stared hard at the floor. Hiding in the kitchen wouldn't be an option forever. Someone would some looking for her, if they hadn't started already. The servants could be punished for harboring her.

Wren stood from the stool and trailed to the exit. She had too many things weighing on her conscience already. Pushing through the door, she wandered through the hallways, trying to remember the way back to the bathing room.

Somehow, she found what she'd been searching for. She'd almost given up at one point. All the hallways looked alike. It was a veritable maze.

Wren pushed open the door and stepped into the room. She froze as she spotted an unexpected woman inside. Queen Astrid sat on a striped chaise lounge. She straightened when she noticed Wren and stood, gliding forward.

"I..." Wren began, though she did not know what to say.

The queen moved toward her and took her hands. "I figured

that when you ran off, you might find yourself back in the only room you knew," she said, squeezing Wren's fingers. It was a gesture Wren's own mother used to do to make her feel better, which hurt her very soul. "It's not safe to wander, my dear."

"So I am told."

Astrid nodded, her deep brown eyes scrutinizing Wren. "You are a princess."

"I am."

"With privilege comes responsibility."

Wren cocked her head. "True." What was the queen getting at?

Astrid sighed and pursed her lips. "Did your mother prepare you for what's to come?"

What's to come...the wedding night. Wren thought she might be sick.

"You are young," the queen continued. "I don't want to shock you."

She shook her head. "I was taken from Lorne on my wedding day," she reminded her. "Trust me, I know what is to come." Not that *it* was *going* to happen. The prince would not be touching her this night. Nor any of them. The queen didn't need to know that.

Astrid's shoulders sagged in relief, and a small smile graced her face. "I'm happy to hear that. I've never had to have this conversation before."

Wren gave the queen a weak smirk. "Not even with your sons?"

The queen's smile turned brittle before it slipped from her

face. "They had their father for that."

She didn't even want to imagine what that was like. A moment of silence lapsed between them, and Wren rocked back on her heels. It was too soon to tell but Astrid might be her ticket out of the palace.

Astrid smiled again, except there was nothing but sadness behind it. She did not let go of Wren's hands. "Come. I shall take you to Arrik's chambers. You can wait for him there instead of returning to the celebrations."

Wren breathed deeply, steeling herself for what really *was* to come.

Let's do this.

CHAPTER TWENTY-THREE

WREN

No matter how much Wren hated the situation, she couldn't help but appreciate the beauty of the Verlantian Palace. Even now, as she stood waiting for her new 'husband' to arrive, Wren was struck with how breathtaking the chambers were that she was expected to share with the prince.

The sun had already set, and the lanterns bathed the room with soft light. One wall was entirely open to a courtyard, which was held up by tall marble columns. Sheer curtains hung from the ceiling and rippled in the soft breeze. It made Wren realize how it must not really get cold in Verlanti. The insubstantial fabric of her wedding dress made more sense against the still-balmy evening. Huge leafy plants grew outside the room, hiding what lay outside but she could hear water running over stone. A stream or pool?

Looking around the room at large, Wren could not ignore the enormous, finely carved bed, the wood gilded in an ostentatious amount of gold to her left. Tables bracketed the bed. Then there was a fireplace across from it which Wren assumed never got lit given how hot it was in Verlanti. Two upholstered, cushioned chairs sat on either side of the hearth, large enough that Wren could, in all likelihood, curl up on one of them to sleep.

All in all, the room was simple, but beautiful. A wide mirror hung on the same wall as the bed, framed in what looked like bone, and standing close to the end of the bed was a circular table covered in food and drink.

A private feast for the bride and groom.

Her nose wrinkled in distaste.

In truth, the food on the table looked far more appetizing than the selection that had been provided at the celebration proper—and there was a pot of tea which smelled rather pleasant—but since Wren had only recently eaten an entire bowl of stew and bread, she was not in the least bit hungry. She edged farther into the room and stared at the plants outside.

"I didn't realize you were so eager to get me alone that you would leave your own wedding celebrations."

She tensed but didn't immediately turn at the sound of Arrik's voice. He'd snuck up on her. Wren walked forward until she stood by the open wall to the courtyard and leaned against one of the columns, looking at the trees and plants. But her entire focus was on the man behind her. She heard the scuff of a boot but that was it.

Wren scanned the plants and attempted to identify their names in order to keep herself distracted from the knife still hidden in her dress. She inhaled deeply and tried to calm herself. Wren didn't want him to see the attack coming...though, given how on every other occasion they had been alone together she'd attacked Arrik, she very much doubted he would expect anything less from her.

But he doesn't expect me to have a knife. He doesn't expect me to be armed.

"Stay silent, then," Arrik muttered.

She glanced over her shoulder and watched him stride across the room to the bed. He sat down upon it, stretching out his arms and then his legs while sighing in satisfaction. The prince glanced her way, the lantern light turning his silver hair gold.

"All these clothes are far too restrictive, wouldn't you say, wife? Although there doesn't seem to be all that much to yours, so I guess you may disagree."

Her jaw tensed at his use of *wife* and the jibe. It hadn't been her idea to wear the bloody dress. She restrained herself from lashing out and kept her tongue firmly locked behind her teeth.

Don't give him the satisfaction of a reaction. Let him tire himself out with insults and innuendos until he makes the mistake of coming too close.

She moved slightly so she could watch him from the corner of her eye. He sat up and unlaced his boots, but he didn't stop there.

Here we go.

The prince unbuckled his belt, removing the rapier and ceremonial daggers that had been part of his wedding attire, before sliding out of his lavishly embroidered tunic and then stood. Wren's heartrate skyrocketed despite herself.

Does he have no fear in removing his weapons? Does he truly have no fear, or is this all a ruse? Is he testing me?

Arrik removed the undershirt he'd been wearing, leaving him in nothing but his doeskin leggings, and Wren temporarily forgot all about his weapons and the fact she was meant to kill him. She turned to face him, ignoring her better judgment, eyes widening at the strange and enticing sight of him.

For the prince's bare skin was of far more interest than the clothes he had been wearing; he was covered in scars and ink, an entire tapestry of interlocking designs in blue and black and bottle green that Wren could make neither head nor tail of.

All she knew was that she couldn't look away. There was something mesmerizing about the tattoos and scars—as well as the canvas upon which they were drawn.

He was completely opposite of Rowen in every way, but despite her loathing for the prince, she found something about him compelling. She eyed his wide, muscled shoulders and chest that tapered to a slim waist. He was immense. Rowen had been tall, but Arrik would have dwarfed him. Rowen had a swimmer's physique: muscular, lean, and graceful. But the prince...

Arrik was all hard muscle in brutal, violent lines...

And she'd married him.

She finally forced herself to match Arrik's stare, as if daring him to acknowledge the horrific amount of damage he had brought upon her. But, of course, Wren saw nothing of the sort in his eyes, nor was she ever going to hear such words of sympathy from his lips. Once again, he was a blank slate. Did the man have no expressions at all?

Nothing he said or did mattered at this point, anyway. Wren did not need empty words from him. He was a demon that was dead inside. All that spoke to him was the lust for flesh and blood.

Arrik took a few careful steps toward the table and its treasure trove of food and drink, as if he and Wren had not just been caught in a tense staring match and as if he was not half-naked. He indicated toward the pot of tea. "I did not see you touch a thing at the ceremony," he said. "Would you have something now?"

"How observant of you," she retorted.

Was he watching me throughout the entire celebration? And if he was...did he notice the dagger his brother gave me with which to slice his throat?

Her hand went toward her chest, but Wren jerked it away at the last moment to rearrange the ties upon her shoulders that kept the dress from falling off.

If the prince was bothered by her stony silence, he did not admit it. Instead, he shrugged and popped a morsel of food into his mouth before washing it down with a glass of amber whiskey. Wren could do nothing but watch him from her position by the open courtyard, wishing she could be alone to enjoy the warm breeze on her face and the babbling of the water. Just one night to enjoy the simple pleasures of life.

Arrik rolled his neck and set down his glass. He stared at the food and finally looked her way once again and approached her slowly. She pushed away from the column and put it between the two of them, the courtyard to her back.

He slowed and eyed her. "We should get this over with."

The prince trailed behind her until she was inside the room. Wren moved until the bed stood between them with the door behind her.

"There is no way I am crawling into bed with you," she said

with a calmness she didn't feel.

"Really?" he murmured, running his fingers along the silk covering his bed.

"I have thought this over today and it doesn't have to be this way."

He cocked his head. "How so?"

Wren licked her lips. "It has occurred to me that you are at the mercy of your father as well. I don't think either of us want this. We can say no. I'll even sleep on the floor."

For a moment, it seemed like he was seriously considering her words. "Be that as it may, we have a duty. My king will not be denied."

"He does not control this."

"Soren controls everything," the prince replied softly. "Come quietly to me and I'll make sure you're safe and cared for."

"I'm not taking one step toward you," she hissed. "You don't deserve to have even an inch of me."

A flash of something she couldn't work out crossed Arrik's face. She thought it might have been irritation. *Or frustration.* She'd struck a nerve. Did the pretty prince not like being told he couldn't have something? Was that how she could rile him?

"So be it," he said, and, with that, he lunged for her.

Wren was not so foolish as to not have expected it, and when he leapt over the bed, she darted around the end in the nick of time to avoid the prince's arms.

"You're fast," Arrik observed, clearly impressed. "But you are weak from all your days spent as a prisoner. Which means..." He charged around the foot of the bed and toppled her to the mattress. She scrambled forward and the prince grabbed Wren's leg by the ankle. She cried out in surprise and flipped onto her back as he yanked her toward him, her skirt sliding up. "That *I* am faster. For now."

She was not going to let her current state of malnutrition get in the way of stopping a degenerate. Reaching out a hand before he managed to reel her in, she grabbed the silver tray, the teapot and food crashing to the floor, and slammed it against Arrik's face with all her might. The metal cracked satisfyingly when it made contact. Wren followed it up with a swift kick to the gut.

He grunted but didn't let her leg go. She growled when he ripped the bent tray from Wren's hands when she tried to hit him again, revealing that she had bloodied his nose and swollen his upper lip.

"I do enjoy a woman full of fire," he said, grabbing for her once more, as if she had not just viciously hit him in the face.

Wren screamed and reached for her blade. He pinned her arms and she yowled as she tried to escape his other roving hand. "Do not—*do not touch me!*"

"Perhaps if you didn't have a knife," he murmured, eyes shining in the twilight as his hand skimmed over her right hip, "I would not have to."

He knows.

Wren fired out a fist, intent on punching Arrik in the nose in an attempt to break it. He responded by throwing his entire weight on top of her. All the air was squashed from Wren's lungs in an instant. She gasped for breath, but no sooner had he slumped onto her than he knelt back up, wrapping several blankets around Wren so tightly and expertly that no amount of wriggling enabled her to get out of them.

By the time Arrik was done, Wren could no longer move an inch. She bellowed in frustration from her soft, unyielding prison. "Let me go!" she demanded, knowing any such plea was useless now. She was at his mercy...and she hated it.

"Stop fighting me!" He slapped his hands against the mattress on either side of her head and glared down at her. "I'm trying to save your fool life!"

What?

She snapped her mouth shut and blinked slowly at him. What the devil was this? Another trick?

His eyes sparked as he leaned close enough that she could count his long lashes. The prince's hair fell around them, forming a curtain. "You'll get us both killed if you carry on."

"So you want to save your own skin," she spat.

His jaw ticked. "Whether you like it or not, we are bound. Our fates are intwined. I didn't take my vows lightly. I meant them when I said I would protect you with my life."

"Lies," she hissed. What was this nonsense?

His expression sobered. "I don't lie, Princess." She held her breath as he continued to stare down at her. "You don't have to trust me, but you must obey me."

No way.

She opened her mouth to retorted when he reached down the front of her dress and pulled the sheathed stiletto out. "That's mine!" she gritted out.

"No, it's not." His mask slipped back into place. "It's my brothers."

Arrik stood up and she felt like she could finally breathe.

"Go to sleep," he muttered before moving to the table. The prince picked up some of the food that hadn't been completely destroyed and placed it on a broken plate, then reclined on one of the chairs by the empty fireplace.

Wren couldn't believe her ears. "You want me to go to *sleep*? Oh, I see how it is. If I am asleep, I can do nothing against you raping me."

His impartial expression slipped and turned to one of disgust. She flinched at the rage and revulsion she saw clear as day written across his face. She expected him to storm back to her side and slap her in the face, but instead the man remained as still as a statue.

"I may be the monster from your every living nightmare," he said, very quietly, "but I would never force a woman to lie with me. *Never*. And besides...I do not take vipers into my bed. So, take my bed from me and *go to sleep*. I know you are exhausted."

Wren did not know how to take this. His words did not sound like lies, but even so, she could not take them at face value.

"I'm not a viper," she replied. "Your people are."

"You'll find no argument from me," he said, fatigue coloring his tone. "Go to sleep."

You cannot afford to sleep a wink with him around. Not with the rumors of his wives.

If Arrik was not the one who killed his wives in the past—and if his three wives being murdered was not merely a story concocted by his brother in the first place—then someone else may very well attempt to kill Wren tonight. For that alone, she could not sleep, regardless of her feelings toward Arrik.

A stalemate it was.

She was unable to move, but not willing to surrender.

The moon rose fully in the sky, and though it grew a little colder, Arrik did not put any of his clothes back on. He sat almost motionless, staring out at the courtyard, occasionally eating from his plate or turning his brother's dagger in his hands. Wren, in her state of immobility, could do nothing but watch *him* do nothing.

"I hate you," she whispered.

"I know," he responded. "I accept it."

It would be a long night, but not for the reasons she originally thought.

CHAPTER TWENTY-FOUR

ARRIK

If one thing had been made clear to Arrik from the moment he had first cast his eyes upon Wren, it was this: she was as wild as the dragons who dwelled in her homeland.

He popped another grape into his mouth, the sweet taste bursting across his tongue. Arrik winced and swallowed it down quickly. He hated sweet things. Tart grapes were his favorite though. A sigh escaped him, and his gaze was drawn back to his wife. Even in the dark, her red hair was like a beacon.

His new wife had wasted no time in trying to attack him the moment an opportunity arose. Arrik could not blame her. Rather, it only served to impress him. Instead of turning into a weeping mess, she'd fought back. He respected Wren, though he highly doubted she would believe him if he were to vocalize his regard. The lass was suspicious, and she had every right to be. She'd entered the house of serpents and it was wise for her to never forget that. Someone would always want to kill her.

The thought caused something dark and possessive to burn in his chest. No one would touch what was his. Not again. He would not fail. She would not die.

You're getting too attached her.

Tearing his gaze away, he focused on the courtyard, on the plants that waved in the breeze. That was the problem. Truly, he'd only spent a handful of days in her presence, but something about her called to him. She had somehow reached inside his heart and made a place for herself. The worst part? He'd felt it happen in Lorne when she'd spat at Shane and then swore she'd never marry his father. It intrigued him. Every woman he'd married before had come to him for any number of selfish reasons, but Wren was the first woman who wanted nothing from him. It was refreshing in a twisted sort of way. But then again, Arrik was twisted. His soul was corrupt but a small part of himself wanted to be better so she wouldn't look at him with revulsion.

Given what had happened to his last three wives, that was a problem.

If she survived the night...he clenched his jaw. *When* she survived the night, the princess would be in even more danger. His brothers were jealous, dangerous creatures with a horrid penchant for depravity and violence. If they suspected that he cared one whit for the princess, death would be a kindness compared to the games they played.

Drawn once more, he cast his gaze over the bed. His new wife had turned her face toward him, the moonlight shining in her eyes as she glared at him. Thoroughly wrapped up and unable to move, her gaze promised vengeance. She'd not spoken one word to him in three hours and refused to go to sleep which she clearly needed by the black bags beneath her eyes. It was a waste of breath to tell her to sleep.

He supposed that Wren had no reason to believe he would not ravish her after she fell asleep. Considering everything that happened to her so far—at his hands, no less—it was no doubt the least she would expect from him. It rankled, but he understood it. Trust did not come easily, and he hadn't earned hers. *Yet.* Once they survived the night, Arrik would start the process of gaining her trust. They were both in a precarious situation and if he played his cards right, perhaps they could be allies. She wanted to go home to her people, and he wanted control of Verlanti. They could both get what they wanted if they worked together.

Only if she survives the night.

From his past three experiences, he was well aware of the mortal danger his dragon bride now found herself in. He turned his attention back to the courtyard. Surely the attacker would come from there. He'd stationed men throughout the corridor and on the roof, but Arrik doubted it was enough. Whoever kept sending assassins to kill his brides hired only the best. He touched his left side, running his thumb along the scar there. The last time, he'd almost died as well.

Arrik never had a chance to know any of the women who were married to him for not even a full night. They had all been arranged marriages—much like this one—only those women had been of Verlantian blood, women seeking money and prominence. Though the marriages had been arranged, that did not mean that he hadn't felt their deaths keenly. It weighed heavily on his conscience.

He had been responsible for them. They'd been in his care. And yet, each and every time he went to sleep on his wedding night, he'd awoken to discover his new wife lying dead beside him.

One had been poisoned. Another suffocated.

The last time, he'd moved his bride to a secret location. Despite all the planning that had been put into place, the assassin still had killed two of his men and slipped inside the small cottage. Arrik had been prepared for the fight, but his new wife had not listened to him. She hadn't stayed hidden, instead joining the fray. The assassin had stabbed him and then slit his wife's throat and disappeared into the night. He could do nothing but hold her and watch as she labored to breathe her final breaths. Even now, he remembered the horrid sound. What was worse was the silence afterward.

That had been the final straw.

He'd thrown everything into discovering who was killing these women...and why. It was obviously a ploy to get to him. But if the assassins had been quiet enough to murder the women lying beside Arrik without him waking until it was too late for him to save them, then why had they simply not killed him too? It wasn't as if there hadn't been many attempts on his life already. It was practically part of his schedule each week.

Eat, train, ward off an assassin, eat again.

Whoever was responsible was trying to send him a message. A bloody, unknowable threat. But what was it? And who was it? The assassins he'd managed to track down had been paid in untraceable coin and had never met their mysterious benefactor.

Quietly, Arrik examined the blade that he'd found in Wren's possession. A quick look over at the bed confirmed she was, indeed, still watching him, but, at this point, he no longer cared. It was clear that, beneath her hatred and revulsion of him, she was deeply curious about what was going on, so Arrik decided it was up to her to finally give in and vocalize that curiosity.

If she wants to know what is going on, then she can ask me. I will not simply hand out the answers she seeks, whether she'll ever admit to wanting them or not.

He held the thin stiletto up in front of his eyes and twisted it this way and that. It was a finely made Vedonian knife, from far down south: too expensive and rare a weapon for most in the nation to be able to afford it.

This was Kalles' work. It screams him.

Of all of his brothers, Kalles was the one Arrik was least sure about. His youngest brother acted just as lazy and as hedonistic as his other brothers, yes, but Arrik was growing more and more suspicious that it was all simply an act. Kalles *did* like to play games—of that he was certain. His brother had so many faces that he wasn't sure which one was genuine.

"What did my brother say to you when he gave you this knife?" he asked Wren, irritated that he had to break the silence between them first to get an answer. But this wasn't merely a tit-for-tat situation: both his and Wren's very lives depended on why she was given the dagger.

She remained stonily silent. This was going to be a long bloody night.

Well, hopefully not bloody.

Smiling grimly and not at all surprised by her reaction, he returned the knife to his lap and stared out at the night. He did not know when an assassin would appear tonight. He was only certain that one *would*. But, until then...

Arrik had a long night of waiting and waiting and waiting in silence, as it stretched endlessly between him and the woman who would never trust him. And though it was clear both of them were growing tired, they both remained alert to the tense electricity in the air. There was a clear and present danger around them both, and it appeared that neither one of them would sleep until it disappeared.

"Are you really not planning on touching me?" she finally rasped.

Her words surprised him. "I have no intention of ever touching you, woman."

"Then why take me as your wife?"

He chuckled. "I live to serve the crown."

"Even when the crown you serve is corrupt?"

"Even then," he admitted gruffly.

"You are no warrior," she whispered. "You are a sheep."

"Go to sleep," he replied, not rising to the bait. Arrik knew what he was.

"If my lord commands it," she grunted, turning her face away from him.

He couldn't help but smile. Her sarcasm was amusing.

You can't afford to find her amusing.

Arrik sobered and pushed back serval braids from his face and settled into the chair. Time passed slowly and the breeze picked up, kissing his bare skin. It had always been too warm in Verlanti for his taste. He preferred cooler temperatures. One could always bundle up but there was only so many clothes a person could take off.

His state of undress bothered the princess. The isles were more of a conservative sort of people compared to the elves. Bodies were a thing to be celebrated and admired amongst those in Verlanti while the dragon people kept theirs hidden behind layers of fabric and fur. Which was ironic since they spent so much time in the water with their dragons. How did that work anyway? Thoughts for another time.

The wind shifted about an hour or two before dawn and with it a sense of foreboding.

He stood and moved farther into the darkness, the lantern light had long since been put out. The princess stiffened, her eyes widening and Arrik held a finger to his lips. She snapped her mouth shut and closed her eyes.

The whisper of fabric against foliage caught his attention the moment before a shadow drifted through the white sheer curtains as silent as the night. One of the slats of the wooden floor creaked and the assassin froze for a second before continuing toward the bed. Arrik had chosen this room because of its faulty floor. It made it more difficult for someone to sneak up on him.

Without a second thought, Arrik slunk from the wall and crept toward the intruder. He crossed the room, Kalles' dagger in his hand as he stepped over the mess of broken dishes from his tussle with the princess. He hadn't cleaned it up. It was just another obstacle for anyone planning on sneaking in. Arrik gritted his teeth as one of the floorboards squeaked again. It didn't always work in his favor.

He launched himself at the assassin who spun to face him. The killer avoided his attack and stepped backward, a blade flashing in the moonlight. Arrik darted out of the way and cursed as the intruder turned their attention back to Wren.

He should not have left her unarmed.

The assassin reached for her at the same moment she levered up and slammed her head into their face. The killer cried out and Arrik grabbed them by the back of their hood and placed a dagger at their throat.

"Don't!" the princess cried out.

He knocked the blade out of the killer's hand. "They just tried to kill you."

"But why?"

Why indeed.

Coming to his senses, he took the intruder to the ground and wrapped his arm around their neck, choking the air from their lungs. The assassin scrabbled, clawing at his arms but soon their struggles slowed and then ceased.

He cursed and released the killer. Arrik tore off the hooded shroud from the person's face and frowned. It was a boy. He couldn't be more than sixteen years old.

"Did you kill him?" the princess rasped.

Arrik placed his hand along the boy's pulse at his wrist. "No. He still lives."

"He's just a boy," she whispered.

He stood up, his heart still pounding. Arrik felt as though he should be out of breath, but he wasn't. The thrill of the fight lingered. The dispatching of the assassin had been quick. He barely had to do anything at all. But now that the immediate danger was over relief crashed over him. He'd saved his fourth wife.

That did not mean she was safe, though, nor him. There would be another attempt on her life.

He ran a hand over his face and paced alongside the bed, Wren's gaze roaming over him. Whoever had sent the boy had chosen him on purpose. Was it another game? Another way to try and break Arrik? All knew his stance on children. They deserved to be protected, cherished, and loved. Not used and abused. It happed too often in Verlanti.

He kicked a piece of shattered dish and sat on the edge of his bed before he could stop himself, not caring that the princess stiffened as he did so. It was his bloody bed. She'd have to get over it.

"Do your own people truly hate you so much that they'd have you killed?" she asked, sounding as if she very much did not believe it. "The reaction of the people in your father's court would lead me to believe that to be a falsehood."

Dark humor filled him as it always did when he thought about the attempts on his life. He chuckled as the deep blue sky began to lighten just a touch. "I have been the target of assassins for longer than I care to remember," he admitted. "They seem to come in waves—an attempt every night for a week or so, then nothing for several months or years. But they have never managed to best me. They always fail." A pause, then Arrik added, "Well, in killing me, anyway."

Wren rolled her eyes, but at least she finally seemed open to engage in conversation. She narrowed her eyes at Arrik, clearly seeing right down to the root of his problem. "Why would they try to kill you? What secrets are you hiding?"

He shrugged. No point in hiding it. "Most of the court do not know I am the eldest of Soren's children," Arrik admitted. "Yes, bastard born, but the eldest. Almost everyone believes me to be the second son. My father had my birthdate changed to avoid any complications...regarding who was the heir to the throne."

Wren said nothing in response, as if she were processing everything Arrik had told her quickly and efficiently, going over everything in her head to work out if he was lying to her or not. And Arrik would know—he did the same thing whenever anyone told *him* anything.

"Not that any of that matters. They weren't here for me."

Her brows furrowed together, and she wiggled in the blankets. "They were here for me?"

"Yes."

A myriad of emotions crossed her face. "Why?"

That was the question of the day. "If I knew, I would tell you." He rolled his neck and stared down at the boy that was out cold on his floor. "You're the first wife I have managed to save."

Wren gurgled. "So you haven't been killing your wives?"

"No."

He peeked at her from the corner of his eye, and she frowned at her lap. "So you're not a rapist or a killer?"

He barked out a laugh. "I am a killer, just not of people undeserving of it."

Her face snapped in his direction. "My family deserved death?" she hissed.

Arrik shouldn't have opened his mouth. "Your family were the unfortunate casualties in a war our sires have been secretly carrying out for years."

"We weren't the ones who attacked and invaded!"

He met her angry glare squarely. "Your father sent an assassin to Soren. He was wounded but managed to survive. That was his first mistake. If you want to kill someone, you do it yourself. Never trust someone else."

"How dare you! My father would do no such thing!"

"You'd be surprised what men will do to protect the ones they love."

"I don't believe you," she said finally.

"You don't have to. The truth doesn't change just because you refuse to accept reality." He sighed. "For what it is worth, I am sorry for the loss of your family. Losing a parent isn't something that ever leaves you." He knew he shouldn't tell her anything, much less all about his secrets. Wren was a prisoner—and the sole remaining heir to a neighboring kingdom.

You're getting too personal.

They lapsed into silence as the sky lightened to navy blue. Dawn was close.

"You're bleeding," she finally said.

He followed her gaze to his arms. The boy had dug into his forearms with his nails. "I've had worse."

Electricity snapped down his spine as her gaze roamed over his arms and chest. "I can see that."

What was it about her that called the primal side of himself?

"What do we do now?" she asked, nodding to the unconscious boy.

"He'll be interrogated."

"You won't kill him?"

"No. Even monsters have their limits."

She nodded, accepting his words. "I suppose that is true. No being can be truly evil in every aspect."

"My father can be."

Wren pulled a face. "He is the exception to the rule." A pause. "What do you want from me, Prince?"

He shifted slightly so he could meet her gaze. "Your cooperation."

"I don't trust you."

"You shouldn't," he volleyed back.

"I am your wife in word only."

"I planned as much."

Something loosened in her expression. Relief? "I can't stay here."

"No, you cannot." He gestured to the boy. "It's too dangerous."

"I hate you."

"Noted, but we're both stuck in this situation together."

She arched a brow. "Which is?"

"Trying to survive my father's court." He leaned closer and her breath stuttered. "We are enemies, but we have a common goal. I promise to protect you to the best of my ability, but you must follow my every command."

"I will not obey you. You are not my master."

"In the eyes of the Verlanti, I own you," he pointed out.

Her jaw set. "No man can own me."

"Society expects you to act a certain way. In privacy, you may do what you like, but in public, you play the good, little wife."

"What do I get out of it? Why would I help you at all?"

"Because you want to return home, to your people. I can help with that. All you have to do is say yes."

The princess wasn't stupid. He was offering a lifeline.

"You are not my friend."

He smiled. "I should hope not."

Her stony expression didn't waver. "Don't lie to me. Be honest and I will do as you ask for my people."

It was in that moment Arrik realized he had *never* lied to Wren, even when he was goading her into reacting to him. For what could he be with his new-found dragon wife if not honest? She made no attempt to hide her true feelings of him, either. Considering how they met, it made no sense to lie. Wren could hate Arrik, yes, and he could continue watching her like a hawk in case she should attack him, yes, but, through whatever bizarre circumstances, he had found a person he could actually talk to honestly.

He slowly reached out and untucked the edge of the blanket, freeing her arms. It was a show of trust. Arrik held his hand out. "A truce?"

She eyed his outstretched palm like it was a snake but eventually took it. Her hand was calloused like his own, not like any highborn lady of the elven court.

"For now," she replied.

He released her hand reluctantly, liking her skin upon his own too much. Arrik turned from her to ensure she did not see the small smile that curled his lips, though he was aware her eyes were on the back of his head.

"You really need to sleep," Arrik told her, before standing and moving back to his chair by the empty fireplace. "I doubt you have slept for days."

Wren clucked her tongue and clutched the blankets to her chest. The giant prison of blankets Arrik had trussed her up in loosened, but she didn't move. She sagged into them and let out a sigh. "I would sleep better if you gave me a weapon," she said innocently. *Too innocently.*

"Demands already? What a greedy wife you are."

She shrugged. "When you can't beat them, join them. It was worth a try." Wren yawned. "If I need to sleep, then you definitely need to sleep, too."

"I'll sleep when I am dead."

"Wouldn't that be a miracle."

Arrik smothered a chuckle. A fiery sense of humor to go with her fighting and her hair. He liked it. Too much.

But despite her words of protest, Wren's eyes eventually grew heavy, and Arrik watched with some relief when she finally slipped into a resistant, unsettled sleep. He rose and made sure to secure the boy's hands behind his back before he called in Shane. His second took in the scene and then had his men remove the young assassin.

Shane eyed the sleeping princess. "Quite a fight she put you through earlier and now she is sleeping? How curious."

"We came to an understanding," Arrik whispered.

His friend eyed him critically. "Be careful. Females are dangerous creatures."

"I always am."

His second left the room silently as the sky turned pink to the east. Curiosity getting the better of him, Arrik moved back over to the bed once more to examine the sleeping face of his new bride.

He did not know when he would next get a chance to, after all.

There were deep shadows beneath Wren's eyes, and there were barely healed cuts and bruises on her neck that her hair had hidden.

Arrik had not had the chance to look at Wren this closely since he had nearly choked the life out of her. Now that she was washed and clean and dressed in the high fashion of Verlanti, he found it easier to take in her features.

It was the wild, red hair that Arrik liked the most. Truly, he had never seen the color upon any other person he had ever met. Even after their tussle, it was still adorned with tiny jewels, which seemed to burn and glow with her hair. It was as if her head was aflame, especially in the burgeoning light of dawn filtering through the courtyard.

He placed a hand over Wren's face, not quite touching her skin. She was not a Verlanti version of beauty—the dress she wore to their wedding had highlighted that. Most women in Verlanti, and most of the men, too, were polished. Perfect. All sharp planes and immaculate, shining hair and clothes.

But there was something natural about the Dragon Princess that Arrik found himself drawn to. He liked it a lot. There was a softness to her, despite the lean muscles of her body that made the swathes of insubstantial Verlantian fabric feel more alive rather than sterile. It was that contrast that pleased him so. He wanted to capture her wildness and keep it for himself.

His fingertips touched Wren's cheek for just a moment, then he retreated from the bed as if he had been burned. He was a fool. Giving in to his attraction was a mistake.

She would sooner kill him than let him touch her.

His new wife was a dragon among vipers and he had a feeling that she'd wreak havoc in the court. Soren should have killed her. She was a dangerous piece to add to the chessboard.

He smiled. It was his father's mistake.

She was Arrik's key to the kingdom of Lorne.

And then he would take Verlanti.

CHAPTER TWENTY-FIVE

WREN

Her eyes snapped open. Wren had fallen asleep within her enemy's chambers.

Is he the enemy after last night?

She didn't know. He saved her life but did that excuse his past actions? It didn't.

Her head was fuzzy and thick, her limbs heavy. She was exhausted—which wasn't a surprise, given that before last night, she had been locked up on a ship for weeks and then thrown in a cell. She knew she'd fallen asleep sometime right before dawn, and going by the way the sun shone into the room via the courtyard, it couldn't have been many hours after that. It still didn't feel like enough.

Wren could not believe she'd slept. Now that she was becoming more aware of her surroundings, she became furious that she'd so stupidly done so, especially after watching Arrik dispatch the assassin. He was cold, clinical, precise.

He hadn't hurt her.

The prince wasn't the one who was meant to kill her like she'd been led to believe. Just some unknown threat. She struggled against the blankets which still held her tight. It was far too hot beneath them. For some reason the idea of an assassin was worse than her husband. At least she knew what to expect with the prince. Wren hated the idea of death creeping around corners, seeking to hunt her down.

The door opened and she bolted upright. Arrik was nowhere to be seen and servants began to file in. She blinked repeatedly as the sun shone in her eyes, the sheer curtains doing nothing to shut it out. A sheen of sweat covered her body as they wordlessly released Wren from the blankets that kept her suffocatingly in place. Guilt pricked her as they began to clean up the shattered dishes and food strewn across the ground. They did not comment on the dented tea tray that lay on the floor.

That wasn't the only thing on the floor.

Her attention snapped to the side of the bed. The boy was gone. Not a spot of blood, nor any other trace that someone had attempted to murder her in the night.

Wren watched as the servants laid out a selection of dresses on the bed for her to wear, each of them airy and gauzy and ridiculous by Lorne standards, but still somewhat more sensible than the wedding dress she still had on.

Just as silently as they entered, they left, closing the door behind them.

Wren gazed around the huge but sparsely decorated room and swung her legs over the bed's edge, her toes meeting the warm wooden floor. She stretched her sore body and stumbled over to a large bowl of water which had been warmed by the morning rays of the sun. A small towel sat beside it, so she dipped it in the water and used it to wipe away the sweat from her skin.

She scurried over to the bed and eyed the courtyard to ensure nobody was watching, then she quickly untied her wedding dress, the fabric sticking slightly to her skin. The air had a wet sort of quality to it that she'd not experienced before. She grabbed the most modest dress from the bed and put it on. It was a soft green color, made of a lightweight silk that would have protected against none of the elements of the Dragon Isles. But, in the already startlingly hot morning of Verlanti, the cool material was welcome.

Her bladder complained and she drifted toward the front of the room to an open doorway. It was dim without the light but she was baffled by what she saw. It was a huge room made of stone and silver. A toilet, not a chamber pot, in the right corner but that's not what intrigued her the most. Wren drifted to the back of the room and ran her hand over the silver levers on the wall and then studied the ceiling. Was this the device her mother used to tell her about? A shower? Where the rain came from the ceiling?

Her bladder complained once more. She'd have to investigate later.

After relieving herself, she washed her hands and exited the privy. Moving over to the table, she sat down and blankly stared at the food. She was not sure if she should eat it or not. Someone tried to murder her last night, after all. What was stopping them from poisoning the food?

But if that was the way it was going to be, then that was the way it was going to be. If someone meant to poison Wren's food—and continued to do so—then eventually they would get to her. She couldn't live her life in fear. Plus, the prince didn't seem like the person to leave things to chance. No doubt he'd had the food tested.

And you trust him?

"Stop it," she muttered out loud. She couldn't go on this way.

If Arrik meant for Wren to die, he'd have let the assassin finish her off. Which meant he wanted her alive...for now. Though she could trust nothing else about the man, she could, at least, trust that he did not wish to see her poisoned or dead. They both had an agenda and needed the other to fulfill it.

So, in the end, she relented to the gnawing in her stomach and began eating.

She watched the trees swaying in the courtyard outside as she grazed on unfamiliar foods that had only been brought to Lorne in the height of summer. Strawberries and honey, with thin, toasted slices of bread slathered in butter. A crystalline jug of apple juice was particularly delicious.

All of it was beautiful. The scenery, the food, the clothes.

But it wasn't home.

A lump formed in her belly as grief struck her heart, and she realized in horror that she was about to cry. But she did not want to risk anyone seeing her do so—least of all Arrik, if he were to return—so she gulped down another glass of apple juice until the tears subsided.

She'd never been much of a crier before, but it seemed like she was seconds from bursting out in tears at all times now. It was bothersome and it made her feel weak.

When Wren was finished, she tucked a silver fork into her corset and began to pace around the room. The sun rose higher in the sky and she felt like she was being baked in an oven. It was so bloody hot. The breeze picked up and she stepped out into the courtyard. Wren paced the circular edge until she arrived back at the prince's room. The courtyard was entirely private, with only the open wall from Arrik's chambers being the entrance and exit.

Next, she pushed through the huge leafy plants, searching for the source of the water. A true smile came to her face as she discovered it. A large round pool sat in the center of the courtyard. A ledge ran around the edge of the pool form a circular shelve to sit upon. Wren turned her face up to the sun and sighed, appreciating the moment of peace.

She dipped her left foot into the water and shivered as the cool liquid lapped at her ankle. A swim would be so nice but too dangerous. Wren gave the pool one last longing look before padding down a winding path with stepping stones that led back to the prince's chamber. She glanced around.

It was gorgeous, but it was still a prison she could not escape from.

Or could she?

Her attention moved to the door. Time to find out.

Wren strode forward and tried the door, not expecting it to be unlocked.

The door clicked open.

Freedom.

She popped her head outside the door, spotting three guards. None of them said as word as she stepped barefoot from the room and closed the door behind her. Keeping her head high, Wren forged ahead when two of the guards peeled away from the wall and followed behind her. Were they there to protect her, or to make sure she didn't do something stupid? Why had she been given free rein in the palace? Sure, she'd married the prince, but she was still the enemy. Anyone who attended the wedding knew she didn't want to be here.

Stop questioning it. You're not constrained.

Something held her back. None of this felt right.

Just what was stopping her from escaping? She could sneak away from the guards if she wanted to.

For several hours, she wandered aimlessly. Wren stumbled across courtiers from time to time, but they only stared and whispered to each other. They never approached her. Perhaps it was her wild unbrushed hair or the glares she tossed their way, but it worked for her. She didn't wish to speak with anyone, and if they started rumors about how savage she was, it worked in her favor.

Eventually, she found her way onto a wide balcony overlooking the front of the palace grounds. The bay was right there in her line of sight, the path between the palace and the water tantalizingly short. If she reached the water and secured a boat, she could make her way back to Lorne on her own.

"Wife," a deep voice said behind her.

Wren spun around, her silk dress flaring around her feet. The prince stepped onto the balcony. His silver hair was pulled back from his face, making his jawline and cheekbones appear sharper. His pointed ears were longer than her mothers had been. Was it because he was male? Or just because of his bloodline?

"I can see your thoughts." She shuttered her gaze and he

nodded. "That's better."

"You want me to hide things from you?" Wren asked slowly.

He smiled and glanced toward the bay, giving her the perfect view of his profile. Blast him. He was gorgeous. Too bad his soul didn't match his exterior.

"I want you to protect your secrets. That is the currency here. You need to guard ours."

Ours. She shivered at the use of the word.

"Do we have secrets?" she murmured.

"We do, and we will." He focused his piercing blue eyes back on her. "Come, wife. There is much to be done this day and you've slept much of it away."

"What would you have me do?" she asked hesitantly. What was the captive wife of a beast supposed to do?

His smile turned wicked. "Please me, of course." She stiffened and he rolled his eyes. "The queen requests your presence."

She pushed away from the banister and walked to his side. He stared down at her like he was trying to figure her out, a small smile lingering on his lips.

"What?" Wren demanded.

"You didn't fight me."

Wren scowled. "I happen to like the queen. It has nothing to do with you."

His smile melted away. "Be careful who you bestow your friendship upon."

She studied him. "Do I have cause to be wary of the queen?"

Arrik held her gaze. "You need to be wary of everyone. No one here is your friend."

"No one?"

"No one," he repeated.

"She seems nice."

"Looks are deceiving."

"Should I not associate with her?" she questioned. Had she gotten the woman all wrong?

"You cannot escape it."

"Then why say anything?"

"Because you're too trusting."

She blanched. "How would you know?"

"You haven't tried to kill me yet, despite the fork you have stashed between your breasts."

"How the devil did you know that?" she demanded.

"I am a tall elf, you are a petite human, and that Verlanti dress doesn't leave much to the imagination."

Wren gasped and covered her chest. "Stop looking. I picked the most modest one."

"So I noticed." He gestured to the door. "Shall we?"

She looked over her shoulder at the bay, wishing that she could escape now. This place was confusing. No one was who they said they were.

"Your expressions, wife. I can read your thoughts."

Wren smoothed out her expression. She really needed to work on that. Wearing her heart on her sleeve was a danger while living with the enemy. To survive, she needed to do better. She needed to thrive. That started with pretending to become one of them. She'd cooperate with the prince and gain his trust bit by bit, but then when the time came, she'd pull the rug from beneath him.

"What am I thinking now?" she asked, batting her lashes.

"Something devious, I'm sure," was his dry reply.

Wren pressed her lips together to stop herself from grinning. He wasn't wrong.

All she needed was a way out of the palace and some jewels with which to barter for everything that she would need to get home.

CHAPTER TWENTY-SIX

WREN

From that day on, Arrik returned to his chambers but slept in his chair each night. Or at least she thought he slept there. She always managed to fall asleep before the prince did despite how he trussed her up.

It was a game of sorts. They ate dinner quietly together and then when it was time for bed, the predator in him came out.

The bloody man didn't chain her to his bed but no matter how much she fought, grappled, and cursed, he somehow cocooned her in his blankets to the point where she couldn't move. Then he left her there to fall asleep.

"Is this really necessary?" she complained at the end of the week. She was sweaty and sticky.

"It's for your safety and mine."

"How so?"

He hadn't responded.

Time passed in a blur of exploring, luncheons with the queen, and a complete lack of contact with the rest of the court. She hadn't seen Soren or his other sons in over three weeks and Wren found herself comfortable in Arrik's quiet presence.

She still didn't trust him, but she wasn't terrified of him.

He'd kept his promises and she'd kept hers. It worked for them both.

What she didn't tell her husband was that she'd successfully managed to hide away several jewel-encrusted hairpins that would hopefully secure herself a ship and provisions. But she was no closer to finding a way out of the castle; all entrances and exits to the palace were heavily guarded, and she had no doubt that the expansive gardens were teeming with spies and guard dogs.

Wren thought back to the dragon and the mad boy locked in prison. It had seemed like such a desperate, suicidal plan to use the dragon to escape, yet now it seemed more and more appealing. The longer she stayed in the palace the more she itched to escape. The castle was enormous, and she hadn't even scratched the surface when it came to exploring, but it was still a prison.

That evening, Arrik stormed into the room and slammed the door.

Wren blinked at him. That was the first instance of a temper he'd ever shown in quite some time. "What's wrong?"

"We are expected at dinner with my family," he said simply. He tossed a green gauzy garment onto the bed and began stripping as he walked out into the courtyard. "My step mother sends her regards along with that dress."

"I have plenty of dresses," Wren called back, getting up from the chair. The plants rustled as the prince disappeared from sight.

"Well, I like this one and it would please my stepmother."

Wren scowled and eyed the dress like it was a snake. She'd

seen what the queen viewed as appropriate clothing over the last few weeks. Lifting it up, Wren sighed. The neckline was higher than any of her other dresses and had a solid fabric beneath the sheer layers so no one would see all of her important bits.

She hugged it to her chest and darted toward the privy to get changed. Not only did she want privacy but she had managed to steal a little bag which she could hide beneath her dresses. Wren kept her filched treasures there.

It was time to become the prince's complicit little wife.

Well, not complete amenable.

Wren slipped on the gauzy emerald-green dress and then exited the privy. She smiled as she ran her hands down the gown. It was stunning. Her mum would have loved it. She swallowed hard, her smile staying in place. It was nice to have a happy thought about her mum.

Water splashed outside; she glanced toward the courtyard just beyond the billowing white curtains. The plants waved in the wind and her eyes widened as she caught a glimpse of toned, wet skin.

Arrik.

The elves had no shame. They even bathed out in the open.

Don't be such a prude. Your people do the same.

Quickly, she adjusted the golden, jeweled straps of her dress on her shoulders and smoothed her hands down the gauzy material. It clung to her curves in a classy way that made her feel beautiful. For the first time since she'd arrived in the elvish kingdom, Wren felt like she was back in her own skin.

In her short time in Verlanti, she'd learned two things:

beauty was valued above all else and women were praised for their sensuality.

Tonight, Wren would use both.

She ran her fingers through her tangled red locks to unknot them and pinched her cheeks to add some color.

This was it.

Gut churning, she padded toward the curtains, the trees surrounding the bathing pool gently rustling. Wren averted her eyes and slung a hip against one of the tall, white marble pillars that bracketed the entrance to their room when Arrik exited the pool. She examined the painted sunset, even as she focused on every sound her new husband made as he approached her.

He paused near her side and Wren glanced at him, relieved to see that he was now covered by a towel. His long silver hair hung in his face, dripping water down his chiseled chest. His weapons were tucked underneath his arm. The man never let her near any of them. He was smart.

"Like something you see, Princess?" he murmured.

She dismissed him, focusing her attention once more on the sky. "Beauty isn't everything, Prince."

"On that we can agree."

"It was bound to happen," she retorted. "Get dressed or we'll be late for dinner. I'm sure that would displease your king."

He grunted and moved into the room. Wren was keenly aware of his movements behind her. Her cheeks warmed as his clothes rustled. What was wrong with her? She'd never been a prude before. A body was just a body. Why did he affect her so? That was part of the problem. Arrik had become a person to her in the weeks that had passed. He wasn't just a faceless monster she could blame her pain on.

You're betraying Rowen.

She squeezed her eyes shut and shoved the ugly thought away. Rowen was gone. The best thing she could do was survive and then take vengeance for him.

"I have something for you," Arrik rumbled behind her.

"A gift? You shouldn't have," she snarked. *Reel it in, Wren. More flies with honey than vinegar.*

Her dress whispered around her ankles as she faced her husband.

"Temper," he murmured.

Wren sighed. "I'm not the only one."

He pursed his lips. "I apologize. It has been a...rough day."

She blinked at him. That was surprisingly honest. They usually kept personal things to themselves. "I am sorry."

The prince shrugged. "It is nothing."

He set an ornately carved box on the bed and opened it, pulling out a headpiece. Raw black crystals were woven together with gold strands to create a crown that looked suited only for the goddess of the underworld. Delicate gold chains hung from the sides and the back was adorned with tiny black crystals.

Her eyes widened as Arrik pulled out a choker from the box with a large black diamond pendant at the center. He approached her in his signature black leather pants and velvet waist coat, his wet hair leaving patches on the silk shirt he wore.

"A few finishing touches," he murmured, nodding toward the full-length mirror to her right. "Turn around and I'll put

253

them on you."

Wren complied slowly and watched him as he approached her. The prince met her gaze in the mirror and then carefully set the crown atop her head. She shivered as he pushed aside her hair and lowered the choker over her head and placed it around her neck. This was so stupid. If he wanted to, he could easily kill her.

Play nice.

He leaned closer and his eucalyptus and leather scent invaded her senses. Wren inhaled shallowly when his breath cascaded over her neck and shoulder, causing butterflies to take flight in her belly.

"Are you quite finished?" she managed tightly. Every brush from his calloused fingers were causing goosebumps to ripple across her freckled arms.

"It's a tiny clasp and my fingers are having a hard time with the task," he grunted.

"I can do it."

"I know." He once again met her gaze in the mirror. "You are very capable."

Was that a compliment?

Arrik clasped the choker but didn't withdraw. He smoothed her hair back into place and settled his large hands on the edges of her bare shoulders. "Now you look like a true princess."

"It's not how you look but a state of the mind," Wren replied automatically. Her mum had repeated those words to her over the years. She never understood them more than she did now.

"True," her husband mused. His thumbs skated over her skin. They gazed at each other for a beat of silence before he said, "Is it so bad to be my bride?"

Yes, she wanted to scream, but Wren kept the words from tumbling free. Deep down she knew it would have been a lie.

"I was sold to you. Did you think gems from my own kingdom would sway me?" Not exactly antagonistic, but not the words of seductress either.

He barked out a laugh. "You're not one to hold back your thoughts, are you?"

Her lips twitched in a ghost of a smile. "So I am told."

His mirth faded. "It is a dangerous habit in this place."

"Are you a danger to me?" she whispered, holding his icy blue gaze.

"I'm a danger to everyone." The prince spoke quietly like he was speaking to himself. He stepped back and held his hand out. "Are you ready to face the wolves?" he asked, changing the subject.

Wren faced him and took his hand. "I was raised with dragons. I can handle a few wolves."

CHAPTER TWENTY-SEVEN

WREN

The dinner was exactly what Wren had imagined it would be: overly opulent and full of snide laughter and too much alcohol. Arrik's brothers kept making comments about her—even Kalles who had tried to help her—ensuring she did not forget how filthy and disgusting she'd been when she had been brought up from the dungeon.

I'd rather all that muck and blood to your laughter.

To her right, Arrik caught her eye, and imperceptibly shook his head. She could tell he knew exactly what she was thinking. But all he did was smile blandly, his expression giving nothing away about what *he* thought. This only served to annoy her further.

Don't make a scene. Keep your head down.

She took a delicate sip of her pumpkin soup. The king's voice rose, catching her attention. Wren tried to focus on her soup and block out his words. She had deliberately avoided listening to him so far.

"Oh, the Dragon Isles have put up far more of a fight than any of us could have expected," he said, waving a casual hand as he spoke, "but they are now completely subdued." A pointed look at Wren. "A dragon in chains is just a beast to be tamed, after all. And now we have many of them! Just look at Arrik's wild bride. All she needed was a strong Verlanti hand to get her in line, just like her mother."

Her head snapped up and Wren acted before she could think. Grabbing her goblet of wine, she tossed it into the king's face, even as Arrik caught her wrist. But it was too late.

The entire room went quiet, all laughter and cruel jibes gone in an instant.

Stupid, stupid, stupid.

It was clear Wren had crossed a line nobody had thought she'd dare to.

She held her breath as Soren opened his eyes, wine dripping from his hair and face. He chuckled, but his eyes were hard as flint when he stared her down. "It seems someone is yet to learn some respect for her betters. Guards, I think our feral princess is better suited to the dungeon than to the dinner table, don't you?"

Wren said nothing.

The prince's fingers tightened on her wrist, and he lowered her hand and the goblet to the table. His expression was like stone. Arrik had promised to protect her but she crossed a boundary. She hadn't followed her side of the deal.

Calm down. You will be okay. The dragon is in the dungeon.

She exhaled slowly and pulled her wrist from the prince's fingers. Wren pushed her chair out and stood from the table. She wouldn't be dragged away kicking and screaming.

"Good evening," she murmured.

The last thing she saw as the guards escorted her away was

the prince, whose blank expression had not cracked but his eyes glared daggers at her.

Good.

She flashed a grin at him the moment before the door was closed behind her.

Be furious. I do not care. I am not your perfect bride who will do what you want.

Then why did she feel so much guilt?

She chuckled as the guards led her down to the dungeons. It seemed that even marriage to the king's favorite son did not prevent Soren from throwing her into the dungeon. It only served to show Wren how false everything in Verlanti was—all she had to do was splash the king with some wine and here she was, back in her cell.

Well, not *her* cell. For whatever reason, Wren was thrown into the cell right next to the mad boy, rather than the one two cells over from him.

"I knew you'd be back," the boy said the moment the door to the prison was slammed shut.

"By the tides," she breathed. "You're still here?"

He ignored her.

"And just as mercurial as before."

"From rags to riches, and riches to rags," he sang back.

"Oh, be quiet," Wren snapped back. She had no time nor patience for his twisted, confusing words. No; she had a pocketful of jewels and the ghost of an idea to escape the hell she'd been placed in.

Feeling bold, she rushed to the very edge of the water and stared intently into its dark and murky depths.

"Watch your toes, watch your toes, oh, watch your toes!" the boy cried in his annoying singsong voice.

"I told you to be quiet." Wren edged just a little farther back from the water anyway, then crossed her arms and considered her options in blessed silence.

The dragon is clearly not trapped in here. The dungeon is too small to house it, and I doubt this strip of water is a narrow, deep pool. And it definitely rose and receded like the tide. It's attached to the sea. The dragon can come and go as it pleases.

The fish definitely hadn't shown up last time when the dragon did. Wren reasoned that its luminous scales served as a warning for the fish to keep well enough away—which was exactly what Wren needed.

Which meant she had to escape alongside the dragon.

No, Wren had to *ride* the dragon. That's if he didn't kill her while she attempted such a thing.

Behind her, the prison door creaked open, and Wren did not have to turn around to know who had deigned to visit. To her left, the mad boy retreated into the shadows of his cell—to obscure his presence or for some other reason, Wren did not know.

"I thought we had a deal," the prince said softly.

Her shoulders tensed up as his dark tone slithered over her skin. "We did."

"You broke it."

"Do not pretend to care about that," she replied calmly. "You're put out that I ruined your plans."

"My plans?"

She slowly faced her husband. "I am not a fool. You gained

much more than I in the deal. You may have not locked me away in your rooms, but I am a prisoner just the same."

But no longer. She'd escape this night. No more waiting. Wren could feel it in her bones: tonight was the night. Soren throwing her into the prison had been exactly what she needed to sneak out of the complacent rut she'd found herself in.

Wren raised her brows as the prince entered the cell and then sat down on the disgusting stone floor a few feet away from her.

"What are you doing?"

He gave her a hard smile. "Sitting, of course."

"Why?"

Her husband sighed and leaned his head against the grate. "Did you really have to throw wine at my father?" he countered.

"No. Well, yes." She tossed her hands in the air. "What else would you have had me do?"

He laughed softly. "I suppose I should be thankful you did not have a knife this time."

Wren hated herself for it, but she smiled. His dry humor would be the death of her. "I'll regret that I did not possess a dagger during that dinner for the rest of my life." Her gut churned as she thought over his words. "The king is a pig."

"As are most men," the prince commented. "But you're not leading a crusade of hate toward them."

"He is a murderer," she snapped back, feeling exposed.

"Do you seriously intend to be so vicious to him, knowing you'll end up in here every time?" Arrik asked, waving a hand around at the cell. "His words don't matter. Just ignore him."

"His words hold *power*," she countered. "How could you

expect me to stay silent when he was speaking so ill of my people, of me? Why did you..." She closed her mouth, halting the flow of words.

The prince's expression shifted as he watched her. "Say it."

Wren glared at him. "You did nothing. You swore to protect me and yet here I am in the dungeon."

He cursed. "You acted rashly before I had a chance to. While my situation is precarious at times, yours is far worse. I told you that I could only protect you if you obeyed me."

"Like an animal," she sniped.

"You crossed a line tonight, Princess."

Wren crossed her arms over her chest. "Do not *Princess* me. I have had enough of all your false politeness. It is clear what your family thinks of me—what you *all* think of me—and I do not intend to put up with it. If you will not defend me, then I'd rather spend my days rotting in here."

She expected him to scoff at the suggestion that he would defend her against his own kin, especially after the blank look on his face during dinner while his brothers were insulting her, but, to her surprise, Arrik sighed, then got to his feet.

"You are correct," he murmured. "Truly, they were shameful tonight, but I cannot protect you from my father if you will not listen to me. I am trying but you are still fighting against me." He glanced away, his jaw ticking in anger. "You'll have to spend tonight in here, but I do promise to keep you from the worst of my brothers' ire and stupidity in the future."

"We do not have a future."

His attention snapped to her, and he stepped into her space, towering over Wren. The prince leaned closer and ensnared

261

her with his eyes. "We are bound, you and I," he whispered. "Our futures are more entangled for every moment that passes." Her breath hitched as he brushed the tip of his nose against hers. "It's inevitable, but I know you. You need to be in control just like me. I can wait for you to choose."

"I won't choose this. Choose you." It felt like a lie, but she desperately wanted it to be the truth.

He cocked his head. "Wife, the choice has already been made."

Her hands shook but she kept her head held high. "I refuse for this to be my future. There has to be more."

The prince nodded. "There is but only if you stick with me. All you have to do is take my hand."

She swallowed hard and looked away. "I need to think."

He nodded slowly and backed toward the door. "A wise choice." He paused and asked hesitantly, "Is there anything I can get you to make your night more...comfortable?"

There was nothing Wren could say in response to what Arrik had said. Just like when he had explained to her that he was, in fact, the firstborn son, Wren knew in her heart that he was speaking the truth. He had not wanted his family to insult her. The blank expression on his face had been a mask.

And yet the prince was still her enemy. He was the man responsible for destroying her family and her kingdom. Rowen was dead because of him.

A small kindness from him now meant nothing.

But Wren *did* need something from him.

"Some lamb, if you would," Wren said, glancing at Arrik from beneath her lashes in an act she hoped came across as reluctant but necessary. "I did not eat much at dinner."

"You never eat much at dinner."

"That's because I do not like the food here!" she fired back, getting annoyed despite herself. Arrik's eyes found hers, and she saw that he had genuinely softened at her comment.

"That is another error on my part. What would you like to eat? Is it the way it's cooked?"

"Roasted on an open flame. Rare, if possible."

A pause. Then Arrik shook his head and laughed softly. "A true dragon. I shall see what I can do."

Time ticked by slowly and half an hour later, a guard came in and reluctantly handed her a bowl of fire-roasted lamb that set her stomach growling. She stared at the meat. That was one thing she could say about the prince: he did not lie.

The mad boy approached immediately. "You cannot possibly eat all that by your lonesome."

"Of course not," Wren replied, rolling her eyes before ripping off some of the meat and pushing it through the bars of the cell to her companion. His eyes gleamed, fixated on the steaming meat.

"You are a true princess. A princess of smoking meat."

She could not stop herself laughing at the comment, nor at the way the boy scoffed down the lamb without taking a breath. Wren ate far more slowly, chewing on the same piece of meat over and over again before swallowing.

After all, most of the lamb was not for her nor for the boy.

Hopefully, the dragon was hungry.

CHAPTER TWENTY-EIGHT

ARRIK

He paced in his room, his gaze moving to the empty blankets and bed. It felt wrong that Wren wasn't here with him. How had that happened? She was a tool to be used to thwart his father. Now, she'd become something else...something Arrik longed to possess.

Even now her scent seemed to permeate the room, driving him mad. He dropped down into his chair and stared blankly at the bed. Tonight hadn't gone like he'd planned. His father had been in a foul mood and as soon as Wren had walked into the room, his attention had homed in on her.

The image of Wren standing in the dungeon in her gown and jewels flashed through his mind. She didn't belong there. Arrik growled and stood back up. He stared at his door. What good was it being the king's favorite son if he didn't take advantage of it? Wren was *his* wife. She'd done nothing wrong and Arrik would be damned if he let her sit for a moment longer in the dungeon.

She belonged here, with him.

CHAPTER TWENTY-NINE

WREN

"A princess in rags, now a prisoner in riches," the boy commented. He whistled. "That is some dress you have on."

"Charming. What of it?" she grouched.

"Do you not wish to tell me how your status changed?"

"Do you actually wish to hear it?"

"But of course!" the boy insisted, jumping to his feet to emphasize his enthusiasm. His eyes gleamed in Wren's direction. "Considering the prince of nothing just showed up for some...*conversation*..."

Wren clucked her tongue, disgusted. "I did not do what you are thinking. Nothing even close."

"So, what, then?"

"It's something even worse."

At this, the mad boy seemed to grow genuinely interested. "What is worse than diving beneath the sheets with one's enemy?"

"Marrying them."

"Oh."

"Oh?" Wren also got to her feet, somehow affronted by the boy's lack of a reaction. "Oh? Is that all you can say to such a horrific thing happening to me?"

"You're surely clever enough to know that being married to the enemy does not have to be a bad thing. The line between enemy and lover is very fine indeed."

So stunned at the comment, Wren took a step backward. What he'd said was not a riddle or a jibe. It was a genuine, sane statement. She narrowed her eyes at him, suspicious. "You are…not what you seem, are you?"

The boy shrugged, then sat with his back against the grille of the cell that separated him from Wren, indicating for her to do the same. And so, though she did not much feel much like sitting, she followed suit so that their backs were to each other with just the iron bars between them. Wren felt the warmth of his skin through the grated, reminding her that she was not the only living thing in the dungeon.

The heat was welcome; between her flimsy dress and the freezing prison, Wren had already begun shivering.

"What do you think of the Verlantian Court?" the boy asked after a while, the singsong nature of his voice still not having returned. "You must have seen it when the guards escorted you out."

"So, you haven't?"

A surprisingly low chuckle, but otherwise no response.

Wren tried to make sense of this. It was clear that if she asked anything personal about the boy, she would receive no coherent answer. But, perhaps, through answering *his* questions about herself, she could discern a bit more about her mysterious, possibly-not-quite-mad companion.

"I hate it," she began. "It's beautiful and wretched and light and evil, and I want nothing more than to escape from it. It's fresh and pure on the outside, but it's diseased down to its very core. Completely rotten. This land is corrupt." Wren took a breath, pausing from her tirade, before adding in a much quieter voice, "Verlanti is the throne of vipers."

At this, the boy barked out a laugh, but before Wren could be angry with him, he said, "They probably think *you* are the viper, Princess of Dragons. Do you miss it?"

"Miss what?" Wren could scarcely keep up with the direction his questions took. She glanced at the water, knowing that, soon, it would rise. She knew she had to make a decision about what to do next. Only now, Wren was beginning to realize that her escape plan may have to include another body. She couldn't leave him.

"Home," the boy said simply.

She stilled at the word, her back going stiff against the boy's. But then she grew slack. "All the time," she admitted. "It's all that's keeping me going; getting home, how I can escape from here and reach it..." She stopped herself before she revealed everything that she had so far kept tightly to her chest. Such as the fact that her sister was still alive. Though the boy seemed harmless, there was no telling what or who he really was. For all Wren knew, he was a spy put down in the dungeon to encourage Wren to talk and reveal all her secrets.

But something about his nature suggested that this was not the case. *Even so, I cannot tell him something so important. Yet, that does not mean he is my enemy, nor does he deserve to rot in here.*

They sat together in companionable silence for a time, Wren

carefully watching the water and picking a lamb's bone clean while the boy hummed tunefully. She thought that she may have recognized the melody, but, whenever she tried to place it, the song escaped her mind.

It was the boy who finally spoke again. "Why eat that bone when you could eat the rest of the meat?" he asked in genuine confusion. "It will be difficult for you to eat it when the water begins to rise, and that will happen...imminently."

On impulse, Wren reached a hand behind her, searching for the boy's fingers between the bars that separated them. She did not expect him to reach out for her, too, and so was surprised when he did. They interlaced fingers, then Wren squeezed.

She'd made her decision. Whether the boy was a spy or not, she would get him out of the dungeon, then leave him someplace safe before she made her way back to Lorne.

"We're getting out of here," she told him, very quietly. "Unless you would rather remain?"

She did not need to see the boy's face to know that he was grinning. "Are you mad, woman? Of *course*, I want out of here. What do you have in mind?"

"The water is about to rise, as you said."

"Yes."

"And then the dragon might appear."

"*Might?*"

"Well, have you ever seen it down here before?"

"There has never been a Dragon Princess in the dungeon before."

"Is that a no?" Wren asked, letting go of his hand and getting to her feet, preparing to climb the bars just as the water began to rise. The boy did the same, and they found themselves face-to-face with each other. He was perhaps several inches taller than Wren, somewhat gawky and awkward with his height but possessed beautiful, wide brown eyes that she had never had the opportunity to see up close before.

A truly innocent face. He is no Verlantian spy. But still, I cannot take him with me to Lorne. I cannot risk him knowing about Britta.

The hem of her green dress floated on the surface of the water below her.

"It means I do not know," the boy admitted. He climbed the first rung of the iron bars, and Wren did the same. "It could have been under the water, out of sight. I would not have much liked to find out, one way or the other, by stepping in the water."

The smallest of smiles curled Wren's lips. "No, I suppose not."

"So, what happens when the dragon gets here?" A flash of concern crossed the boy's face, which only made Wren's smile grow larger. He was nervous. It was only natural. No one outside the Dragon Isles dealt with the dragons.

"We'll deal with that if and when the dragon shows up...and hope that the fish do not."

He reached out and flicked one of the crystals hanging from the crown she wore. "So sparkly. What did you do to get theses?"

"Nothing."

She tucked the bone away in her pocket. The two of them climbed the grille until they were as high up and as secure as they could be, and, when the water stopped rising, Wren began to sing.

Instead of a sorrowful, calming tune, this time Wren sang a fighting song. Bright and vibrant and daring, to encourage the dragon to show up. But, after fifteen minutes, there was no sign of the water stirring, and she felt her heart sink.

You have to show up.

The dragon was her last chance. She'd burned a bridge tonight.

Wren sang louder and more fervently with every passing second. Her lips hurt from humming, and her hands grew slick with sweat, despite the bitter cold. Wren knew, in her heart, that if she could not get the dragon to appear tonight, then that would be it for her.

She would be doomed.

When she was mere moments from giving up, a set of spines finally broke the surface of the water, and she let out a sigh of relief.

Opposite her, the boy looked down at the dragon with wide eyes. "I'm not going to like this next bit, am I?"

Wren grunted and tried to calm down. Whether it was because she was no longer responsible for just her own life but for his, too, Wren herself no longer felt scared or uncertain. Slowly, she climbed down the bars and into the water, closing the distance between herself and the dragon with careful, calculated steps. Her dress pulled on her frame as the fabric soaked up water.

The creature growled as she approached. But still, Wren was not scared. She dropped to her knees with a splash and held out the lamb as an offering, holding her hands a mere inch from the dragon's dark yet luminous snout.

"Go on and take it," she murmured. "It's a gift for you."

Air stuttered from her lungs as the warmth of its breath wafted over her hands as it finally took the meat gently from her hands.

"Get ready," she told the boy—just as the door to the prison opened up.

"Wren?"

Arrik's surprised voice washed over her as she stared down the dragon.

No.

"Get back," he commanded. "It's dangerous."

She ignored the prince and her heart raced in her chest. This was it. Wren continued her song, and when it was clear the creature would not attack her, she launched herself onto its back. The prince yelled as water lapped over her legs as she straddled the dragon. She exhaled slowly and silently rejoiced. The dragon had not attacked her nor rejected her. Instead, it now lowered the spines on its back so that she could position herself more safely.

"Don't you dare," the prince said lowly.

Wren finally lifted her gaze to her husband. His chest lifted up and down with his breaths as he gazed at her. His normally stoic face was pinched in anger and worry. Arrik waded farther into the water and held his hand out to her.

"It doesn't have to be this way," he gritted out.

The dragon slid forward to the next cell and her traitorous heart clenched at the heartbreak on the prince's face.

"Get on," she demanded of the boy, knowing they had mere seconds before the prince came to his senses and attacked.

"Are you crazy?!" the boy cried; mouth wide open at the sight of Wren atop the glowing, dangerous dragon.

"Between you and I, I am not the one who is mad."

The prince cursed and launched himself through her cell door to get to the boy's.

"Get on. Now!"

The boy jumped on behind Wren, having no qualms about wrapping his arms around her waist to secure himself.

Wren glanced behind her. "How well can you hold your breath?"

A pause. "Hopefully well enough not to die from this."

The boy's cell door swung open and the prince strode through it. His livid gaze locked on her. "Don't make me your enemy."

"You have always been my enemy," she whispered.

"I thought we agreed not to lie to each other." His ice blue eyes narrowed. "I will hunt you."

"You can try," she retorted as the dragon slid forward once more.

The prince smiled. "You know I love challenges, Wren. I'll be seeing you soon, my queen."

A shiver ran down her spine. It wasn't so much a threat but a promise.

"Take a deep breath," she commanded the boy.

A quick kick to the dragon's side, and the three of them dived into the murky water. The last thing Wren heard as they disappeared under the surface was Arrik calling for the guards.

The boy tightened his grip around Wren's waist so hard it hurt. He was clearly terrified for his life and unsure whether he truly could hold his breath for as long as was needed to survive. *Please let us make it.*

Wren realized half a minute later that she herself had not taken perhaps as big of a breath as she should have before diving into the freezing water, though there was little she could do about that now. No, all she could do was cling to the dragon just as the boy was clinging to her and hope to still be alive when the dragon finally chose to resurface.

Hopefully far away from the palace.

The dragon hurtled through the water at frightening speeds. *He might even be as fast as Aurora had been.* She could sense it more clearly now that she'd touched him, instinct telling her that she was right. There was some comfort to Wren that the dragon was male whereas Aurora had been female—to ride a female dragon after what happened to her felt wrong, somehow.

Wren was growing light-headed. She didn't want to imagine how the boy behind her was faring. But his grip on her waist hadn't loosened all the way yet, so Wren had no choice but to assume he was still at least semi-conscious.

Just as her lungs began to burn for air, the dragon abruptly changed course and jolted upright, swimming straight as an arrow until Wren could see traces of moonlight upon the surface of the sea.

And not a moment too soon.

She gripped the boy's arm with her left hand to stop him from slipping off.

And then, a moment later, the dragon broke through the surface, and Wren heaved in as much air as her lungs could carry. She took in some water, too, the salt of it stinging her throat and making her sputter and spit as the dragon snaked along to a small, wooden pier. When he got there, Wren tumbled off his back and onto the pier, taking the boy with her. She extricated his arms from her waist and turned to check on him, relieved to see he was breathing.

"Open your eyes," she whispered to him, not knowing who might be around to hear them. "We're alive and breathing."

"I'm not so sure about that," he coughed, but then he struggled into a sitting position, and Wren knew he would be all right.

She rolled onto her knees and faced the dragon, holding her hand out to his snout before whistling a thank you. "You are a true treasure trove," she told him, meaning every word. For what was treasure if not freedom and life? The dragon had granted both back to Wren—and her unlikely companion.

With this, the dragon slipped beneath the surface of the sea, his scales glowing faintly before he disappeared from sight entirely. Wren watched him go while her skin turned clammy, then wiped a hand across her brow when she realized she was sweating. *How...?* she wondered, before taking note of just how hot the Verlantian evening's air was. Locked up underground in the dungeon, the air had been frigid; Wren had completely forgotten that it was, in fact, the height of summer.

Wren adjusted the gold clasps of her now ruined emerald dress. Against all likelihood, she hadn't lost the crown. It was now knotted in her long hair.

Time to work out where they were.

Scanning the darkness, Wren spied a cluster of houses a little way past the pier. Another pier lay in front of her on the water, also with houses at its end, then another and another.

A trading port?

"Wow, that dragon got us all the way to the international market," the boy murmured, clearly impressed. He touched a hand to Wren's shoulder. "I know of a place we can hide and recover."

She raised an eyebrow. "*You* know a place? How?"

The boy could only laugh. "I was not captured in Verlanti because I am mad, Wren."

It was the first time he'd said her name. The first time he'd acknowledged his own so-called madness. Wren was wary as much as she was intrigued.

"Who *are* you?" she asked, but the boy merely grabbed her hand and pulled her to her feet.

"Later," he said. "For now, we must be quiet."

The pair of them tiptoed down the pier and past the houses, through the market and the first alleyway they came across. The boy led Wren beneath stone bridges and through narrow corridors with practiced ease, which only served to fuel her suspicion that she had completely underestimated him.

"Where are we going?" Wren whispered after another ten minutes of twisting and wandering through the midnight streets of Verlanti. Luckily, anyone around ignored them.

"Here," was all he said, before leading her through a large wooden door which opened silently on its hinges.

Inside, the building was so dark Wren could not even see her hand in front of her face, but then one lantern after another lit up all around her—revealing that she and the boy were surrounded. A dozen masked people, all wielding swords or spears or daggers, formed a tight circle around them, and Wren's heart sank.

This is not happening. I did not escape the Verlanti Palace and all of its barbaric people just to die like this.

"Leif? Leif, is that you?"

"Aye," the boy said, grinning. "So please don't skewer me. *Or my companion.*"

The person who had spoken—a woman—took off her mask to peer at Wren.

She froze, not believing her eyes as she stared at the woman. It was her mother. *It can't be.* "You died," Wren rasped.

The woman's eyes widened in surprise. "I am not your mother."

"Then are you a spirit here to torment me for my failure?" Wren whispered, not taking her gaze off the apparition

Sympathy filled the woman's expression. "My dear, I am your aunt, Vienne. I'm so glad Leif was able to get you out."

Aunt?

"*She* got *me* out," the boy who was called Leif replied. He sounded pleased about it. Proud. "On the back of a dragon, no less. It was bloody terrifying."

Wren was beyond confused about what was going on. She focused on the woman who'd removed her mask. Vienne was petite and the same age as Wren's own mother, with lines on her face that suggested she'd seen more than her fair share of hardships.

"What have I been brought into?" Wren asked, her voice slow and soft and steady—unlike her throbbing, nervous heart.

Her aunt smiled and opened her arms wide. "Welcome to the Kingdom of Myths, Dragon Princess. We'd sincerely hoped to run into you."

Wren frowned. "The Kingdom of—"

"Myths," Leif finished for her, squeezing her hand before letting go of it. "It's an order designed to balance out the world. And damn if it's out of balance right now."

"We seek to take out and replace those who are corrupt," Vienne added, when it was clear Wren was no wiser about what the Kingdom of Myths did.

And then it clicked.

"Like...taking out the High King of Verlanti?"

Vienne's smile became a feral grin. All around her, the masked faces of the people grew wild. "Of course. Why else would we be here? And so, the only question I have for you, Princess, is this: won't you join us?"

Wren hesitated. Running back to Lorne had never been a good solution to her situation—not when Verlanti had taken the country over. But dispatching King Soren...

That would free the Dragon Isles for good.

Verlanti and its king will pay for what they've done.

"How do I know I can trust you?" she asked.

"You don't, but if it helps, I have a letter for you from your mother," her aunt said softly, pulling a sealed letter from the pocket of her skirt.

Wren straightened. What the devil "How?"

"She knew what decisions your father was making for the

Lorne, and she'd supported them. Anneke knew that they were dangerous and reached out. She always had a feeling for misfortune."

"I don't know you," Wren pointed out. "Why would she reach out to you?"

"Who do you think got her away from the poisonous lord who abused her?"

"You," she breathed. The Leif shifted and Wren glanced at all the other silent occupants of the room before taking the letter from Vienne. "I have much to think about, but I have a question. Why wait to pull me from the palace?"

The smile her aunt gave her was chilly. "We needed to know you were strong enough for the task."

"What task is that?"

"Bringing Verlanti to its knees."

It sounded too good to be true. "I can commit to nothing."

Vienne bowed her head. "Spoken like a wise woman."

"I have more questions."

"Which I promise to answer, but not here. I'm sure the Beast is already searching for you."

Wren's stomach swooped. Was it anticipation or foreboding she felt?

The door opened and an elf with blond hair stepped inside. His gaze snapped to her and held for a moment. Wren's jaw dropped. It was one of the guards that had tailed her most days.

"He's—he's," she stuttered.

"Welcome, princess," he murmured, closing the door behind him. "I'm happy to see you made it."

"This is Josenu. He is one of our spies," her aunt supplied.

Josenu nodded once and then turned his grey gaze to Vienne. "He has already dispatched soldiers. We must seek a more secure shelter. You need to move now."

The masked people burst into action.

Wren gathered up her wet, soiled dress in her arms, watching in silence as her aunt barked out orders. Leif slipped his hand into her right one and she blinked at him.

"What do you think you're doing?"

He eyed her; his expression serious. "Giving comfort, like you did for me in prison."

She dropped her attention to their laced fingers and something in her chest cracked. When was the last time she'd experienced a touch like this? It felt like years.

"Thank you," she whispered.

"No need for thanks among friends," he murmured back.

"Wren." She focused on Vienne. "It's time to leave. Will you come with us?"

Leif squeezed her fingers.

She swallowed. "If I choose not to help you, will you leave me here?"

"No," her aunt replied, her lips thinning. "You have a place with me for as long as you like."

"I will go."

"Follow Josenu. I'll be right behind you."

The palace guard waited by the back entranced and opened the door. The masked rebels slipped out. Leif darted forward, not letting go of her hand and she hauled more of her dress against her chest as she hurried after him.

"Do not leave my side," Josenu whispered, the moonlight

turning his gaze silver. His eyed her dress. "Will you be able to run in that?"

"I can." It wouldn't be easy.

The spy must have spotted something in her expression. He knelt and cut off two feet from the hem, exposing her legs to the night air. She muffled a squeak when he yanked on the dress twice, forming a high slit over each thigh before placing his blade back in it sheath.

"Leif, where she goes, you go."

The boy nodded his head and Wren almost rolled her eyes. "I can handle myself."

Josenu nodded once. "Which is why I have not thrown you over my shoulder."

Her eyes narrowed as he turned his back on her and ran down the cobbed alley. Leif dropped her hand and urged her forward. Wren sprinted after the spy. They clung to the shadows, weaving through the labyrinth of streets. Her thighs began to burn as the trekked to the north, away from the bay.

The spy, cursed and darted to the left. She and Leif followed suit.

Josenu crept to the barrels and climbed the nearest one.

"What are you doing?" she whispered.

"The commander's men are blocking the roads. We must take to the roofs." The spy launched himself upwards and caught the edge of the building and climbed up, his cloak disappearing from view.

"You next," Leif said.

Wren grumbled underneath her breath. While she wasn't afraid of heights, scrambling across roofs in a gown, barefoot didn't seem like the best idea.

You can do this.

She took a running start, using the boxes and barrels to help with her jump. Wren grunted when her fingers caught the edge. Her arms shook as she managed to pull herself up some but not quite all the way. She slipped and her heart pounded faster.

Blast it.

She was going to fall.

Josenu grabbed her forearms and lifted her onto the terracotta roof as if she weighed nothing. Pulse pounding in her ears, she nodded to him on hands and knees "Thanks."

Leif scrambled up after her, not winded in the least.

"Let's move," the spy commanded.

Hauling herself to her shaking legs, Wren ran after him, trying not to think about how slippery the soles of her feet were against the roof. Josenu lept to the next building, and she didn't give herself another chance to second guess herself and jumped. A scream caught in her throat as she cleared the dead space beneath her. She landed a little too hard, and her ankle twinged but she kept going.

The immense palace lay to her right and she balked when the spy lead them in that direction. Wren cleared another roof and grabbed Josenu's cloak before he could move out.

"We are going toward the danger?" she hissed.

He crouched down next to her, scowling. "The prince has already set up a perimeter farther out. If we go east, we'll be caught. The only way to get out is to move toward the palace and then disappear into the forests. Then we'll double back into the city. Now that your curiosity is assuaged, may we continue?"

She waved her hand. "By all means," she said, sarcasm lacing her voice. What a dolt.

A dolt that's helping you escape.

Her skin prickled as they slowed their pace and began making their way west, closer to the palace. They made it to another building. Josenu sprinted across the top and then dropped to the ground on the other side.

Wren ran to the edge and gritted her teeth. It was a far drop. There was no way she'd make it.

"I'll go down first," Leif said. "Josenu and I will catch you."

She nodded as the bard jumped down, hardly making a sound.

The hair at the nape of her neck rose and goosebumps erupted down her arms.

Wren lifted her head and once again look at the palace looming to her right. Her attention focused on marble stairs that lead to the entrance. A lone figure stood atop, dressed completely in black, his long sliver hair waving in the breeze.

Arrik.

She froze as he stared back her. She could *feel* his gaze on her, running over her skin. Angry, possessive, and... *hurt.* Time stretched and she heard Leif hiss her name, but she couldn't tear her eyes from the prince.

He nodded to her like he was accepting a challenge.

Her belly quivered. She had thrown down the gauntlet when she'd tricked him.

Wren blinked and the spell was broken.

The prince ran down the stairs, and she could hear him

shouting.

"Wren!"

She didn't think twice and jumped from the roof. Her breath whooshed out of her as Josenu and Leif caught her. "We have a problem," she breathed. "The prince saw me."

"What?" both men said at the same time.

"He was standing at the entrance of the palace."

"Rot it," the spy growled. "We must go to the sewers." He ran to a round iron cover set in the cobbles and lifted it. "Leif, you first. You know the tunnels better than anyone."

"That I do," Leif sang. He skipped over to the hole in the alley and jump inside without hesitation.

Wren followed him and peered down into the hole. It smelled something horrible.

"Come on, dragon princess, I will catch you," Leif called softly.

She looked up at Josenu. "You're coming behind us?"

His jaw set. "No, I must close the cover and make sure to get back to my patrol."

"May the winds be with you," she whispered, then sat down and swung her legs into the hole.

The spy nodded. "Be careful, princess. His reach is far. Never assume you are safe. Trust no one."

The prince had said something similar to her. She took one last look at Josenu's face and then jumped. Leif caught her easily and set her down. Her feet sunk into water that was slimy and she gagged.

Don't think about it.

The cover scaped against stone as Josenu began to push it

back into place. Wren glanced up at the moon a second before the cover was settled in place, cutting off the light.

"What do we do now?" she rasped.

Leif reached from her, his fingers running along her arm until he grabbed her hand.

"We run."

CHAPTER THIRTY

ARRIK

She'd seen him.

Even now as he thundered toward the last place she'd been spotted on his mount, Rage; his heart beat quicker than it should have. His dragon princess with her flame red hair had looked like a warrior queen, haloed by the moonlight. She exuded power. Power that he wanted to collect.

That isn't the only reason.

Arrik gritted his teeth. She's crawled beneath his skin and left her mark. Everything thing had gone according to plan, except for that part. He couldn't allow himself to feel, to care. It put too many at risk. He wouldn't be a selfish creature like his father.

Shane rounded the nearest inn, his giant black stead tossing its head. Arrik slowed as did his second in command.

"Any sign of her?" he rasped.

Shane shook his head. "My men are searching the area, but there isn't anyway they could have gotten past our blockade. They took to the sewers."

Then she was as good as gone. He growled.

This is what you wanted.

Arrik cursed. He'd always planned on getting her out of the palace. There'd been too many assassination attempts on her already. Plus, he wanted, no *needed* her cooperation. With the dragon princess at his side, they would hold the power of the world in their hands.

They would be *free*.

"Send Josenu to me," he bit out before wrestling his passive mask back in place.

Shane nodded and wheeled his horse around then galloped away.

No one approached Arrik as he sat on Rage. His horse pranced, feeling his anger. Eventually the guard appeared, his stride brisk.

"My lord," the blond guard murmured, bowing slightly as he reached Arrik's side.

"Is it done?" he murmured, so only Josenu could hear.

Josenu nodded.

Wren was with the rebellion. While it hadn't been his first choice, at least she was out of the grips of his father and brothers.

"What would you have me do?" the guard asked.

"Keep watch over her. If she is harmed, you will rue the day you were born."

"Noted." Josenu backed away.

Arrik watched him leave. The spy was a wily one, but he hated Soren almost as much as Arrik did, so they made a good team. Wren's escape had surprised him. Rarely was he surprised. What was the worst part was the *fear* he felt when she'd sank into the water with the dragon and rebellion supporter. She'd unnecessarily risked her life. If only Wren had been a little more patient, Arrik would have been the one helping her escape and gaining her trust. He would have been able to tell her that he'd put on a good show of hunting her down for his father.

He clicked his tongue and Rage spun around, moving back toward the palace. Now she would think he truly wanted to hunt her, to chain her to his side.

You do want those things.

Arrik wanted her to willingly come to him. It was foolish but he couldn't help it.

A spark of excitement ran up his spine. The coming days would be interesting.

He was used to playing the monster. It was a part he excelled at.

His princess wouldn't see him coming. She was caught in a web of his own making with nowhere to go but back to him.

And her surrender would be all the sweeter.

"Run, little dragon," he whispered.

CONTINUE THE SERIES WITH:

QUEEN OF LEGENDS

NOTE FROM THE AUTHOR

Court of Dragons has been such a wild ride.

It's been a few years since this idea came to me and it really came to the forefront when The Rise of Skywalker released. If you didn't know already, I'm a HARDCORE Reylo shipper. I've made no secret of the fact that I adore the enemies-to-lovers trope (25 + books show that).

While I was vindicated by the ending of the most recent Star Wars movie, my poor heart was crushed when Ben died. Honestly, it was a fitting ending. I don't know how they could have absolved him of his crimes, BUT it got me thinking. What if he'd come around a bit sooner? What if Rey had been a bit darker?

Then the ideas really came.

What if it was set in Viking times? What if there were wicked dark elves determined on taking over the world? What if there was a boy and a girl on opposite sides who were blinded by prejudice but were forced together?

The story seeped into my bones, and I *needed* to tell it. One night, I was sitting by the fire with one of my best friends and she asked me what I was working on. I told her I had an idea, but I wasn't sure if I should give it a go. She told me to write what I love and if no one read it, who cares, I was happy. That struck a chord. It had been a long time since I had written something for myself, not for my readers.

This story was born from passion, love, and a little bit of

obsession.

Thank you to my editors who helped take this manuscript from a lump of coal to a sparkly diamond. I couldn't have done it without you.

To my PA – you are the bomb. I love you so stinking much. Without your help, I wouldn't be able to do what I love.

A million thanks to my husband and Robert who let me bounce ideas off them. Y'all are the best. Thank you for answering my million hypothetical questions, listening to me rant, and making dinner while I continued to write.

Thank you to my readers who have stuck with me this entire time. There are some days that I want to quit, but y'all always encourage me and give me support.

Much love,
Frost

About the Author

Thank you for reading Court of Dragons
I hope you enjoyed it!

If you'd like to know more about me, my books, or to connect with me online, you can visit my webpage https://www.frostkay.net/ or join my facebook group FROST FIENDS!

From bookworm to bookworm: reviews are important. Reviews can help readers find books, and I am grateful for all honest reviews. Thank you for taking the time to let others know what you've read, and what you thought. Just remember, they don't have to be long or epic, just honest. <3

ALSO BY FROST KAY

THE AERMIAN FEUDS
(Dark Epic Fantasy)
Rebel's Blade
Crown's Shield
Siren's Lure
Enemy's Queen
King's Warrior
Warlord's Shadow
Spy's Mask
Court's Fool
Prince's Poison

THE TWISTED KINGDOMS
(Epic Fantasy/Fairytale Retelling)
The Hunt
The Rook
The Heir
The Beast
The Hood

DRAGON ISLE WARS
(Epic Fantasy)
Court of Dragons